D0384602

PERFECT
GALLOWS

BY THE SAME AUTHOR

NOVELS

The Glass-Sided Ants' Nest
The Old English Peep Show★
The Sinful Stones
Sleep and His Brother★
The Lizard in the Cup
The Green Gene
The Poison Oracle★
The Lively Dead★
King and Joker★
Walking Dead★
One Foot in the Grave
The Last Houseparty★
Hindsight★
Death of a Unicorn★
Tefuga★

CHILDREN'S BOOKS

The Weathermonger
Heartsease
The Devil's Children
(Trilogy republished as *The Changes*)
Emma Tupper's Diary
The Dancing Bear
The Gift
The Iron Lion
Chance, Luck and Destiny
The Blue Hawk
Annerton Pit
Hepzibah
The Flight of Dragons
Tulku
City of Gold
The Seventh Raven
A Box of Nothing

★AVAILABLE FROM PANTHEON

PERFECT GALLOWS

A
NOVEL
OF
SUSPENSE

PETER DICKINSON

PANTHEON BOOKS
NEW YORK

Copyright © 1988 by Peter Dickinson

All rights reserved under International and Pan-American Copyright
Conventions. Published in the United States by Pantheon Books, a
division of Random House, Inc., New York.

Published in Great Britain by
the Bodley Head, Ltd., London.

Library of Congress Cataloging-in-Publication Data
Dickinson, Peter, 1927–
Perfect gallows.
I. Title.
PR6054.I35P47   1988   823'.914   87-43047
ISBN 0-394-56311-5

Display typography and binding design by Jessica Shatan

Manufactured in the United States of America

2 4 6 8 9 7 5 3

PERFECT
GALLOWS

The door had been forced.

Poachers after dove-meat? GIs from the camp? Lovers desperate for a place — but the nights had been fine and warm and the woods were private enough. He tiptoed up the narrow spiral stair.

No one in the loft, and the doves apparently unalarmed. Shafts of almost horizontal sunlight shot through the flight-slits above and below the nest-boxes, bright golden dusty bars which made everything else dim. The ladder . . .

It was loose, its slant line just visible across the chamber, beyond the dazzle of sunbeams. Last time he'd been in the dovecote — a couple of weeks back — he'd left the ladder bolted in place with its foot by the stairhead. That made it look as if the intruders must have been poachers — they'd need to swing the ladder round to reach the nest-boxes — though to judge by the stir and mutter there were plenty of birds left.

Stooping beneath the jut of the nest-boxes he picked his way round outside the mess of droppings to reach the ladder. A rope — new, strange, never there before — was knotted to the third rung up and rose in a slant and straining line, angling inwards toward the central pole round which the ladder pivoted. Stiff with the menace of it, he forced his head back so that he could follow the rope towards the golden bars of light above. Their lines were broken by a dark blob. The blob itself was marked by two pale patches.

For a moment the shapes were unreadable, in another moment not. The patches were the soles of two bare feet. The blob was black not only because it was silhouetted against the sun-shafts. It was black of its own nature. Black clothes, black skin.

5

"Samuel?"

Silence. His voice had stilled the fidgeting birds. He gulped, controlling his shock and waiting for the hammer of his heart to calm, then climbed. The transfer of his weight pushed the ladder a few inches further on its circuit and the body moved beside it. Five rungs up he reached out and laid his fingertips on the nearer ankle where the weight of the limb stretched it below the pin-striped trouser-leg. Cold as a raw sausage.

So Caliban was dead. There would be no more performances. Last night's had been the only one, the single chance, given and taken. Meant.

Apart from the questioning tilt of its head the body hung straight, respectable and respectful. The rope ran from the knot beside the neck up over the beam which connected the ladder to the central pole and then down to the rung where it was fastened. Samuel could have tied that bottom knot first, climbed and slung the rope over the beam, put the noose round his neck, jumped . . .

No. The pink soles of the feet were clean. So were the rungs of the ladder. It was more than six weeks since Andrew had mucked the dovecot out with Jean. Unless the doves had stopped spattering their droppings . . .

He glanced down. The floor of course was the usual mottled mess, dark khaki flecked with white and black, fresh droppings on top of old, all streaked with bright light where the sunbeams shot through the lower flight holes, each pock and hummock casting its tiny shadow. And stamped clear in the streak immediately beneath him, a footprint. The familiar pattern of a GI boot. You might never had spotted it, except from above, in this special light, but now that he'd seen one he saw three more — all over the mottled floor, dozens!

No, not all over the floor. In a rough ring, just inside the swing of the circling ladder.

A picture swept into his mind, half a dozen men facing outwards, drunk faces lit and vanishing in the waver of torch-beams, whoops of glee echoing up the chamber, the axle-bearing groaning with the turn of the ladder, fast as it can be spun from hand to hand, and the body circling overhead, its legs still dancing to their tune . . .

"There's guys homesick for a good lynching."

6

Would a lynch-party clean the ladder-rungs?

The bottom door scraped on its flagstone, the noise huge in the silence. Andrew scuttled down the ladder and round beneath the nest-boxes to the top of the stair.

"Jean?"

"Coming. Couldn't you find a key?"

"Don't come up! Wait!"

He glanced back. His rush from the ladder had moved it again so that now the body hung with the head directly lit by one of the sun-shafts. The eyes were open, the angle of the neck asked its question.

"*And if, before you go . . .?*"

Stiffly he turned away, drew a deep breath, squared his shoulders. Forget it. That's all over. It's part of the past, part of Andrew. Andrew's finished.

He made himself Adrian, put on a face of horror and rushed down the stair.

Adrian was used to the glances, the faint frowns of not-quite recognition. He responded by seeming not to notice them. Much later, driving home perhaps, these people would suddenly exclaim his name. They would then tell their friends that of course they'd known he wasn't specially tall, but they'd never imagined . . .

Now they were in any case distracted by his companion, fluttering and fingering among the numbered lots, young enough to be his daughter and obviously not, monkey-faced but delectable in her pale grey mink, an embodiment of youth and warmth in the big dead rooms.

"Look," she said. "They've got your initials on them. Would you like them as a prezzy? They're almost good as new."

She turned one of the ivory-backed hairbrushes over and pressed the yellow bristles with suede-gloved fingers.

"Not surprising," he said. "The old boy was bald as a coot."

"Who? You knew him!"

"I acknowledge him as my great-great-uncle."

"That's why the initials are the same!"

"Indirectly why."

She didn't hear him — another thought had intervened. "That's why you were so keen to come!"

"I also thought it might amuse you to add a modicum of junk to your squirrel-hoard."

"Ooh, yes. I want it *all*! But you can keep the hairbrushes."

"No, thank you. I am going to look at the books. I'll meet you at the foot of the stairs in forty minutes."

She folded back her glove and held out her arm for him to set the timer on the man-sized wrist-watch. He stroked the skin as he finished, kissed a finger to her and turned away.

8

The Viewing Day was more crowded than one would have expected, judging only by the interest of the lots on offer. When Sir Arnold Wragge had returned from Kimberley with his millions and rebuilt The Mimms he had furnished it by instructing his agents to "Buy modern — best you can get and bugger the cost." So everything down to the bootjacks was excellently made and had worn so well that the objects had tended to resist the batterings of the years, and thus often had the look of fakes, the too perfect props of a costume-drama. With the less functional pieces the agents had, perhaps rightly, assumed that Sir Arnold would accept cost as the criterion of excellence, so these all in their various ways tended to be excessive.

The house itself colluded, though more interestingly. Someone had told Sir Arnold that the best architect in England was a young fellow named Lutyens. He had designed a series of rooms which were indeed grand, in a fashion likely to be gratifying to the client but rather differently satisfying to the ironic outsider. The same kind of ambiguity was apparent in the family group of the Wragges, by Sargent, which hung above the fireplace in the Saloon, the room Adrian was now leaving.

The Lutyens revival accounted for some of the crowd. As he reached the door Adrian caught by the elbow and prevented from falling a man who had tripped over the legs of a young woman who was kneeling to sketch the door-fittings. The woman snarled at the man for a clumsy sod and the man swore back and turned, as if to the witness of a traffic accident, to where Adrian had been; but without having seemed to hurry he was already out in the corridor.

Pursuit of him was blocked by two middle-aged couples who were teasing out of their joint memories the details of the Wragge inheritance, that true-life romance that had intermittently occupied corners of the scant post-war newspapers of their youth. They represented another type in the crowd at the Viewing Day, intending at most to leave a bid for some curio to keep as a souvenir of this contact with once-newsworthy riches.

"Wanted to cut her off with a shilling," one of them was saying, "and then the poor lad went and got killed in Italy."

"Wasn't there some kind of nephew?" said one of the women. "Couldn't he have put in a claim?"

9

Adrian slipped past them, unnoticeable almost to the point of being invisible, the family ghost. He turned into another huge room, its walls lined with leather-bound books, series after series of the necessary authors, mostly unread but present because a room designated in the architect's plans as the Library has got to contain books. The lighter furniture had been moved elsewhere and the floor-space filled with trestles on which were ranged volumes brought in from other rooms, the random acquisitions of a mainly unliterary family. Members of the public would come in and nose through a row or two, but since most of the books were to be sold in lots of forty or fifty together they soon left. Three men who looked like dealers were working systematically along the trestles, watched by a young woman from the auctioneers.

Adrian at first glanced casually at the books, picking out the odd item that caught his eye, reading a paragraph or two and putting it back. After a few minutes he reached a pile of scrap-albums and began to look through them. They contained newspaper-cuttings, playbills and programmes, photographs of performances, mostly out-of-doors. He put two volumes aside after a quick inspection and turned to the point in the third at which the entries ended and a series of unfilled pages began. Having studied the single item on the last completed page — a programme — he closed the album and put it back beneath the others.

Now he began to search the trestles more systematically, running his finger along the titles, clearly looking for one particular book. The process brought him up against a dealer working in the opposite direction.

"Have you spotted a copy of *Nada the Lily*? Rider Haggard?" he said.

The man, round-faced, woolly-haired, looked at him with bored eyes.

"Don't think so. Wouldn't have noticed, unless it's a first."

"It might be, but it's not collectable. It got some fairly heavy handling."

The man shrugged and returned to the books. Adrian continued his search, but had done little more than half the room before he looked at his watch and saw that his time was almost up. He considered a moment, then crossed to where the woolly-haired dealer was working, now close to the pile of albums.

"Do you do theatrical material?"

"We've got a section. I've seen that lot. It's rubbish."

"You are mistaken."

No recording equipment could have picked up the alteration in Adrian's tone, but the dealer paused in his work. Adrian pulled out the third album and flipped the pages, pausing three or four times to point to names in programmes. The dealer attempted to conceal the symptoms of interest.

"She had a very good eye for young talent," said Adrian. "I bet some of these are not recorded elsewhere."

"Can't tell."

"I can, however, tell you about this."

Adrian turned to the final programme and pointed to a name.

"First appearance on any public stage," he said. "This is probably the only copy in existence. There was one performance — the others were cancelled. The spare programmes would all have gone for scrap."

"Same fellow?" said the dealer.

"Myself."

Without moving his head the dealer swivelled his eyes to stare. Affability was evidently not his style. He now seemed to think that some kind of trick was being played on him.

"If you find me that copy of *Nada*," said Adrian, "I will do you a signed manuscript note on the production to put with the album. That particular copy, mind you."

He took out his wallet and produced a card. The dealer read it as though suspecting a forgery. By the time he looked up Adrian was halfway to the door.

The girl was waiting. She ran to meet him, seized his wrist and dragged him back to the room they had been in before, to a corner where the working equipment of a late Victorian household was laid out, brass coal-scuttles, mahogany sweepers, cane carpet-beaters, crumb-trays and so on, things which twenty years before would have gone to the scrap-dealer or bonfire but which were now classified as "Bygones". The girl, eager as a leashed dog straining after an odour, hauled Adrian to one of the tables.

"Lookie! Lookie!" she whispered. "Please, A."

11

She was pointing at a small flat drawer which lay in the middle of a mass of material from the butler's pantry. In it were a dozen wooden objects, most of them flat discs about two inches across with turned knobs at the centre.

"Butter-moulds," said Adrian.

He picked out a squat hollow cylinder and fitted one of the discs into it, knob down. There was a flange at the lower end which held the disc in place. The inner surface of the disc was incised with a carving of a cart-horse.

"You wet it," he said, "fill it with butter, turn it over and press it out. Presto — and you have a suitably rural picture on your butter."

"Will you leave a bid?"

"They aren't a separate lot. I will endeavour to make arrangements."

"Darling A. But look at these ones. Aren't they funny? And tiny?"

At the back of the drawer was another set of moulds, less than half the size and very different in style, different in fact from most other lots on display. The large ones were made of fine-grained box, turned on a lathe, their images chiselled out with the deft strokes of a craftsman on piecework. These others were only crudely circular, whittled (perhaps from beech) with a knife. Instead of pictures, letters were incised on their inner surfaces. Their maker had not tried to copy the lathe-turned knobs of the large discs. One had a square block, but the other four had whittled human heads. Small though these images were, their nature was unmistakable. They had nothing to do with Western civilization, that billion-celled complexity whose spirit informed and shaped even such trivial objects as the moulds in a butler's pantry. No, they quite clearly belonged instead with the stuff now on display in the Billiard Room, the mementoes of Sir Arnold's life in South Africa, assegais, knobkerries, Zulu shields and head-dresses, ceremonial stools, and such. Within the conventions of that very different culture it could be discerned that these were not generalized representations but attempts at individual faces — two women, an old man and a young one.

"Aren't they funny?" she said again. "But they're alive. They say something, don't they? What are they saying, A.?"

She looked up when he failed to answer. His face was blanker than ever.

"Put my foot in it?" she whispered.

He shook his head and took the mould out of her hand. For a moment his face, without a muscle stirring, seemed to become that of an individual, somebody one of the other people in the room might have recognized next time they met him. After a couple of seconds the mask reassembled itself. When he gave her the mould she took it without looking, her eyes still on his.

"Something dreadful?" she said.

"Fairly dreadful. You are a remarkable child. I was rather fond of the chap who made them, my uncle's black butler. He died in an unpleasant fashion. I found the body. Perhaps I'll tell you some time."

"How sad . . . If it's going to remind you . . . I don't have to . . ."

"Rather us than someone else."

"Oh, you are a darling!"

"Perhaps they'll bring me luck in the new show."

"Barney thinks the rehearsals are terrific."

"He would say that whether it was true or not."

"Of course it's true!"

"I wish I had your confidence. Anyway, I will leave a bid for the moulds."

"Goody goody. I dote on them. Why did he make them so tiny, A.?"

"Because the others were too large to hold a butter-ration. For part of each year it was only two ounces."

"Really truly? You mean I can cut down to two ounces a day and you won't whinge?"

"A week."

ONE

Cousin Blue sighed, a gentle, helpless, charming sound.

"I gave a brother for my country," she said. "I never thought I should also have to give a nephew. And my maid."

"You have merely lent Doris," said Cousin Brown. "She is making machine-guns, Andrew, and by all accounts having the time of her life."

"In the circumstances I do think it hard that I should be expected to eat margarine," said Cousin Blue, hardening the hardness by the way she pronounced the G.

"You are not having any of my butter," said Cousin Brown. "Nor of Andrew's."

"I expect Andrew is used to margarine."

"That is as may be, but what he has in front of him is on loan from me. He will pay it back when his own ration becomes available. I have lent it to him for his sole use."

Cousin Brown enunciated the separate syllables in a ringing tenor voice. Mentally Andrew provided the stage — the back row of the audience could have heard every word.

"But you *are* used to margarine, aren't you, Andrew?" said Cousin Blue.

"Stand up for yourself, Andrew," said Cousin Brown. "Don't be a mouse."

"Mum mixes our butter and marge together," said Andrew. "She says you get a butter taste with all of it that way."

"It is very, very hard," sighed Cousin Blue, holding her butter-knife in feeble mittened fingers to chip at the little yellow cylinder in front of her. In front of Andrew on a small silver dish was a slice cut out from a similar round, but a slightly paler yellow. He also had his own set of condiments — twinkly silver and dark blue glass like a Milk of Magnesia bottle — and his

14

own bowl with about three spoonfuls of sugar in the bottom. It was the same with all four places. There were silver candlesticks too, but no candles of course, as well as other bits and bobs on the shiny mahogany table. Two knives, two forks, two spoons at each place. Glasses for wine and water . . .

"If you put it by Father's stove it will soften," said Cousin Brown, clearly misunderstanding her sister on purpose.

"I was thinking about Doris," said Cousin Blue. "It really is unfair. After all, this is not truly my country, for which I have given so much. Last night I dreamed about the Wynberg."

"Do not be absurd," said Cousin Brown. "South Africa is also in the war, and in any case Father was born in Southampton, weren't you, Father?"

Uncle Vole, huddled in shawls at his end of the table, may not have heard. Andrew and the Cousins had finished their soup, but he was still eating his, not with a spoon but by dipping in hunks of bread and sucking at them until they disintegrated. Each suck was a squelch permeated by a thin whistle, a bit like Mum's snoring. The noise must have made it impossible for him to follow the conversation, though he gave no sign of wishing to. Cousin Blue timed her remarks to coincide with the dipping process but Cousin Brown spoke firmly through the squelches. She turned to explain to Andrew.

"We children did not come to England until I was ten and it was time for Charlie to go to Eton, so we still tend to talk about the Cape as 'home'. Until this dreadful war we used to go back every other winter."

She swayed to one side to let a hand — dark-skinned, pink-palmed — snake past her and remove her soup plate. The body to which the hand belonged was almost invisible outside the dim pool of light shed by the central chandelier, which had only three bulbs working in its twenty-odd sockets.

"Not nearly so amusing as the Riviera, and *Diamond*," said Cousin Blue. "That was Father's yacht, Andrew. So beautiful. Such parties."

"Perfectly dreadful," said Cousin Brown. "Imagine, a pair of horse-faced girls — too old because of the first war . . ."

"Oh, that war spoiled everything. If only it hadn't happened. Darling Charles. Oh dear."

"My brother Charles was killed at . . ."

15

"We cannot be sure that he was killed."

"Of course he was. Nor do I think there is the slightest sense in referring to him as darling Charles. The only attention he ever paid us was to tease or bully."

"*I* worshipped him."

"Distance lends enchantment, and death more so. Be that as it may, there we were on this useless steamboat, totally unseaworthy . . ."

"But so pretty . . ."

"Father playing poker with his cronies in the saloon and us on deck pretending to feel comfortable in short skirts and shingles and knowing perfectly well that any young man who looked at us twice . . ."

"They could be so amusing . . ."

". . . was estimating the time before he could decently divorce us and weighing that against what Father might stump up by way of settlement. If there had not been a male heir, perhaps the prospect . . ."

"And now the Germans have killed him too. I do think they have a lot to answer for, really I do."

"Not that Father had the slightest intention of allowing us to marry anyone, had you, Father?"

Again there was no response, though by now Uncle Vole had finished his soup and the darkie had removed his plate. The main course appeared slowly, like something happening in Chapel. A plate slid silently into each place. Rissoles (one each) were handed on a silver dish. Mash. Sprouts. Gravy in a silver boat with a ladle. The Cousins abandoned their cross-talk act — food was more important. Andrew himself was almost desperate with hunger and cold. Though the distance, as the crow flies, was only a bit over twenty miles, he'd had dinner at twelve, then lugged his suitcase down to the bus station in Southampton, getting there an hour before his bus went to be sure of getting on. That bit of the journey had been ninety minutes, snaking to and fro between the villages up to Winchester. More than an hour to wait at the bus station there, but the queue had been forming for his next bus before he'd got in, so he hadn't dared leave it to look for a snack, and then this bus had been the sort that towed a gas-bag, so it had really doddered along for almost two hours through the icy dusk. Last of all

16

there'd been half an hour in an open pony-trap up from the village.

There'd been no heating on the buses of course, and the bus stations had been open-air stands, but as the frozen minutes crawled by Andrew had held in his mind a picture of the island of wealth and warmth he was going to. It turned out that The Mimms was colder still — not really, of course, but it seemed like that, and you couldn't wear your overcoat indoors. These huge rooms, how could anyone heat them on a coal-ration? Uncle Vole had a paraffin stove either side of him, but it was an enormous table and Andrew was at the opposite end. A log fire glowed in the grate behind Cousin Blue, but all it seemed to do was suck in a draught from the door.

Though Andrew could feel no warmth from Uncle Vole's stoves, he could smell their oily fume. It seemed quite wrong with the silver and the mahogany and the butler, even if the butler was only a darkie. Mum wouldn't use paraffin if she could help it. She said it made the house smell poor. She usually managed to scrounge coal from somewhere, but of course with the docks so close that was easier than it would be right out here. Andrew was used to a good fug while he ate.

These people weren't. Uncle Vole was wrapped in shawls and wore a tasselled smoking cap, but he kept swivelling round to hold his trembling claws in the updraught from one of his stoves. Cousin Blue wore a shawl and mittens, and Cousin Brown a thick velvet dress, almost the same colour as the table, buttoned close at neck and wrists. Her large raw-looking hands did not tremble as she sliced her rissole into sections.

Andrew did his best not to gobble. Mum would have sniffed at what he had on his plate, not half enough for a growing lad, never mind he's small for his age. He'd given himself a double go of mash to make up for the one rissole. The rissole was very tasty, what there was of it, and the mash was far better than Mum's — not a lump anywhere. The sprouts weren't bad and the gravy had something in it which wasn't Oxo or Bisto. Wine, too. He'd never tried wine before, not counting Mum's Christmas port once, early in the war, when you could still get it. He'd almost finished what was on his plate before the others were halfway through, so he pushed his last two sprouts around and studied his new relations under his eyebrows.

17

The names weren't bad, though he'd chosen them when he was too cold to think. He'd met Cousin Brown — Miss Elspeth — and Cousin Blue — Miss May — in the big room they called the Saloon for a few minutes before the meal, which he'd have called tea but they called supper. He'd named them from the colour of their clothes, just to go on with till he knew them better. Uncle Vole — Sir Arnold — had come shuffling in to the dining-room when the other three were already there and waiting. He was tiny, bent, poisonous-looking. He'd given Andrew a furious quick stare when Cousin Brown had introduced him and then gone shuffling on to his place without a word.

Cousin Brown ate steadily, first the mash, then the sprouts with the gravy on them, last of all the rissole, all in small mouthfuls chewed thirty times. Cousin Blue pecked, hesitated, sighed at the unfairness of being made to choose. The darkie had dished for Uncle Vole and then taken a fork and mashed everything into a uniform mess which the old man shovelled into his mouth, holding his head so close to the plate that he could just as well have licked it up direct, like a dog. Again he took ages, but this time the conversation didn't start up when the other three had finished. Instead, to Andrew's amazement, the darkie came back with second helps. Two more rissoles. Cousin Brown took half of one, but Cousin Blue almost snatched the whole one. The last half appeared at Andrew's elbow. He hesitated — there was still Uncle Vole.

"May," said Cousin Brown. "Andrew is a growing boy."

"Oh, I *am* so sorry. I forgot. I thought it was only us. But there is plenty of potato, isn't there, Samuel?"

"Plenty in dish, miss."

The darkie's voice was not at all like Robeson's, but light and a bit squeaky. Andrew took the half rissole, and more of the veg and gravy when it came. The darkie brought more wine, but he asked for water instead. Silence fell, apart from Cousin Blue's sighing and the rattle of Uncle Vole's spoon. Now Andrew watched the others with a slightly different feeling, less jumpy, more detached. There'd been something special about that last bit he might be able to use one day — and now the way Cousin Blue had cut her rissole up and buried most of the bits under her mash, trying to pretend she'd never taken more than half in the

18

first place — and the shining huge table and the silver and wine and the butler — all that money!

They can't buy me. No one can ever buy me. They can't buy me . . . During the endless, boring, icy journey Andrew had fallen into a sort of trance, with the same words repeating and repeating themselves like a spell, until he'd at last stumbled down out of the second bus. Three other passengers had used the same stop, but they'd known where they were going. Their hand-torches had dwindled into the black-out.

"Mr Wragge, sir?"

"Yes."

A bent, leather-smelling gnome, almost invisible, a darker bit of dark.

"Take your cases, sir. Just the one, is it? This way, then."

Two yellow oil-lamps, glisten of brass and varnish, stir and snort of a horse.

"Step's on the high side, sir. Got it? Dessay you'll be feeling the cold. There's plenties of rugs."

A thick, soft fur over the knees, thick wool round the shoulders, Andrew huddling into himself, nursing his last faint inner warmth. *They can't buy me. No . . .*

And they couldn't even buy two rissoles all round! Mum would have managed, scraping by on Dad's half pay. She'd have sensed when the butcher had a bit on the side and coaxed it out of him. But these people, with all their money, they didn't know how! The knowledge was like magic, a spell that changed things. He even started to feel less cold, and then almost warm when the afters came, a sort of pancake, only one each but decent size, with black jammy stuff inside, hot and sweet but with something extra in it sharp enough to be interesting. There must be a cook too — you couldn't imagine either of the Cousins making a meal this stylish. And the darkie butler and the bloke who'd driven the pony-cart and the bent old maid-servant who'd showed him up to his room. How many more?

"What do you propose to do with your life when the war is over, Andrew?" said Cousin Brown.

He looked her straight in the eyes.

"I'm going to be an actor."

He had answered questions of this sort the same way since he was five, and knew how to deal with all the usual responses, the

19

laugh of disbelief, the smirk, the suppressed shrug. This time he got a surprise. Cousin Brown's mouth fell open and her severe face went orange-red.

Cousin Blue giggled.

"Elspeth hoped to go on the stage," she said.

"Did you really?" said Andrew. "You've got the voice. I can see you in Flora Robson parts."

"Until this war I saw every play she appeared in."

"I sometimes think I saw every play *anyone* appeared in," said Cousin Blue. "We used not to be let go alone, so she sometimes forced me to come to the same play three nights running — dreadfully boring."

"I hitched to London twice last year to see Lehmann's *Ghosts*," said Andrew.

"I caught a matinée," said Cousin Brown. "Rather a disappointment, I thought."

"Oh, but . . ."

"Such a mistake to play Ibsen as though all parties expected to have a thoroughly gloomy time from the first. I believe that with a less wooden translation than poor old Archer's . . ."

"Of course Elspeth's always wanted to be a man and play Hamlet," said Cousin Blue.

"I've mostly played girls in school plays," said Andrew. "I tried to make them let me do Lady Macbeth last summer."

"May is talking nonsense," said Cousin Brown. "Of course I have my ideas about how I would play Hamlet, but who has not? I am aware that it would have been absurd for me to have attempted Helen of Troy, but, for instance, Juliet. There is nothing in the text to inform us that she is conventionally beautiful. All we know is that Romeo thinks she is, and that depends on the actors and the production."

"Romeo was devastating," said Cousin Blue. "Everyone knows that."

"I see no reason," said Cousin Brown. "I think one might stage it rather interestingly with a very ordinary couple. Let Mercutio be the glamorous one, and that other girl, with whom Romeo thinks he's in love . . ."

"Rosaline, but she doesn't come on," said Andrew.

"She does not have a speaking part, but let her come on. Let her be as beautiful as Helen. But Romeo and Juliet are two quite ordinary children, caught up in their passion, while all their families can think of is their own pride and wealth. Romeo and Juliet are heirs. *That* is the point. Let it be not simply a play about doomed love, let it also be a play about *money*. Let that be what dooms . . ."

She was interrupted by a noise, an almost animal yelp, somewhere between a swear-word and a sneeze, from Uncle Vole. She turned to meet his glare, then rose, the darkie drawing her chair aside as she did so. Andrew had seen enough high-society films to guess what happened next. He helped Cousin Blue with her chair, then went and opened the door. He'd been expecting to follow the Cousins out, but as she passed him Cousin Brown whispered, "Father wishes to talk with you," so he closed the door behind them and went back to the table.

The darkie was holding a chair for him just round the corner from Uncle Vole. He sat down, feeling on his right the soft warmth of the stove and on his left the chill of the air sucked in by its updraught. The old man gazed at him with gummy, red-rimmed eyes under scurfy brows. The lower part of the face was just like a rodent's, with no real chin, bluish lips under a ragged sandy moustache streaky with the black jam. The nose was small and sharp, the eyes surprisingly wide-set. Above them the forehead bulged like a mushroom, blotched grey and khaki and purple. Uncle Vole's body was shaken by a continual shudder which made the tassle of his smoking-cap dodder to and fro, but when he spoke the words came perfectly clearly, showing he simply hadn't bothered before.

"Port, Samuel."

"Coming, Baas. 1927 Dow."

The darkie moved away to the sideboard and returned. There was something about the silence of his footsteps that caused Andrew to glance down and see, instead of shiny black shoes below the pin-striped trousers, naked dark brown feet.

"I hate to see a nigger in shoes," said Uncle Vole.

He stared at Andrew, challenging him to disagree, but also challenging him to meet the malice of his glare. Andrew did so, smiling. He had a trick for dealing with this sort of encounter. What you did was turn it into a scene from a play, with yourself as an actor and the other person — unwanted caller, schoolmas-

21

ter, playground thug — also an actor playing his part. You could then perform, doing whatever was needed, while your true self stood off-stage, untouched. It helped to give the other people play-names — Cousin Blue, Uncle Vole. You had a secret name of your own, too. In some ways it was more like a spell than a trick. There really was something magical about the way it worked, how you could outface the schoolmaster, dominate the thug, smile at Uncle Vole.

The encounter lasted only a few seconds before Uncle Vole lost interest and turned to snatch at his glass. He sucked and sluiced the wine to and fro across his palate, then swallowed.

"Might just as well be sow's piss," he said. "Can't taste, can't fuck, can't get warm. Never thought I'd have to face another winter in bloody England. Drink up, boy. Let's see what you're made of. Samuel, you clear out."

"Going, Baas."

Andrew sipped at his port. He hadn't enjoyed the wine much, but this was pretty good, not as sweet as he remembered Mum's, but with a rich strong juicy flavour. He sipped again.

"So you want to be an actor," said Uncle Vole.

"That's right, sir."

"You're a bugger, then."

"No, sir."

"Horse shit. All actors are buggers."

"I prefer girls."

"Had any?"

"Not yet."

"How old are you?"

"Eighteen in March."

"Drink up. Let's see what you can hold. What did they tell you about me? Black sheep of the family?"

In fact until Mum had suddenly decided that Andrew had better accept the out-of-the-blue invitation, Andrew had known practically nothing about the other branch of the family. Dad had never mentioned them. Mum, being Mum, couldn't resist hinting, but not in Dad's presence. Before sending Andrew off she'd tried to explain, in her rambling and excitable way, but he'd soon realized she didn't know much either, and was mostly guessing and hoping.

"You quarrelled with Great-grandfather Oswald, didn't

22

you?" he said. "And then you went to South Africa and made some money in the diamond fields and came back and built this house."

"Tell you what the row was about?"

"No. My mother says Great-grandfather was very strict, and so was Grandfather, so I suppose they didn't try to make it up."

"Whey-faced, tight-fisted, canting, sermonizing, hypocritical, yellow-bellied, bootlicking, brass-arsed Judas. Your great-grandfather, my respected elder brother. Same goes for my dad. Drink up. Let's see the glass tilt. Six quid a bottle this, if you could buy it. Opened it for you."

One day, Andrew thought, he would be able to buy wine at six pounds a bottle and drink as much as he felt like. Not yet. Deliberately he only half-filled his glass.

"Right up."

"That's as much as I want, thank you."

"Got you placed. Pansy little runt who can't hold his liquor."

"No, sir. All you know about me is that you can't make me do what I don't want to."

"Don't know what you're talking about."

"You can't bully me and you can't buy me."

(Mistake. He hadn't meant to say that. Good thing he'd stopped drinking.)

"Buy you?" drawled Uncle Vole. "I only buy the best available."

"Perhaps I'm the best Wragge available."

"Where's your father then?"

"In a Jap POW camp, but we haven't heard for more than a year."

"Ain't he too old to fight?"

"He was mate of a merchant ship. They got caught in Singapore."

"Gimme some more port."

Adrian poured. That was the third glass, and there'd been at least three of wine with the meal. Of course the old man was used to it . . .

"Chapel?"

"Yes."

"But you sneak out of it when you get the chance."

"No. I don't mind it."

23

(Watching the others — families, with their suppressed twitches of help and rejection; attempts to assume the spiritual look; the give-away tensions of necks.)

"Scared to tell them you ain't coming again?"

"No."

"You're scared. You'd have said. You're not the Chapel sort, no more than I was, but I wasn't scared, though my dad leathered the hell out of me and my whey-faced brother held me down while he did it. You ain't got a brother, eh?"

"No, sir, and no sisters either. Dad's the same."

The old man nodded, as though he already knew that. A shudder shook him. He twisted his chair round and shrugged it across the carpet till the cylinder of the stove rose almost between his knees. When Adrian passed him his glass he cradled it in shivering hands as he crouched into the rising warmth. The flame, shining through the pattern of holes in the stove-top, cast yellow oval blobs on to the mottled face.

"Done a job yet?"

"Only war-work in the hols. I got a scholarship to the grammar school and I'm staying on to take Higher Cert in the summer. Then I'll be due for call-up."

"I left school when I was twelve. What's the good, once you've learnt to write a hand and add up? Time I was your age I was digging on the Vaal. Time I was twenty-one I had three hundred thousand pounds in the bank. You going to beat that, acting?"

"I might strike it lucky as you did."

"Horse shit. What I struck was fellows less sharp than I was. I learnt my lesson on the Vaal, up to my waist in water, rocking a cradle six hours a day, nothing to show for it beyond a pile of gravel. When I trekked out to the dry diggings I promised myself that then on I'd see to it that some other bugger did that sort of work for me. Heard of Cecil Rhodes?"

"Yes, of course."

"He was a gent. Liked to make a show of it. Read the books and you'll find not more than a couple of lines about Arnold Wragge, the writer-johnny wondering how a gent like Rhodes could have given the time of day to a bounder like Wragge. They wrap it up, of course, or I'd screw them for libel, but it's there, and it's true. I tell you, Rhodes would never have got

24

started without me. He wanted to keep his hands clean, so he'd got to have a partner didn't mind paddling in the shit. I didn't, and I don't. Gimme some more port."

He drank without bothering to sluice the wine round for the taste. The glass was empty in three gulps. He held it out again.

"I built this house by paddling in the shit. What makes you think I intend to leave one brick of it to a pansy little actor?"

"I don't."

"Don't what?"

"I don't expect you to leave me anything, sir."

"Horse shit. The moment I whistled, there you were on the doorstep."

It wasn't true, but it must have looked that way. In fact Andrew had fought against coming, because Cyril had half-promised him a job helping with the panto. It was only going to be a semi-professional production, two weeks' run in St Michael's Hall, because all three theatres had been bombed flat in the blitz, but it was what Andrew wanted. Then the letter had come with the last Christmas cards, and Mum had said better go. Now that that poor young man had gone and got himself killed in Italy, Andrew was the last of the line. Stupid to pass up a chance like that. And so on. She had got really worked up about it. He'd even thought of pretending to set off and sneaking back to take the job at St Michael's, and sleeping rough somewhere, but of course the Wragges would have started asking where'd he got to. In the end he'd given in, but there was no need to tell Uncle Vole any of that.

"I don't want you to leave me anything," he said. "I'm going to make my own way."

"Horse shit again. You live in Fawley Street. I remember Fawley Street."

"It's been bombed since then, but not our end."

"Shut up. I tell you I know Fawley Street. One cut above a slum. Front parlour, snug, back kitchen. Two rooms up, neither big enough to swing a cat. Outside shit-house. Right?"

"We're on main drains. Dad put the plumbing in when I was born."

"You'd give your right arm to be shut of it."

"I will do that myself."

"Acting? I know actors. I knew 'em at the Lanyon in

25

Kimberley. If the diggers didn't like the play they'd flip gravel on the stage and watch the actors crawl about picking it up, case it might be diamonds. Actresses, now. They could get diamonds. But not like that."

"I think that's what you're trying with me."

"Don't know what you're talking about."

"Flipping gravel on to the stage to see if I'll crawl. Well, I won't. I'm going to make my own way, by acting. To the top. I've got it in me."

"How d'yer know, when you've done nothing more than put on a long skirt and simper. Oh, la, Sir Jasper. How d'yer know you're not a bugger when you've never had a woman?"

"I do know. To me, it's obvious. I'm the only person who *can* know. In both cases."

"Cocky little bugger. All the answers."

"I expect they said the same about you, sir."

"Horse shit. They could've carved six of you out of me."

"I think I've got about an inch to grow. I'll be five-foot-four then."

His height used to bother Andrew. Until he was twelve or so he'd invented exercises, such as hanging from the kitchen door lintel with his toes hooked into the handles of two of Mum's flat irons, to stretch his joints. Then he'd noticed how boys a couple of years older suddenly shot up, and had waited for the magic moment. The moment had come with its odd magic, but not the extra inches. He still did exercises, teaching his body to be fit for the most exhausting roles, but nowadays told himself that his shortness didn't matter. Part of his power would lie in making the audience not see it. The line of his heroes ran from Garrick to Olivier. Six-foot players had to be hams.

Uncle Vole sneered. He had an A1 sneer, worth copying.

"Know what the gents called me at the diggings? 'Wragges-to-riches'. Meant it as an insult, but when I had this place built I half thought of having it carved on my gateposts. I built this house and no man else, and I did it spite of all the nobs and Holy Joes and snivelling politicians in the world. But *you*, Mr Andrew Wragge, you'll never carve that anywhere. You'll be Wragges-and-Tatters, more like, poncing around in flea-pits till you drink yourself into a pauper's grave."

"As a matter of fact my stage name is Adrian Waring."

26

It was the first time he had ever told anyone the secret, since he had chosen the name three years ago, a sudden but fixed decision, made while Mum was out serving at the NAAFI and he was sitting at her dressing-table trying out mouths with the last of her pre-war lipstick. He was startled to hear his own lips speaking it aloud, and the effect on Uncle Vole was startling too. The old man poked his head forward like a darting terrier. A froth of spittle, purple with port, appeared at the corner of his mouth. He snarled. The sneer a moment ago had been calculated, intended to rile Andrew. The snarl was involuntary, real.

"Clear out!" he said. "Clear out and don't come back. I'm through with you."

Andrew pushed back his chair and stood looking down, while the old man huddled himself back round the stove, so close that a smell of scorching cloth prickled the air. Pity. It might have been useful to stay long enough to see him get properly drunk. He wouldn't have been an ordinary drunk either. There was something extra about him, something rare — personality, energy, rage at being so near the end. Andrew knew he mightn't be able to watch anything like that again.

But at the same time he felt triumphant. He'd got exactly what he wanted. He could go home. It was the naming of his secret name that had done the trick.

He bowed politely.

"Thank you for your hospitality, sir," he said. "I will leave first thing tomorrow."

TWO

The bugle call began in his nightmare and ended with him lying awake, stiff with the terror of it, slowing realizing the meaning of the soft, warm, unfamiliar bed, but baffled still by the sound, fairly distant but oddly loud and distorted. The distortion had been part of the dream. A war-film, first war, playing the young doomed officer about to lead his men over the top. Some of the time he was in the film, on set, and some of it he was in a cinema, watching the screen. The bugle call for the attack came through the cinema loudspeakers, but at the same moment came the understanding that the director had taken advantage of

27

a real war to save money on extras and sets. One of the bullets now beginning to whine on the sound-track was going to kill the young star dead.

The terror continued as real as the sound. A secret name was no protection in dreams. Andrew lay unable to move until the bugle call ended and the music began. "Oh What a Beautiful Morning", also horridly distorted by the loudspeakers. Soldiers, somewhere out in the dark. Reveille. Yanks — Andrew recognised the tune from having heard it on AFN — you wouldn't get music like that in a British camp.

He sighed and slowly relaxed. Terror subsided into the usual, permanent, unspoken dread of call-up, some time next autumn. Adrian would be no protection there, either.

To push the thought out of his mind he reached into the icy air outside the Lanaircell blankets, pulled his clothes off the chair beside the bed and teased them down either side of his body. Waiting for them to warm through he considered the problem of getting away before Cousin Brown was up and about. He'd need something to eat. It must be three miles to the village, lugging his suitcase, and then God knows how long before a bus came. He didn't want to argue with Cousin Brown about leaving, though he would if he must. Sometimes you had to hurt people. It was necessary.

He thought about the end of yesterday evening. He'd come into the Saloon and found the two Cousins huddled either side of a log fire, most of whose heat must have gone up the huge chimney. There was a portrait of the whole family over the mantelpiece, painted in this very room, but that had been summer, about fifty years ago, to judge by the clothes. Now Cousin Blue was playing patience on a sort of tray hitched to the arm of her chair, but Cousin Brown had got out three albums and made Andrew sit beside her on the settee to look through them. Programmes, photographs, newspaper cuttings, all of productions by something called The Mimms Players. Kids at first, dressing up on the garden lawn. Then growing up, and a stone stage, still outdoors, with yew hedges behind it. The obvious plays, *Dream*, *Rivals*, *As You Like It*. Elspeth and May Wragge in the cast list, and sometimes Charles Wragge. A gap for the first war, and then only Elspeth. Big parts for her — *Electra*, *Ghosts*, the Scotch play — *Ghosts* indoors, on a special

28

stage in what Cousin Brown said was the Ballroom. Money spent on scenery, costumes and lighting. And real actors, names Andrew knew, people he'd seen, though they must have been just beginning then. Grander and grander . . . And then the war, and back to unknowns. Village halls. You couldn't get an audience out to The Mimms in wartime, Cousin Brown said. Last production *Dear Brutus*, 1940.

Andrew had started to look through the albums both bored and wary. Kiddy-plays, amateurs, Bottoms and Starvelings. Soon he'd seen that though The Mimms Players might have begun like that, Cousin Brown had made it into something different. It wasn't only because she had the money. She was obsessed with the theatre. It was the most important thing in her life. She was, Andrew realized, the first person he'd met who actually understood what he meant when he announced he was going to be an actor, took him seriously, knew that it mattered. When they'd finished looking at the albums they talked about other productions — she'd of course seen dozens of plays he'd only read, or read about — until long after Cousin Blue had gone sighing off to bed. There had been no further sign of Uncle Vole. Andrew hadn't told her what had happened in the dining-room. As soon as he got home he would send her a letter, explaining.

When his clothes were warm he eased himself out of his pyjama bottoms and into pants, socks and trousers. Then the top half. It was a game, but also an exercise in muscular control. A watcher in the room must not be aware what you were up to, so you must make only the visible movements natural to a sleeper, including getting your head right under the blankets in order to push it through the neck of your vest. He varied the imaginary play from which the scene came. This time he was in a prison hospital, about to escape and prove his own innocence . . .

He flung back the bedclothes and sprang forth. Phee, it was cold! Uncle Vole had sneered at Fawley Street, but all his millions couldn't buy that snugness. Andrew eased back the heavy curtain. Still almost dark . . . But now from somewhere down in the house he heard a rhythmic click and clump. A carpet sweeper. The servants were up. There'd be someone he could ask about food. He switched on the bedside light, stuffed his pyjamas into his already-packed suitcase, laced his shoes, crept out. None of the door-fittings rattled. Not a plank creaked, nor any of the treads in the staircase. He used the banister to feel his way.

A yellow light shone in the main downstairs corridor, off which all the big rooms opened. Beneath it an old woman was working the sweeper, some kind of housemaid, though she wasn't wearing the smart black-and-white uniform the other old girl had who'd shown him his room yesterday. Or perhaps she was, only it was hidden beneath her thick tweed overcoat and shawl. Her frosted breath rose in a cloud as she thumped the sweeper to and fro. Intent on her work she didn't notice his approach.

"Good morning," he said.

She looked up — wispy hair, puckered lips, sunken pale cheeks. She glanced at the suitcase.

"Going, then? Thought you was here till Monday."

She wasn't wearing her dentures.

"Sir Arnold changed his mind."

"How many'd he had?"

She tilted an imaginary glass to her lips.

"I was wondering if there's any hope of a lift to the village."

"No bus, Tuesdays."

"Oh."

"Jack's taking Hazel down for the choir-treat, mind you. Suppose you'll be wanting early breakfast. They don't have it till nine, upstairs."

"Well . . ."

"You'll have to see Mrs McHealy. Green baize door and down the stairs. Follow your nose — she's baking."

The door was next to the dining-room. Just inside it on the left was what looked like a pantry, with a scrubbed table bearing compartmented trays of cutlery, cruets, candlesticks, glasses, decanters. Beyond that a wide flight of stairs with slate treads descended, apparently underground. At the bottom a lino-floored corridor led left and right. The smell of baking bread was easy to trace. He followed it along into a large square room with a huge Aga cooker on the further side, and on the right two tall barred windows, their glass reflecting the room because of the dark outside. So he wasn't in the bowels of the

30

earth — the house must stand on a hill which sloped away at the back.

In the middle of the room was a long scrubbed table at which sat the man who had driven the pony-trap last night, with a steaming mug in front of him. He was older than Andrew had realized in the dark, with a gipsy-looking face, very coarse grey hair and strong brows, a slight hunch to his shoulders. He looked up as Andrew came through the door and coughed unconvincingly. The woman standing at the Aga turned at the signal.

"Good morning, sir."

"Mrs McHealy?"

"That's right, sir. Breakfast for upstairs isn't till nine."

Her voice was soft country Hampshire, not the harder Southampton accent which Andrew could do in his sleep. The "isn't" was "idn't" and the "r"s had a burr to them. Mrs McHealy's eyes, pale blue in a flattish, doughy face, had glanced at the suitcase and back. Andrew tried anxious charm.

"Won't someone be driving to the village before that?"

The man at the table stirred but said nothing.

"And I think you've got my ration-book," said Andrew. "Sir Arnold asked me to leave, you see. I said I'd go as soon as I could."

"Where's my Sambo?" said Mrs McHealy. "Give him a shout, Jack. You'll be wanting a bit of breakfast in any case, won't you, sir?"

"Sammy! Oi, Sammy!" called the man.

Andrew put the suitcase down. From along the corridor came the sound of dragging footsteps, a sinister, quiet, approaching shuffle.

"Nice and warm in here," he said. "Like home."

"You're missing home, I expect, sir," said Mrs McHealy. "Not been away before?"

"Not much."

"Weren't you ever evacuated?"

"Just for the blitz, but only out to Upton. My school's still there, but most of us skived off home as soon as the bombing stopped, and nowadays I bike out to school every day."

Mrs McHealy nodded. She was a strong, slightly chilling presence, apparently making conversation not out of friendliness but in order to stop him asking about ration-books and such.

"Our Hazel, she's evacuated from London," she said. "And I wouldn't have it otherhow."

The footsteps reached the door. The darkie came in, wearing a linen jacket over his butler's uniform, and on his feet a weird pair of shoes, a bit like carpet-slippers but with inch-thick pads of felt for the soles, which were far too wide and long for the uppers. Andrew guessed it was a way of polishing the floor as he went about his duties, but it was also a way of keeping his feet warm without breaking Uncle Vole's rule about shoes. He smiled at Andrew, saw the suitcase, looked inquiringly at Mrs McHealy.

"Now, love," she said. "The young gentleman's been saying how Sir Arnold told him to go home."

"He never meant it," said the darkie. "He's always telling people 'Clear out.' "

He too had a slight Hampshire accent, nothing like the pidgin darkie-talk he'd seemed to be using in the few words Andrew had heard him speak last night in the dining-room.

"He said he didn't want to see me again," said Andrew.

"How many times Sir Arnold told you that, Jack?" said Mrs McHealy.

"Lost count," said the groom.

"Lay a place for Master Andrew, love," said Mrs McHealy. "Or maybe you'd rather eat by yourself, sir. There's the parlour."

"It's nice and warm in here," said Andrew. "We eat in the kitchen at home."

"Start you off with a bit of porridge?"

Mrs McHealy bent creakingly to one of the lower ovens. She was older than Andrew had thought — they all were. Anyone younger would have gone off to war-work, like Cousin Blue's maid. She spooned two rubbery lumps of grey goo from a large brown casserole. The darkie brought the bowl over to the table. Jack passed the milk and sugar, and Andrew, mindful of ration-manners with the three of them watching him, helped himself stingily.

"Spare a bit more than that, eh, Mary?" said Jack.

"I'll have to take my ration-book with me," said Andrew.

"If'n you're set on going," said Mrs McHealy. "Still, spare you a full spoon — seven below stairs, we've a bit of slack."

The porridge was grainy, chewy, piping hot, quite different from Mum's tepid slop. While he was eating Mrs McHealy took a tray of bread rolls out of another oven and flipped them on to a wire rack to cool.

"When Mum tried baking it was more like bricks," said Andrew.

"Daresay it was," said Mrs McHealy. "This wartime flour's no earthly. How'd you fancy your egg, sir?"

"Soft but not gooey, please."

"Sammy has his getting on raw," said Jack. "Don't see how he can stomach 'em."

The darkie grinned. His presence seemed to make the atmosphere more welcoming, and Andrew thought he himself had helped by judging the charm-flow right, but there was still a sense of caution, of wary inquisitiveness. He could feel the old groom watching him, but then switching his glance away the moment he looked up. The attention of the other two, though more tactful, was also perceptible.

"Sammy says how you managed Sir Arnold was very nice last evening, sir," said Mrs McHealy.

"I did my best. I didn't realize anyone was listening."

"You think we didn't ought, sir?"

"I don't mind."

"Getting on fifty years Sambo's lived in this house. Thirty-nine I been here, and now we've got our Hazel too. Nineteen-twenty-two you come, wasn't it, Jack, and Florrie was here afore that, and Mabel soon after, not to mention others as live in the cottages, like Mr Feather, and Mrs Oliphant up West Lodge — her George was under-gardener when I come. My way of thinking, we've as good a right as any to know what's coming to us. Sir Arnold, he's not got long to live . . ."

"Lucky to see another winter, 'cording to the doctor," said Jack.

"Florrie was polishing outside the door while he was telling Miss Elspeth and Miss May," said Mrs McHealy. "You see, while Master Nick was alive we all thought it was going to him in the end, spite of everything, but then he went and got killed in Italy, poor lad . . ."

33

"Isn't Sir Arnold going to leave most of it to my cousins?" said Andrew.

"Sambo says no. He'll never leave the house to a woman. There's one up in London, in Charles Street, he might leave them that. But this house here and the money to go with it, that's got to go to a man."

"Not that we know for certain sure," said Jack.

"But that's what Sambo thinks, and he knows Sir Arnold better 'n most, don't you, love?"

"Baas never took any account of women," said Samuel.

"So you see, sir, when Sir Arnold takes it into his head to have a look at the next heir, after Master Nick, that is, and there isn't nobody else far as we can find, it's only natural we'll be taking an interest. And pardon me saying so, my mind you'll be making a big mistake skulking off home. You stood up to Sir Arnold last night. Can't do yourself much harm standing up a bit more by hanging on, can it?"

Mrs McHealy hadn't stopped cooking while she talked, working at the stove and speaking over her shoulder through the sizzle of frying. The lovely hot-lard smell filled the room. Now, before Andrew could answer, there was a clatter of running steps along the corridor and a girl about ten years old dashed into the kitchen. She had wiry dark hair and skin the colour of milky tea.

"Morning, Gran," she said.

"There's some'll be late for their own funeral," said Mrs McHealy.

"Few minutes yet," said Jack.

Ignoring them the child ran to the darkie and slung her arms round his waist. He bent to kiss her forehead. His grizzled hair and her black tangle had exactly the same texture. Mrs McHealy stumped over to the table with a plate in each hand — fried bread, bacon, egg — nifty though Mum was at wangling extras and bringing odd bits home from the NAAFI it was still only bacon *or* egg in Fawley Street.

"You go and eat," said the darkie, turning the child round and pushing her towards the table. She came a few steps, saw Andrew and stopped in her tracks.

"It's only Master Andrew, ducky," said Mrs McHealy. "And this is our Hazel, what's off to the panto with the choir, and if

34

she don't start now she'll get either no breakfast or no choir-treat."

"The panto in Southampton?" said Andrew. "How are they getting there?"

"Coach from the Golden Harp," said Jack.

"D'you think there'd be room for me? I'll pay. I don't mind standing."

Jack didn't answer, but looked for directions to Mrs McHealy. She shook her head, not in answer to Andrew's question but at the whole idea of his going.

"You see," he said. "I hope you don't mind me saying so, but I don't think I want to inherit this house. I've got my own life I want to live."

"It isn't only the house," said Jack. "There's a pile of money goes with it. How much, Sammy?"

"Nine and a half million pounds."

"That's before death duties, acourse."

Andrew was lifting a carefully composed fork-load of toast, bacon and egg towards his mouth as the darkie spoke. His hand didn't quiver as it rose. He chewed, enjoying the perfect mixtures of tastes, and shook his head.

"You're being very kind," he said. "But, well, I know it sounds stupid but I don't want the money either. And I really do want to go back to Southampton. There's something I want to do there."

"You don't know what you're saying," said Jack.

Perhaps that was true, but Andrew didn't care. Perhaps it was the drama of the refusal, the immense sacrifice for the sake of his career, that appealed to him. Logically there was nothing impossible about starting rich, in fact there were obvious advantages, but his long-planned chart of his rise to stardom didn't include them. Perhaps tomorrow he would curse his choice, but for the moment the notion of the coach to Southampton with a load of children actually bound for the panto where he could have been helping was far more solid in his mind than the fantasy of wealth. In any case, there was no certainty that Uncle Vole would leave him a penny. These people were only servants. What did they know? He shook his head again, smiling.

"What do you say, Sambo?" said Mrs McHealy. "Wake up,

35

love. Gone into one of his moods."

Andrew looked up. The darkie was standing where he had been a moment ago, but was waggling his head from side to side with a slow, loose, lolling motion, as though his neck were broken. I might use that for something one day, Andrew thought.

"I said what do you say," said Mrs McHealy more loudly.

"This house is a trap," said the darkie in a bloodless mutter. "Baas, he built it for a trap."

"Cheerful," said Jack.

"Wake up," snapped Mrs McHealy.

The darkie blinked, pulled his head straight and nodded.

"You give Master Andrew his ration-book, Mary," he said.

Mrs McHealy snorted and seemed about to argue. The snort became a sigh and she waddled round the table to the dresser that ran most of the length of the inner wall, displaying on its shelves enormous oval plates made to carry whole roast joints. She lifted the lid of a soup tureen, groped and brought out a wad of ration-books tied together with pink tape. Slowly she undid the knot and took Andrew's book from the top of the pile, but instead of handing it over she began to leaf through it, holding it at arm's length, like old Mr Singleton studying a pawn-ticket.

As Andrew was cleaning the last salty bacon drippings from his plate with a corner of toast his eye was caught by the ration-book at the top of the pile. That odd knack which somehow picks out letters which don't make sense before one's started to read the paper on which they're written — a misprint in a theatre programme, for instance — made him look again. MARY JANE MK——. The pink tape lay across the rest of the name. Mrs McHealy chuckled as he moved it aside. MKELE.

"There's a lot get caught that way," she said. "Thinking I married a Scottie whenas it was really that big buck nigger over there. Do you a couple of rolls for the journey? Marge and Bovril, but better than an empty belly."

"Thank you very much. And thanks for breakfast."

"Don't mention it. But mark my words, you're making a big mistake, running off. Not too late to change your mind."

"I made up my mind when I was five."

(It had been at another panto, in a proper theatre — he wasn't

36

sure which one — in peace time. He could have shut his eyes now and seen the glitter of the fairy queen.)

"Time we was off," said Jack. "Where's that Hazel?"

"Gone into a dream on the what-not, I'll be bound," said Mrs McHealy.

But at that moment the child, who had gobbled her egg and stolen away a few minutes earlier, came clattering back. All attention was now on her. Andrew picked up his case and waited, then followed the others down a long corridor and out into a courtyard paved with blue-black brick where the pony, covered with a blanket, waited enduringly between the shafts of the trap. From some distance beyond the house music, just discernibly 'Pistol-packin' Momma', penetrated the freezing grey dawn.

THREE

Children were playing in the ruins of the bombed houses at the eastern end of Fawley Street — evacuees who'd been allowed home, or simply sneaked home, for Christmas. Some of them would contrive to stay on for a bit when term began, till their absences from school were noticed and officials came to collect them. A few would escape even that net. Andrew paused for a minute to watch them scooping up the sprinkling of snow and trying to mould snowballs from it. As the snow was half brick-dust the snowballs spattered apart on the way to their targets, but the children still screamed when an icy fragment touched flesh, shouted at a hit and hooted at a miss.

Mum would be at the NAAFI, so he could slip in and dump his case — hide it for the mo — then go and see Cyril and come home to present her with the *fait accompli*. Then there'd be the problem of what to tell her about The Mimms. First part easy — amuse her by acting the parts, Cousin Blue's sighings and probings, Cousin Brown's boom, Uncle Vole's gobblings and spite. She'd take his side over all that. But second part . . . Did he have to tell her anything about the scene in the kitchen? The money?

Mum would love to be rich, not because she was greedy for money but because she was greedy for life. She'd always been

37

like that, even before the closing-in of the war. He could remember her doing the pools back then — secretly, if Dad was ashore, and then secretly sneaking down to meet the postman on mornings she was expecting a win (£6. 17s. 4d. had been her biggest). Andrew had grown as used to Dad's absence now as he was to Mum's presence, before the war the strangest times had been when there was this intruder in the house, with Mum hustling into practices she'd slipped out of while he'd been away — grace before dinner, serviettes on the table, shoes in the house and not slippers, little hidden gestures to Andrew to fit in — like a French farce when the husband comes home. How much had Dad noticed, smoking his thin black cigar and reading the *Gazette* in what Andrew regarded as *his* chair?

It was only since the news had come about Singapore that Andrew had learnt to think of his father as a character, half a married couple with one son. A strong character, with secrets. No smiles. Anger, sometimes, if that was what it was. Now, as so often before, Andrew brought the Mae West episode out of its mental cupboard and looked at it again. It had been seven years ago, almost. Dad, just home, tanned and alien. Andrew, longing to impress, beginning his new-learnt imitation. He'd done it for Mum only the week before and she'd laughed and laughed — why hadn't she warned him? She must have known the other meanings in the lines . . . In order to think about it calmly he made it a scene from a play. Strindberg or someone. Dad's relish in his own anger, in his power, but also some secret in *his* life that had put the crack of pain into the whistling belt. You'd find out in Act Three — a visiting sailor would let slip about the yellow house behind the harbour in Veracruz, with the shutters always closed, where Dad lived a quite different sort of life, where the Mae West lines would seem harmless as fairy-tales . . .

It had hurt like hell of course, and Adrian was only a name then. He still hadn't discovered his other uses. Not that he'd have been much help against pure pain. Now, though, Andrew could take pleasure in the discovery that there was an echo of the scene right back in Uncle Vole's boyhood. No elder brother to hold him down. No need to vow revenge, either. It was all outside himself now, part of a play. And he was going to make his own success, which you couldn't measure in money, not even in millions. OK, so he wouldn't tell Mum about that part of it. He picked up his case and walked on.

Fawley Street? One cut above a slum? Rubbish, if you didn't count the bombed bit. Most of them had electric doorbells, and till the war there'd been a woman come twice a week to scrub out, and to black the stove. Of course they didn't look so hot after five years of war, though Mr Toomey had smuggled a bit of Cunard red out of the docks and done his front door over Christmas. Apart from the yelling children the street was empty.

Andrew put his case down on the doorstep of Number 19, turned into the tiny front garden and lifted the upside-down flower-pot behind the hydrangea. No key. He'd half expected that — she'd have taken it to the NAAFI as she wasn't expecting him home. So he'd have to go round and leave the case in the coal-shed. Question was, had he best write a note for Mum telling her not to lock up, in case Cyril took him on for that evening's performance, in which case he'd get home at all hours? He needn't explain, not till after . . .

While he thought about it his hand, unordered, tried the door handle. The door moved. It wasn't locked. Forgotten? Still at home? Sick? The key was on the inside of the lock. Silently he put his case down in the hallway and tiptoed on into the kitchen.

The stove was hot. The kettle, drawn to one side, had an inch of tepid water in it. Plates stacked by the sink, unwashed, two lots. Someone in for tea last night, then.

Upstairs, footsteps and the click of a door. More steps. The hiss of water into the toilet — not Mum's gush and dribble. The doctor? No, the feet had worn no shoes. The footsteps moved back and the door clicked again. Before it closed he heard Mum's sleepy murmur, and the man's chuckle.

He stood mindless. He didn't ask Adrian to occupy his surface, to smile an ironic smile and nod, but that was what happened. Yes, she'd got very worked-up about him going to stay away for a week, wouldn't take No for an answer. Stupid Andrew. People don't exist solely for you. They have lives of their own.

Leave her a note, letting her guess he knew? What was the point? She wouldn't be glad to see him back next day, either,

not till Monday tea, when she'd be all hugs and laughter . . .
He'd need some money.

There was three-pounds-something in the pewter tea-pot on
the mantelpiece. He helped himself to a ten-bob note and two
half-crowns — she never bothered to count what she'd put by
— then went softly back into the hall, picked up his case and
left. The children were still shrieking among the ruins.

Cyril was delighted to see him, as flu was raging and last night
they'd gone on with only five dwarfs, raising a bit of a laugh by
saying the other two had gone to be Bevan boys. Two bob a
performance and he could sleep under the makeshift stage, but
keep a look-out for a stage-hand called Toby. He liked boys.

There were matinées six days of the week and evening
performances four. At least you got a full house matinées,
shrieking kids bused in for their Christmas treat from villages
miles around, never mind it was only a church hall and not a
real theatre. They understood about one line in three and
drowned half those with squabbles over their sandwich-packs.
The main cast was professional, but otherwise as makeshift as
the theatre. Snow White was fifty, though she managed to look
ten years younger under the greasepaint. Prince Charming had
the voice of a bad-tempered mouse, having been cast for her
legs. The Wicked Queen might once have had promise; now
she brought sailors along, different ones each time, and chattered audibly with them in the wings. The Dame could perform
with real gusto when he'd found enough to drink, but at that
stage was apt to veer off into *Aladdin* or *Jack and the Beanstalk*.

Evening performances were dire in a different way, the front
seats only half full, with older and prissier children than the
afternoon ones, balanced by a couple of dozen adults in the back
rows who'd been attracted by the posters of Prince Charming,
all thigh and tooth and bust; these became rowdy with boredom
unless the Dame placated them with lines that tended to make
the parents nearer the stage start hustling their children into
overcoats and taking them away in mid-scene.

For Andrew it was the appallingness that made it so satisfying. It was the real thing, the bottom rung. His chart of the
future showed him climbing from the insignificance of Fawley
Street to world-wide stardom, missing nothing on the way. He

40

would never retire. He would die on stage (Our revels now are
. . . ended . . .) but before that last, spell-binding instant he
would dictate his autobiography, a summation of the theatre in
this century, so it had to be all there — tolerant but telling
anecdotes about famous colleagues, the applause of Broadway
and the West End, the mad tycoons of Hollywood tamed, and
so on, but also the dragon landladies of Doncaster, Blackpool
nights, Hamlet on one cheese sandwich, and this, including the
first tiny triumph that when Dopey came palely back from his
sickbed the producer sent him packing because his replacement
was getting laughs.

Still, dire it was, reaching its nadir on Friday night with the
back rows fuller and rowdier than usual. Just after the interval
the Dame came weaving on and tapped Snow White on the
shoulder just as she was reaching for a high note in "Somewhere over the Rainbow". Snow White spun round and socked
him.

"Lay off, you silly bitch," said the Dame. "I got a nounce-
ment."

The audience were yelling to Snow White to finish him off
but he raised his arms in a priestly compelling gesture and got
them half-quieted.

"Announcement from the management, ladies and gents," he
said. "Sirens have gone for an air-raid warning. Those as want
to leave, nearest shelters are in Houndwell Park, left and left
again as you go, duckies. Those as want to stay, well, *we're*
staying. We never closed, not for that fat bugger Goering, at
any rate. Now, just to give them as are going time to clear out,
before we get on with this elegant entertainment we are laying
on for your benefit, you unappreciative drunken slobs, I'll tell
you a little story, shall I? Talking of sirens, that reminds me . . .
Any sailors in the audience? No, *thank* you, I don't want you up
here now. *After* the performance, Jack, and I'll be only too
happy to oblige you . . . Now did any of you maritime heroes
ever happen to meet a real genuine siren, the sort that sits
around on rocks, singing her head off, with nothing to wear but
a bit of seaweed? I'm going to tell you about some as did. It
seems there were these three shipwrecked sailors floating across
the great big empty ocean on this raft . . ."

Not more than half a dozen of the audience had left but the

story lasted twenty minutes. Andrew had been on stage when it began, being sung to about rainbows. He listened and watched, rapt. The story was rubbish, its plot just an excuse for anatomical extravagances, with the back rows bellowing encouragement at each variation, but despite that something thrilling took place. Like Samson being given his strength for an hour to pull the temple down on the Philistines, so the battered old Dame was given this last spurt of theatrical energy to do whatever he wanted, winding the tension of laughter up and letting it unreel, at the height of the uproar commanding silence with one crooked finger, then tossing a hiccup into the pool of silence and allowing the ripples to fade and fade until, at the exact and necessary instant, he plunged on.

It was an impossible act to follow. Snow White, almost as old a hand as the Dame, must have seen this in the first few minutes. She went home to her digs, giving the assistant stage manager, a fat woman who wouldn't take her specs off, time to dress and take over. The rest of the performance was drowned in cat-calls except when the Dame was on stage, and then shouts for more of the same. He obliged with ancient blue lines, but the God Hercules had left him. By common consent the cast cut most of the remaining scenes, performing what they chose in front of the wrong sets, so despite the interpolation they finished five minutes before the usual time. The audience went out to the sound of the All Clear.

Toby was a gentle, sad, elderly man who had worked in theatres since he was a child. The only trouble with him was that he kept hoping. While he was supposed to be clearing up after the first evening performance he would find excuses to enter the cave which Andrew had made for himself under the stage, talking about long-forgotten stand-up comics and patter-song artists, settling on to the end of the mattress and trying to progress from there. Once he'd finished his work he went home, so Andrew had found it simplest to leave with the cast, taking a key with him, and wander about till midnight.

The first night he tried going south-east, into the bomb-flattened heart of the city, empty now but not silent. The docks were working all night, and the trains rattled to and fro across the wilderness of cleared rubble. A few buildings and half-buildings still stood, but blind, their shattered windows boarded. He walked quickly, because of the cold, and it was only by luck that he didn't run into the arms of a couple of bobbies on patrol; he spotted the flicker of a torch-beam before they could have heard his footsteps and had time to hide among the gravestones of a roofless church. Anybody found wandering down here would be stopped and questioned. He didn't want that. It struck him that by now a letter might have come from The Mimms, and Mum would be worrying because he hadn't turned up. In a day or two the police might be looking for him.

So the next night he walked north-west and slid a note under the door of Number 19 — "Everything OK. Having fine time. See you Monday. Love, A." Then he zig-zagged back to St Michael's, giving Toby time to clear off. From then on he did his wandering through still-inhabited areas, though about every street had the odd bomb-gap. Here he could walk as if he was going somewhere definite, with a confident officer-voiced "Good-night" for any bobby or warden he ran into. He found these places better suited to his mood in any case, the unlit streets and the still, inward-turned houses, thousands of bed-rooms each with its dreamers, individuals all with their own names, identities they would never leave, while among them, unnoticed walked Adrian Waring — Adrian who had no identity, let alone an Identity Card, and who thus was able to become anybody, by the power inside him — magic-seeming but real as an electric current — was able to step forth for three blazing hours in the face of an audience, to show them a whole human being, rounded, complete, known like an old friend — and then, as the curtain fell, vanish!

On the Friday of the Dame's extravaganza he walked the streets in a trance. It was a frosty night, with a half-moon coming and going behind the light clouds, but he didn't notice the cold. His mind was full of the episode. He recreated it, detail by detail, trying to analyse how the old boy had achieved his effects, the switchings of pace and volume, the varied pauses, the apparent hesitations, the tone at times of joining his audi-ence in a glorious conspiracy against common decency, and at others of silent outrage that they should find anything amusing in the obscenities he was uttering, all with the faint but thrilling undertone of contempt for them that they should have brought a man of the Dame's abilities down to pig it at their level. The slave's contempt for his master, the mob. Adrian would have that too. The slave's contempt . . .

"And where are we off to, lad?"

Enthralled by his vision Andrew hadn't noticed the bobby. He blinked into the shaded torch-beam. He had no idea where he'd got to in the city. He shook his head and put on a friendly but adult smile.

"I seem to have got a bit lost," he said. "I was trying to get to Fawley Street."

"You're right off track for that . . . sir. Got an identity card, then?"

Andrew took out his wallet and produced the card. The bobby studied it under the torch-beam.

"Heard there's been a bomb in Fawley Street?" he said.

"No! Are you . . . which number?"

"Don't know that, sir. News in just as I was leaving the Station. Wasn't there a bit of bombing there in forty-two?"

"That was the other end . . . I suppose . . . How . . . I mean, from here . . ."

"Steady now, sir. Just the one house hit, I heard. Let me see, Fawley Street — you want to go back the way you come far as . . ."

Neat as a missing tooth. The roof-ridge snapped out between the two chimney-stacks. Clear sky now, and the moon shining on to the far wall, so that Andrew could see (or think he saw, knowing it so well) the tulip-pattern of Mum's bedroom wallpaper. Her mantelpiece hung in mid-air, swept clean of its clutter of knick-knacks and photos. A beam-end poked out of the shadow below. Faint smoke, white in the moon, drifted away. Some shaded hand-torches gleamed in the blackness, defining by their movements the invisible mound of debris.

The street was roped off either side of the gap. A few spectators lounged on the further pavement, their attitudes somehow suggesting that nothing new was going to happen. It was cold and late. They had almost made up their minds to go home.

Andrew stood and stared for a moment. His only feeling was emptiness. He knew he ought to have grand emotions churning

44

inside him, horror and grief and outrage, but they weren't there. He ducked under the rope and crossed towards the shadow, but a man in a steel helmet, an ARP warden, immediately came out of the darkness.

"Other side of the line, sonny."

"Excuse me. Can you tell me? Mrs Wragge . . .?"

"Goner, I'm afraid. Dug her out half an hour back."

"Oh . . . was there . . .?"

"Anyone else? We're still digging. The boy's bed was empty. He's staying away, from what the neighbours say. Pal of yours?"

"Well, yes."

"Happen to know where he's staying?"

"I might find out."

"You do that, sonny. Any news, report it to the police station. Father a POW, right?"

"Yes. I could get his address too."

"Good lad. Back across the rope, now."

Andrew did as he was told. He knew quite well why he had lied to the warden — so that he could go on playing Dopey in the panto till the end of the run, which had been almost the only thought in his mind. But the lie had been a strange relief, giving him not just something to say but something to feel, worry for his friend Andrew, sympathy, anxiety to help. Now the thought struck him that with Mum gone Andrew might go too. Andrew's bed was empty, but he might still have been up. The searchers might have missed the body . . .

The idea lasted only an instant. His ration-book. His identity card. Anyway, he wasn't ready. One day . . .

As he crossed the rope one of the spectators, a bulky man made squarer by a fur-collared coat with padded shoulders moved to meet him. The man's face was invisible in the shadow of his hat-brim.

"Real bit of bad luck, that," he said.

"Yes."

"Just the one little bomb, far as I hear. Only one plane, too, on a sneak raid to Gloucester or somewhere, found this little buckshee bomb they'd forgottten to drop, chucked it out when they saw the Solent. Waste not, want not."

"I expect so."

The man had continued to move while he talked in his soft purr, until he was a black silhouette against the moon. His idea, obviously, was to take a good look at Andrew. Andrew was ready.

"Step over this way a bit," said the man.

"I'm not interested."

The briefest of pauses, then the man laughed, getting the point, but not minding.

"Not what I'm on about," he said. "Other way inclined, I am, and you can say that again."

He turned and started to stroll off, pausing in his stride to let Andrew catch up.

"Heard what you told the warden," he said. "None of my business, but you're young Andrew, aren't you?"

"Yes."

"Recognized you from the photos."

There had been two, one on the pianola in the front parlour and one on Mum's bedroom mantelpiece, Polyfoto enlargements, a present from Mum to herself this Christmas, less than a fortnight back. The man had seen them both.

"I didn't want a scene," said Andrew.

"Know what you mean."

"Were you one of Mum's lovers?"

"What you mean, one of?"

There was a note of aggression in the purr. Andrew shrugged.

"She said as I was the first," said the man. "You telling me she was pulling a fast one?"

"No. I mean I don't know. I've only been away once before, when we were evacuated. I don't see how, apart from that she could have . . ."

"There's ways and means. What gave you the idea?"

"Saturday morning I came back when she wasn't expecting me. There was someone with her upstairs."

"That'd've been me. Fact, now I think of it, she fancied she heard someone moving around, but I told her it was the neighbours. Listen, Andrew lad, your mum was a bloody fine woman. She wasn't a whore. She was a bloody fine woman, in more ways than just the one. I'm going to miss her."

"Me too."

Andrew said it because it was expected of him. He didn't yet know if it was true. They walked on in silence, now through the flattened area towards the docks. The man seemed to have a definite idea where he was going.

"Take it you found somewhere to sleep," he said. "She showed me your note."

"I won't feel like sleeping for a bit."

"Same here. Let's find ourselves a mug of tea."

"There won't be anywhere open."

"If you know, there will."

It was right inside the docks, a sort of makeshift shed in a nook between two warehouses. Two dim bare light-bulbs, a few rickety tables and chairs, packing-cases. Dockers, a dozen or so, sat around smoking and talking in low voices. An old Chinese woman went to and fro with a brown enamel tea-pot. The milk was condensed, poured straight from the tin. There was greyish sugar in jam-jars. Smells of frying came from behind a curtain of canvas at the back of the shed, and sometimes an almost-pretty Chinese girl brought plates of sausages and chips out to the men at the tables.

The place was illegal. Andrew could feel it in his bones. The dockers were skiving off their shifts — you could tell from their low voices, their poses, their gestures. The tea and the sugar were sweepings out of a warehouse, the milk was missing from its consignment, the sausages too — a fortnight missing to judge by the cooking smells.

But Mr Trinder was at home here. That was the man's name, he said, Stan Trinder. He had other names, obviously. He'd brought Andrew to one of the railway-gates and stood in the shadow waiting, listening to the dock noises. There'd been a sentry on the gate, stamping to and fro with his rifle on his shoulder in the frosty moonlight. A train had come clunking up from the quays and the gates had opened. As the train churned through Mr Trinder had strolled over and spoken to the soldier on the near gate, then signalled to Andrew to join him. Nobody'd even looked at them as they slipped along beside the clanking trucks into the dockyard, and then on, keeping where possible to the shadows but walking with a casual, OK-to-be-here gait, to this den.

47

"Didn't hit if off with Sir Arnold's lot, then?" said Mr Trinder.

Of course Mum would have told him. You couldn't imagine her not.

"Too nobby?" said Mr Trinder. "You've got the voice, though."

"Fuckin' right I 'ave. When I wannit."

Mr Trinder raised his horse-shoe eyebrows. He was pale-faced, balding, with a big wet mobile mouth and soft brown eyes. He laughed his pleasant laugh but his eyes sharpened for a moment.

"Full of that type of trick, according to your mum," he said. "Try it on Sir Arnold, then?"

"No. He just told me to clear out. He said it was because I refused to get drunk and I couldn't talk women, but really he took against the idea of me becoming an actor."

"She told me about that too."

"It's all I'm interested in. In fact I was glad Sir Arnold chucked me out, because I had a job lined up at the panto."

"How's it going?"

"Fine. I was only expecting to help back stage, but I've got a part. That's where I'm sleeping, as a matter of fact."

"Ah. Having any trouble with Toby?"

"A bit."

"Heard how he was out. Stupid sod — never learns. You mention my name, though. That'll cool him off."

"Thanks."

"What are they going to do about the house, then?"

"I'm sorry?"

"Got a stupid sort of name. The something."

"Oh, The Mimms. I don't know."

"Cost a quid or two to run, place like that."

"There's plenty of money. Nine and a half million pounds before death duties, somebody told me."

"Now that is what I call money."

Part of Mr Trinder's style was the steady softness of his voice, as though nothing in the universe could shake his inner citadel. Now the tone did not change, but he spaced the words out, showing that a tremor had got through. Andrew sipped at the sticky orange tea. It would have been disgusting anywhere

48

else, but here it was part of the experience.

"Worth letting the old bugger have his way for that lot," said Mr Trinder.

"No. Acting's the only thing that matters. I'm not even sure I want the money anyway. Nobody'd take you seriously. They'd always be saying you'd bought your way in."

Mr Trinder tilted his chair and gazed at Andrew, nodding slowly.

"You'll change your mind," he said. "Only then it'll be too late. The old bugger will've copped it."

"The servants told me he won't get through next winter, according to his doctor."

More meditative nods.

"There was these two brothers, way back, your mum told me."

"Oswald and Arnold. They had a row and Arnold went to South Africa and made a lot of money in diamonds. When he came back he built The Mimms."

"Let's take Oswald's side. He had just the one son, your grandad, right?"

"That's right, and the same with Dad and me. Three onlies in a row."

"Clear enough. But old Arnold made more of a go at it."

"He had a son and two daughters. They're still alive, Elspeth and May, but the son went missing in the last war. He was called Charles."

"Missing? Your mum said as he was killed."

"That's what I thought, but he was only missing. I suppose it comes to the same thing, though my Cousin May talked to me as if she thought he might still be alive. I don't think she believed it, just wishful thinking."

"I know the sort. Now, according to your mum young Charles had gone and got married before he bought it. Had a son, what's more."

"I didn't talk to my cousins about this, so I only know what Mum told me, and she didn't always get things right. I expect she told you too, anyway."

"Carry on. She could've left something out."

"OK. Charles got married on his last leave. She was a VAD who'd nursed him when he was wounded the year before. They

49

didn't tell Sir Arnold till after the wedding. Then Charles went back to France and went missing in one of the big attacks. The son was born next year. He was called Nicholas. Sir Arnold tried to have him made a Ward of Court but Charles's wife fought him off. She took the baby to Australia, and married again. Nicholas joined up with the Australians when this war started. He was killed in Italy last year."

"No funny business about that?"

"I don't think so."

"No secret marriages either?"

Andrew shrugged.

"Right, so then the old bugger sends for you to give you the once-over, but he takes a scunner against you for wanting to be an actor. So all he's got left is the two old pussies."

"The servants say he won't leave the house to them, not if he can help it. It's got to be a man."

"And you're the only one going, only you don't want it. Stone me. Poor old bugger. After all that palaver."

Mr Trinder laughed and stretched, then cocked his head and glanced at Andrew.

"You must be getting on for call-up," he said.

"Next August, probably. Why?"

"Strikes me you're going to need to watch your step. Not that I'm what you'd call superstitious, but there's no denying things happen in threes. There's two heirs to the old bugger's fortune have gone and got themselves killed, fighting. Maybe you're doing right after all, saying you don't want it."

Andrew summoned Adrian to smile at the fancy. Inside him the well of nightmare opened. It had been there for months now, but he had taught himself to keep the lid on it most of the time, except in dreams. It wasn't for himself, Andrew-now, that he was afraid. He could have put up with any amount of discomfort, exhaustion and pain if only he could magically have been given the promise that he would come through alive and start on his career. It was terror for Adrian-to-be that filled the well with its cold slow-churning mass, all that glorious future smashed, mown down by a machine-gun-burst trying to cross some bloody ditch. And the way that Mr Trinder had put it had added to the suddenness of the inward ambush, the casual tone, the argument not from solid provable daytime facts but un-

50

graspable powers of luck and ill-luck. Mr Trinder stretched again, widening the gesture into a yawn.

"Trouble is," he said, "I'm missing your mother."

"So'm I."

"Not what I meant. There was I, wandering along under the moon, licking my lips a bit, anticipating, if you get my drift . . ."

"Yes, of course. I don't mind."

"You're a good lad. Point is, if you won't think it heartless, I'm going to have to go and do something about it."

"That's all right. If you'll just help me get out of the docks. Toby'll have gone home by now."

They rose together. Mr Trinder shrugged himself into his coat and put his hat on. He laid a pound note on the table — far too much for a couple of mugs of tea — and weighted it with the sugar jar, but still made no move for the door.

"Pity you couldn't've kept the old bugger happy with a bit of chat," he said.

"I could have if I'd wanted, in theory."

Mr Trinder shook his head, dead serious.

"Much better do a bit of the practical. It's a lot different from how you imagine it."

"Well . . ."

"I know a nice house. Girl there just right for a beginner."

"I don't suppose I've got enough money."

"This is on me. Owe it to the family, you might say."

"All right. Thank you very much."

FOUR

It had snowed again, rather more than a sprinkling this time, enough to make the search through the rubble of Number 19 an even more hopeless task. Still, there was just a chance, seeing the shelf which held the tea-pot had been on the very back wall of the house. The wall might have bulged out, and the tea-pot would only have been squashed a bit, being pewter, not broken. Andrew calculated the position and eased out a couple of bricks, inspecting their sides for the yellow kitchen distemper. No luck. He tried again, further right.

51

There'd been a bobby watching at the front, to keep scavengers off, but Andrew had walked straight past him and round through the back alley between the coal-sheds and the old outside toilets. The mound of rubble hid him from the street. He worked patiently, barely noticing how his fingers numbed and blundered. He was thinking about last night.

The girl had been called Minnie. A darkie, much blacker than Samuel Mkele, he thought, though it had been hard to be sure in the dim and smoky light. She wasn't at all pretty and reeked of sweat and cheap scent, but she'd giggled and squirmed and given every impression of liking what he did, and when it was over she'd said in broken English that he was very nice, very strong, very good. That was part of her job, Andrew guessed, but he'd also known in his bones it was true. From his side the experience had been thrilling, not because of physical enjoyment, which had been there all right, but something more important to him. It had been a parallel event to the scene earlier last night when the Dame had told the story about the siren and the sailors. He had been aware of this even at the time, and more and more so as he looked back. There was the same sense of mastery, of mysterious energies focusing into a moment, of the other partner (the audience, the black girl) being made by those energies to melt, to become so malleable that they answered to a whisper, to a touch — and also, with all that, with the pleasure and excitement, the dominant will detached and watching, chilly, contemptuous, amused.

Mr Trinder had said it wasn't a good idea for beginners to strain the machinery by trying too often, but Andrew was certainly going back soon. That was why he needed Mum's teapot. He had just bent to try a fresh place when a voice spoke above his head.

"Ullo-ullo, and what have we here?"

The bobby who'd been guarding the street side was looking down at him from the top of the mound. He stood up, not bothered at all, and let Adrian take over.

"This is my home, sir. I mean, it was."

"That so? Tell us your name, sonny."

"Andrew Wragge. I've got my Identity Card."

"Told us you were staying away."

"I've just come back."

"Reported yourself at the station?"

"No . . . I thought . . . well, I wanted . . . something to remember her by."

He'd judged it spot on, the stumblings, the catch in the voice, the courage.

"Poor lad. You won't find much. They've started to put a few bits and bobs in the coal-shed. You're not supposed, but I'll nip back over and watch the street a couple of minutes, give you a chance. Then mind you clear off down to the station and report yourself alive."

"All right. Thanks. Thanks very much."

There was a little heap of near-rubbish on the coal-shed floor, the Mickey Mouse clock with its glass smashed but still ticking, the twelve-armed brass dancer from India, one brass bowl from the scales, two black enamel saucepans, a flat iron, the lace table-cloth for Sundays, the tea-pot. Something had hit the teapot making a dent across the top and wedging the lid tight, but he used the dancer's top-knot to lever it open. Far more notes than when he'd been in on Saturday. A couple of ration-books too. He counted the money — £19. 10s. 0d. Where . . .? Of course, Mr Trinder. She wasn't a whore, but she wasn't above a bit of a present, either. The ration-books were new. They had no names or addresses on the front and none of the coupons was gone. You could be sent to prison for that. Mr Trinder knew about prison. He'd talked about Toby being "out".

Andrew put two of the notes in his wallet and the rest in his shirt pocket, right in under his coat and pullover, then stood weighing the ration-books in his hand and thinking. Suppose one of them had been a blank identity card . . . Andrew, dead in the bombing after all, disappears. Adrian begins his existence. He has a ration-book and identity card, but he has never been registered for call-up. He is invisible to the war-monster. The machine-gun waiting at the ditch will clatter its bullets through blank space . . .

Too late. He'd already told the bobby he was alive. And in any case it wasn't worth it. The most important thing was to stay clean. Just the same way you kept your body fit with exercises every morning so that you'd be up to the physical demands of any part you might one day play, so you kept yourself fit in other ways. A career was like Dad's ship, sliding through the ocean but liable to gather as it went encrustations, trailing growths, slowing it down, clogging it almost to a standstill. You wanted as little of that as you could manage, no alliances, no obligations. Perhaps Mr Trinder could have found a blank identity card for Adrian, but in finding it he would have suckered himself on to the hull, trailing unseen lengths of his other interests behind. There must be none of that. Andrew wasn't even going to give him back the ration-books, because then there'd have been a slight connection. He wasn't going to hand them in at the police station either. There'd be questions.

On his way up the back alley he lifted the lid of Mrs Arlott's dustbin and stuffed them well in under the mess, then used a stick to rake a pile of potato peelings on top. Passing down Fawley Street he stopped and showed the bobby the brass dancer, which he'd taken for that purpose.

"Very nice," said the bobby. "You got something to remember her by, then. Off to the station with you now."

His voice was gruff with emotion. Andrew thanked him again, with a choke in his own voice. A couple of streets further on he tossed the dancer up into a static-water tank and heard it splash. No alliances, no obligations, no memories, no regrets. Clean.

He pushed through swing doors into the Woodbine-reeking fug of the police-station front office. Four or five people were waiting, crouched on hard benches in the long boredom of war. A woman wearing a fur coat and a pork-pie hat like a man's was at the counter watching the desk-sergeant write in a ledger. At the movement of the doors she turned.

"Andrew!" she said. "Oh, thank heavens!"

It was Cousin Brown. The sergeant stopped writing and looked up.

"Found him already?" he said. "There's service for you."

"Oh, my poor boy," said Cousin Brown. "How dreadful for you about your mother, but how wonderful that you are alive. Of course we believed that you must have been at home when the bomb fell but they had failed to find you. They had telephoned The Mimms, thinking you were still with us, so I came in to see what I could do. You will come home with me,

54

won't you? There is no need to pay the slightest attention to what Father says — in the evenings, that is."

Andrew shook his head. His dazedness was real. He felt exhausted, too feeble to summon the protective presence of Adrian to act for him.

"Half a mo, madam," said the sergeant. "That's not how we do things in the police force. I'll have a few particulars from the young gentleman, *if* you don't mind."

Fetching a fresh ledger he wrote with deliberate slowness. Andrew let Cousin Brown spell out the address of The Mimms as his new home, but as soon as they were out on the steps he said, "It's very kind of you, Cousin Elspeth, but actually I can't come back to The Mimms now."

"Oh, but . . ."

"I've got a job. Acting. It's only Dopey in the panto, but it's something."

"My dear boy! I *quite* understand. You have somewhere to live?"

"Mrs Habermas — she's the stage manager's aunt — she's got my ration-book so I can eat there. I'm sleeping under the stage."

Cousin Brown stopped in her stride and turned to face him. It had started snowing again, crumbs of whiteness dribbling through the grey air. Her breath rose in a cloud. Her eyes glittered.

"How too lovely for you! And of course you cannot tell the authorities lest they try to prevent you. I shall not. I know you are doing precisely what you should. Perhaps I shall come and see the show this afternoon."

"I suppose I'll need somewhere to live when the run ends. It'll be term again then. I don't want to swap schools — there's Higher Cert this summer."

"I shall have to think about that. We have several connections in Southampton — old servants and so on. We shall look after the rent, of course, and I must talk to Mr Oyler about making you an allowance . . ."

"But . . ."

"Nonsense. You positively must have independence. Now, Andrew, I have a proposal to put to you. To anyone who did not think as we do it might seem heartless, raising such a matter

55

so soon after your poor mother's death, but I know you will understand. I barely slept following our talk last week and was quite disappointed to discover when I rose that you had already left. The thing is, I have decided to revive the Players this summer. I shall put *Tempest* on. I want you to help me."

Andrew gazed at her, saying nothing. The feebleness which had overcome him in the police station was back, worse. He'd had two dry Bovril sandwiches between performances last evening, nothing since then except the orange tea in the dockers' den. He hadn't got to bed till quarter past four and Toby had come to sit on his mattress at seven. Mr Trinder's name hadn't had any effect, so he'd had to get up. He should've gone to Mrs Habermas for breakfast, but he'd wanted to get to Fawley Street and look for the tea-pot before anyone else found it. He'd seen Number 19 in rubble. He had spent other energies with the black girl. The croak and bark of the Dame echoed in his mind. He seemed now to understand what Cousin Brown was saying, but to have no feelings about it, no answer, either way. *Tempest*. They'd done scenes from it for School Play, two years back. He'd been Miranda, of course. The summer. Call-up. She'd done *Tempest* before, she was saying, almost got Gielgud . . . Samuel had been first rate, most unusual, as Caliban. Was she giving him Ferdinand? All Ferdinand had to do was persuade an audience that Miranda wasn't stupid to keel over at the sight of him — Adrian could do that — any woman. Ariel? Come unto these yellow . . .

"It is a tremendous risk," Cousin Brown was saying. "Anyone else would say you were far too young, but I am fully confident that you can take Prospero."

Uncle Vole?

Out of the icy sky, unwilled, Adrian floated down and cloaked him round — not just a fantasy version of himself but a real person, definite, different. It had never happened before. Now Adrian smiled with his lips, spoke with his voice, serious, modest at the honour, confident in his powers.

"I'd love to try," he said.

The room was almost as famous as the face, designed for Adrian Waring by David Mlinaric, and therefore having featured regularly in all the glossier supplements and decor mags. Despite the fame it shared something of the face's willed anonymity, a lavish domestic setting for almost any male star from the more intellectual end of the spectrum. The logs that burnt in the wide fireplace were cedar, the Baksts were originals, the modern water-clock whispered and tinkled in a niche framed by a miniature proscenium arch — a fancy perhaps of the owner's, not the designer's, with its suggestion of time being as fluid and transient as a stage performance, and vice versa. Any actor might have had such a notion. The one element in the room that spoke of particular choices was contained in the niche that balanced the one with the water-clock. There the three shelves were crowded with a clutter of small objects, porcelain pigs and shepherdesses, souvenir mugs, glass knick-knacks, treen, a brown stoneware ink-bottle, a Japanese doll with a parasol, lace-makers' tools and so on. Not only the choice but the clutter of the arrangement seemed foreign to Adrian. He had his own knick-knacks, mostly mementoes of his career and other dramabilia, disposed about the room, but in a far more composed and orderly fashion.

Adrian, in a black tracksuit and training-shoes, was lolling in the corner of the immense white sofa, flipping to and fro through the pages of an elderly and rather battered book, its linen cover embossed with a picture of a Zulu warrior picked out in black and gold. The girl who had been with him at the preview came in wearing a blue butcher's apron, looking no less appealing in it than she had in her furs. She was carrying a saucer which she held in triumph under his nose.

"Olive oil," she said. "You told me water but it kept sticking."

On the saucer was a large round of butter embossed with the representation of a sheep.

"That was my Cousin May's," said Adrian. "Elspeth's was a horse and old Arnold's a bull. No doubt Samuel had selected them as appropriate when rationing started."

"Which was yours?"

"I never had one of these. The ration would not have filled them by the time I came on the scene. That's why Samuel made the little ones."

She turned to the left-hand niche, probed with a spider's delicacy among the clutter and brought back one of the smaller moulds.

"You mean this is you?" she said, holding it out on the flat of her palm. He glanced at the whittled scrap and nodded.

"Was me," he said. "Now, listen."

As he started to read from the book his voice changed, became creaky, sing-song, intense. It was light in tone and without any apparent tricks or distortions was unmistakably African.

Look now, my father! There on the plain far away is a place of the white men. It is called Stanger. There, where is the white man's town, stood the great kraal Duguza. I cannot see, for my eyes are dark; but you can see. Where the gate of the kraal was built there is a house; it is the place where the white man gives out justice; that is the place of the gate of the kraal, through which Justice never walked. Behind is another house, where the white men who have sinned against Him pray to the King of Heaven for forgiveness; there on that spot I have seen many a one who had done no wrong pray to a king of men for mercy, but I have never seen but one who found it. *Ou!* The words of Chaka have come true: I will tell them to you presently, my father. The white man holds the land, he goes to and fro about his business in peace where Impis ran forth to kill; his children laugh and gather flowers where men died in blood by hundreds; they bathe in the waters of the Imbozamo, where once the crocodiles were fed daily with human flesh; his young men woo the maidens where other maids have kissed the assegai. It is changed, nothing is the same, and of Chaka are left only a grave yonder and a name of fear.

"Please stop," she said. "I'm sorry, but it's horrible. I can smell the blood in your voice . . . What's wrong? I mean you can go on if you want. Of course you were doing it beautifully. Only . . ."

He closed the book and laid it aside, then put up his hand and took hers. She laid the saucer of butter on the floor and sat, snuggling in against him. His fingers caressed gently at her neck.

"How long have you known you had second sight?" he said. "I'm not sure I approve. Perhaps I shouldn't have taken you to the sale."

"But I loved it!"

"Perhaps I shouldn't have gone myself."

"What are you talking about?"

"I used to read *Nada* aloud to Samuel while he was whittling the moulds. He was illiterate, though he had a remarkable verbal memory."

"Good as yours?"

"Different. When I revive a part I have to relearn it. We read through *The Tempest* before we started rehearsals. Samuel did Caliban from memory, having played the part once, some twenty years earlier. He scarcely needed a prompt."

"What did you mean about second sight?"

"Samuel used to say that he could smell the blood in my voice. I don't think he can have been a Zululand Zulu — I gather that very few of them went to the diamond diggings — but Zulu was his language. He thought the voice I used appropriate, at any rate. *Nada* is a rum concoction — I didn't then realize how rum. No doubt as history it is very highly coloured — *Richard III* blacked up, and to something of the same effect. One thinks of Haggard as a writer of mildly mystical adventure yarns — *King Solomon's Mines*, and the rest nowhere."

"Daddy read us that. The old witch gave me nightmares for weeks."

"Gagool. *Nada* might be described as an attempt to tell a story from the point of view of a male Gagool."

"Ghastly."

"Successful, in my opinion, and also in old Samuel's. He can have been only a few years younger than my uncle, so the reign of Chaka would have been fairly recent history to him. He had come to the mines when he was sixteen, intending only to earn enough money to buy himself a gun and then go home, but my uncle got his claws into him and kept him, and eventually brought him back to England."

"And he made this?" she said, taking the butter-mould out of the pocket of her apron. "I wish I could try it, but I haven't got a thingy to fit."

"A cylinder. We should be able to find something of the right diameter — take it to Dowley and Dowley and beg an inch of plastic water-pipe off them. If nothing's right I'll get one made."

"Darling A. I've a nasty feeling it's going to stick — it isn't the right wood."

"Samuel managed, and he wouldn't have been able to get hold of olive oil. That must have been pretty well unobtainable."

She half lay, leaning against him, moulding her body to his and responding with faint cat-like movements to the rhythm of his caress. Her own fingers turned the buttermould to and fro to let her inspect every facet of the wizened little object.

"It *is* you, A.," she said. "I can see. Are you cold? Shall I warm you up?"

Folding her hands together with the mould between the palms she blew gently into the hollow. Adrian reached out and wrenched her grip open.

"Ow!" she said.

"You must be more careful what you do and say, my dear."

"Please don't call me that. It makes me think you might send me away."

"Not unless you force me to. I have a particular talent which has enabled me to achieve what I have, and that is the most precious thing in the world to me. I am prepared to be entirely selfish about it, and to sacrifice anything and anyone in order to preserve it."

"Oh, yes. I've always known that. Only . . ."

"Now, my dear . . ."

"Please, A.!"

"I am doing it deliberately, in order to force the lesson home. I am beginning to believe that you possess some kind of psychic knack, at least where I am concerned."

"It's only because I love you so much."

"Possibly, but it would make no difference. There are certain things . . ."

"Like Bluebeard?"

"In a sense."

"All right. Only . . ."

"Be careful."

"I'm trying — really I'm trying. Only I don't see how I can be careful when I don't know what I'm supposed to be careful about! You said you'd tell me, but . . ."

"Did I?"

"Well, you said perhaps."

He took the mould from her, glanced at it and then pushed it out of sight in the pocket of her apron.

"When you were at the sale did you look out of the front windows?" he asked.

"Oh, yes! That peculiar little tower!"

"The dovecote. I found Samuel's body hanging there early one morning. The previous evening had seen our first performance of *The Tempest* Samuel was a naturally gifted actor. Given other circumstances he might well have been a major force in the theatre of his day. Even as it was I would number him among the handful I have worked with whom I regard as having talents equal to my own."

"And he spent his whole life buttling!"

"Yes. He took a few minor parts in some of my cousin's other productions, and did a remarkable Caliban for her in the later Twenties, the role he repeated the night before he died."

"What happened?"

"I was not at the inquest. I gave my evidence of finding the body by affidavit, because I had by then been called up. I believe other evidence was given of his having been depressed and at least partially estranged from his wife and the other servants in recent weeks. That was certainly the case. The final straw, it was thought, was that he had been dismissed for a piece of gross impertinence just as the performance was about to start. In the circumstances a verdict of suicide was pretty well inevitable."

"He didn't, though, did he?"

"What do you mean?"

"Only I can't imagine you . . . whatever else was happening in your life . . . I mean after a good first night . . . you don't have to tell me, A."

"What are you talking about?"

"Just the way you haven't said what *you* thought. I can feel you sort of pushing it all outside you . . ."

His fingers froze in their caress. His arm disentangled itself. With a slow but lithe movement, dance-like in its control of every muscle, he slid himself forward along the sofa, stood and turned. She had shrunk back against the sofa's arm and was staring up. It would have been impossible to tell whether his countenance of patriarchal sternness expressed real inward anger or some other emotion, or whether it was a further step in what he had called "forcing the lesson home", or perhaps no more than a move in the game of dominance and submission on which their relationship to some extent depended. At any rate the pause before sentence was, for once, mistimed. He made his face blank and looked down at his right foot. She followed his glance.

"Ooh!" she squeaked. "I'm terribly sorry. I put it there. It's all my fault."

Still in silence and still with the same muscular control he bent and standing on one leg unlaced his shoe, to which the saucer of butter now adhered. He peeled them apart and used the saucer's rim and the toe of the shoe to scrape each other and thus ease the main mass of butter into the fire — all of this with the calm movements of a priest at the altar, so that you would have thought he stood on a pat of butter every day of his life. The fire hissed and the butter began to burn at the edges with a soft unwavering flame. Watching it with his back to her he spoke, now clearly acting, indeed hamming.

"Upon such sacrifices, my Cordelia, the Gods themselves throw incense."

"Is it all right?" she whispered. "Oh, A., I wish I understood you!"

He turned, shaking his head.

"And I do not wish you to make the attempt," he said. "In fact, I forbid you to do so."

"It's too difficult. I *can't* help thinking about you, can I?"

"Then you must think about me as I am now. I am going to put *Nada* away in a drawer. You may keep the butter-moulds, but you must not play with them any more."

"But it was your idea going to the sale."

"It turns out to have been a mistake. I thought . . . no, never mind what I thought. I now think it is time for bed."

She rose and put her arms round him. They stood in front of the fire rocking gently to and fro, like a couple on a dance-floor too crowded for circulation.

"It's going to be all right, isn't it?" she whispered.

"How much butter was there in that saucer?"

"A bit over half a brick. It's surprising how much you can squidge in."

"Five ounces, say. Almost three weeks' ration. That should be enough."

ONE

"I say by sorcery he got this isle," croaked Samuel Mkele.
"From me he got it. If thy greatness will revenge it on him —
for I know thou darest, but this thing dare not . . ."

"Wake up, Stephano," said Cousin Brown.

"Me? Oh, sorry," said the flabby bald young man one along
from Andrew. "Dreadfully sorry. Where are we?"

Andrew leaned across and pointed at the line.

"Oh, yes. That's most certain. What's most certain? I do
wish I understood what was going on."

"Caliban is persuading you to murder Prospero so that you
can be king of the island," said Cousin Brown. "He has just said
that he is afraid to do it himself, but that you are not. You are
drunk enough to agree."

"Roger. Like this? That'sh mosht shertain!"

He glared at Cousin Brown with quivering jowls. She smiled
encouragingly and nodded to Samuel to continue. The cast
were new to each other as actors, though all, except Andrew,
being local were at least acquainted in other ways. Cousin
Brown was planning four open-air productions, two under the
cedar on the vicarage lawn and two in a similar garden in a
neighbouring village. There was no likelihood of attracting
audiences the extra miles out to the stage in the garden at The
Mimms. The read-through was taking place in the Village
Institute, a barn-like hall used as a British Restaurant at mid-day
and still smelling strongly of Woolton Pie and non-egg custard.

Most of the readers were as dire as Andrew had expected,
or worse, stumbling, wooden, uncomprehending. Stephano
(available after being invalided out of the navy — his unhealthy
look was the result of his illness, Cousin Brown had whispered)
had just shown a flash of promise and Trinculo (the old boy

who with his daughter kept the post office) had the right clown face, bunch-cheeked and gleaming. Miranda was a strapping, freckled land-girl with hair between mouse and ginger who read in a whispering monotone. The courtiers and sailors, apart from the bosun, were all going to be played by women, some of whom gave every appearance of having been press-ganged — indeed Antonio, cast no doubt for her permanent sulk, seemed already on the edge of mutiny. Cousin Brown was playing Gonzago, which she read with energetic clarity, and since she had not yet managed to cast a Ferdinand or an Ariel she took those parts too.

The star turn was Samuel Mkele. He knew his lines, having played Caliban twenty years before and barely forgotten a word. When he was in a scene he rose from his chair and spoke with full energy, as though already on stage, accompanying the words with wild, expressive gestures. Andrew had intended to read his own part with some reserve, deliberately not committing himself to it. To do so, he felt, would be to fall in completely with Cousin Brown's plans, to accept her idea that he should stay at The Mimms the whole of the Easter hols (today was their first Friday, and the read-through had been timed to coincide with the arrival of his bus from Southampton) and make a start on the immense series of rehearsals which she said were going to be necessary to "lick the cast into shape". Since his first dazed acceptance of Cousin Brown's proposal outside the police station that icy morning, the project had become more and more forbidding, in its absurdity, in its difficulty, but mostly in its boringness. She expected him out here not only all these hols, but almost every weekend of the summer term. Andrew had spent most of his bus-ride considering possible ways of explaining to Cousin Brown that he wasn't going to do it. The problem boiled down to one question, whether or not to tell her about Lily Butt.

Lily lived a few doors down from his new lodgings in Itchen Way. She was a bus conductress, a dyed blonde with green eyes, no chin, and a small mouth made up into a scarlet pout. She had a big bust and wide hips, and strapped her uniform belt in as tight as she could to show them off. Off duty she let her hair down over one eye, like Veronica Lake. Andrew had spotted her in the street almost as soon as he moved into Itchen

65

Way. A week later the three-speed on Dad's old bike had finally jammed so he'd had to take the bus to school. It had been Lily's. He caught it the rest of the week, worked out the return times and caught them too. Thursday, standing on the platform, waiting for the stop, he'd asked her if she'd like to go to the Saturday hop with him. She'd stared and started to laugh. She was twenty-three and he didn't look more than sixteen. But he'd laughed with her and her tone had changed. Later she swore that she'd only agreed as a way of getting into the hop and picking up a Yank — they wouldn't let girls in alone so as to keep the tarts out — but he knew it wasn't true. He had made it happen. He had made her see, not an optimistic little twerp, but what? . . . amusement, fun, fizz, novelty . . . Adrian. At any rate she had stayed with him all evening, dancing closer and closer and when the doors closed she had taken him into the bus depot by a side door and used the back seat of her bus. She'd obviously done it before, often, with lots of blokes, but he didn't mind. Despite the cold and the smell of sweat and oil and Craven A it was much better than the brothel. Andrew had only gone back there twice more after that first time with the black girl before realizing that wasn't what he wanted. Paying was cheating, cheating your own powers, your private magic, the magic that had made Lily say yes. Not that she wasn't almost a tart herself. She wouldn't have had much time for Andrew if he hadn't been able to afford her tickets for the Saturday hops, and drinks and fags when you could get them, and visits to the flicks other evenings. He needed Cousin Brown's allowance for that, which was one of the things that was going to make it difficult to explain. But he had come to the reading certain that he was going to back out of doing any more than he absolutely had to.

In his opening scenes, with Miranda and then with Ariel, Andrew had expressed this lack of commitment in his voice, simply reading his lines in almost impersonal tones. But then he had called Caliban from his cave and everything had changed. Samuel had risen from his chair into a half crouch and with spread hands and bulging eyes had croaked his first curses with such energy that Andrew had been forced to respond, to rise too, and gesture and answer with equivalent power. The current had immediately flowed between them, that thrill of

66

contact and response which Andrew had read about but only partly and faintly experienced in school plays when one of the other boys had been sparked by Andrew's own energies to act above himself for a few lines, or even a whole scene. This was different. The energies didn't have to be supplied, because they were there already. As Caliban had slunk back to his chair the rest of the cast clapped.

"There!" said Cousin Brown. "Now you can see what it is *all* going to be like, if only we put our backs into it. Enter Ariel. 'Come unto these yellow sands . . .' "

It had somehow been impossible to go back. From then on, without trying to match Samuel's total involvement, Andrew spoke his lines with definite commitment. Tedious though the whole idea had seemed, he was going to do his best to make the play work. If it meant spending most of the hols here, just getting back to see Lily once or twice a week, missing some Saturday hops next term, well, too bad. He was, he realized, a bit bored with Lily anyway. She was too easy. She was like the sailors in the back rows at the panto, who had laughed at anything the Dame gave them.

". . .As you from crimes would pardoned be, let your indulgence set me free," he said and snapped the book shut, smiling.

"Capital!" cried Cousin Brown. "Absolutely capital! You know, in spite of everything we are really going to make a go of this. Now, one of the convenient things about *The Tempest* is that apart from Caliban and Ariel there are three sets of characters who do not meet until the final scene, and this means they can rehearse quite independently. So now we will split up and make some preliminary arrangements, to see what will suit everybody best. Prospero and Miranda, if you would go over and wait under the memorial tablet . . ."

Andrew rose and crossed to the far wall, where a panelled plaque declared that this Institute had been given to the village as a memorial to the glorious dead by the generosity of Sir Arnold Wragge of The Mimms. In a useless, momentary attempt to harden himself against his own terrors Andrew forced himself to look at the list of names. A dagger marked the ones who were missing, presumed killed. There were four others, besides Lieutenant Charles Wragge.

"Such a stupid waste," sighed a voice.

He turned. It was the Miranda girl.

"Hello," he said. "I'm Andrew Wragge."

"I know. I'm Jean Arthur."

He laughed with surprise. She blushed.

"I was trying to remember where I'd seen your face," he said. "Why aren't you in Hollywood?"

"Oh, it's stupid. Don't tease me. Mr Mkele was terribly good, wasn't he?"

"Yes."

"So were you. And Miss Elspeth's clever, putting on that man's voice. I'm terrible. I wish I'd never agreed. I know I'm going to let you all down."

"There's lots of time."

"I just can't think of myself saying the stupid sort of things I'm supposed to."

"It isn't you saying them, it's Miranda. That's what makes it exciting. I mean let's say you're actually not the type to keel over at the sight of a handsome shipwrecked prince . . ."

"I'm certainly not!"

"By the way, it looks as if I might have to bring you out a Ferdinand from school. My cousin Elspeth doesn't seem to have found anyone round here. What do you fancy, blond or dark?"

"Neither."

"Bald is going to be difficult."

She took him seriously for an instant, then laughed with his laughter. The tension between them altered. He realized that in spite of her robust, no-nonsense look she was probably very shy, and had actually forced herself to speak to him in much the same manner that he had been forcing himself to read the list of names. When she laughed her green eyes crinkled at the corners. He felt a tingle of interest.

"I suppose you're going to have to wear a beard to make yourself look old," she said.

He shrank, craned, thinned his lips, put a tic into his cheek.

"A beard!" he spat. "What do I want with a beard? D'yer think I'm Father Christmas, gel?"

She backed off a whole step from his glare.

"But that's Sir Arnold!" she whispered.

He straightened and became easy-going confident Adrian. Cousin Brown had a very good eye, he thought. There was something Miranda-like there, a directness, an unhandled innocence, a sense of never having seen — well, *looked* at — a man. Her shyness was like her uniform, an outside layer, contrasting with what lay underneath, making it seem more exciting — if you could get there.

"I've half a mind to play Prospero like that," he said.

"Isn't Prospero supposed to be a nice old man?"

"I wouldn't fancy a dad like that — peeping round rocks, planning everything for me, rubbing his hands because it's working out the way he wants it."

"Oh . . . I haven't seen Daddy for more than three years. Three and a half now, I suppose. He was caught at Dunkirk."

"Mine was caught at Singapore."

"Oh, isn't it ghastly!"

"Worse for a girl, I expect. What about your mum?"

"She's all right. I suppose."

The change in tone, from yearning warmth to chill was very marked. You didn't talk about Jean's mother. What had she done? Taken a lover, probably. Andrew considered a moment whether to mention what had happened to Mum. No, save it up. He'd be seeing quite a bit of Jean. No point in wasting ammo.

"Where are you working?" he said.

"At Mimms Home Farm."

"Handy for rehearsals — you and me and Caliban."

"It's only just behind the plantation, though it's more than a mile round by road."

"What's it like, being a Land Girl?"

"All right, I suppose. Better than being an AT or something."

"They have quite a bit of fun, I gather."

She blushed, and then, visibly, forced herself to keep the conversation going.

"Not my kind of fun. I was in a hostel at first with eight other girls. All they could talk about was the boys they'd met at the last hop. I hated that, so I put in to be a cow-girl. You mostly have to live on the farm for that, because of early milking. Mrs Althorp — she's the tenant at Home Farm — wanted a girl.

69

Really she should have had two. We aren't supposed to be alone, but she persuaded them Dolly counted and I said I didn't mind."

"It sounds a bit lonely."

"Well, I suppose so. Mostly I'm so busy I don't notice. I hope Miss Elspeth isn't going to be much longer. She did say half past six, and I promised I'd be back to clear up after milking."

"How are you going?"

"I've got a bike."

"OK. You push off. I'll explain. It's just you and me and Ferdinand and we haven't got him anyway. I'll come over to the farm tomorrow and see if we can fix some times. Otherwise we'll just have to say our lines to and fro between the udders."

"You appear to have made an excellent start with Miranda," said Cousin Brown. "Oh, do get on, Brutus, it is not that steep. How I long for my Lagonda at times like this. I noticed you jollying her up. She is going to need a good deal of that. But she has the potential, don't you agree?"

"I said I'd go over to the farm tomorrow and try and fix something up about rehearsals."

"Ah, now. I was in any case going to talk to you about the farm. You will no doubt consider that you should be doing some war-work during your holidays."

"I suppose so."

"Mrs Althorp, Jean's employer, is a somewhat intransigent woman. She has come through a difficult time with her husband's death, and other things, so one must not blame her too much. I have had trouble persuading her to release Jean for what I would regard as a minimum of rehearsals, but if you were to work, say a few mornings a week, at the farm, then we would be in a position to argue that we had made up for Jean's lost time, and we could get that first difficult scene at least blocked in before you need to go back to Southampton. That would be a satisfactory solution, don't you agree?"

There was an odd emphasis on the word "satisfactory" which suggested that Cousin Brown was thinking of more than simple convenience, that she took a personal pleasure in the neatness of the solution, the arrangement of other people's lives. It was a moment of decision. If Andrew agreed, it would mean saying

70

good-bye to Lily. A fortnight till term. She would certainly find another bloke. And farm-work was not his idea of fun. But he had called Caliban from his cave and more than a voice had answered.

"OK," he said. "How do you see Miranda?"

"It is the relationship between you that really concerns me, and that in turn depends on your relationship with both Ariel and Caliban."

"It all depends on how beastly you want poor old Caliban to be."

"Exactly. That is the nub. We have to start from the point that Samuel is very strong in the part. Bestial but noble. Old, too — after all he is in fact only a few years younger than my father, at least Prospero's equal in age. This affects the balance of the play in what I hope will prove interesting ways . . ."

The pony plodded between the hedgerows. The blackthorn buds were swelling, pale dots in the watery evening light. Andrew had not yet fully adjusted to double summer-time, which had just come in, and the uneasiness added to the strangeness, the sense of moving between worlds which did not quite belong in the same space–time. Cousin Brown, absorbed in her plans for the production, seemed to forget that Samuel was sitting in the back of the trap and talked about him as though he weren't listening. Sometimes she forgot about the pony too, and let it drift almost to a halt and lower its head to try and browse at a patch of fresh-sprung grass on the verge.

"I see Prospero as really a bit potty," said Andrew. "He's got his magic power, but the power has done things back to him. Sometimes you can see it shuddering through him. I'd like to try that."

"My thought exactly! He is a shaman — the text says he falls into a trance in Act Five . . ."

"And Miranda when she's explaining to Ferdinand . . ."

"Of course. So those awkward moments in your first scene with her . . ."

"Not *her* losing interest. *Him* going dopey and shaking himself out of it . . ."

"*Dragging* himself out. The dark backward . . ."

"She'll have to feel it too — be a bit scared?"

"Perhaps . . . yes . . . but soothing too. Used to his fits. She

71

says so to Ferdinand. They must know each other extremely well, as well as I know my own . . . Dear me, is that a motor? It is extraordinary how some people manage to acquire the petrol."

The trap had heaved out of a dell of coppiced hazels. Just over the crest was a Rover Fourteen, black, facing towards The Mimms with its side-bonnet up and a man bending into the engine-space. He straightened and turned at the sound of hooves. Cousin Brown reined the pony in, but Andrew had recognized the coat and hat before he saw the face. Mr Trinder raised the hat.

"May we be of any assistance?" said Cousin Brown.

Mr Trinder held his hat over his heart, like a war veteran at an Armistice Day celebration. He glanced quickly at Samuel and Andrew, but with no sign of recognition.

"Would you be going anywhere near the camp, ma'am?" he said.

"The Americans? Yes, indeed. We pass the gate. But I fear a fourth passenger would be too much for Brutus. It is barely half a mile to walk."

"Perhaps the young gent would do us a favour and ask after Sergeant Stephens in Supply. Tell him how Mr Trinder's stuck out this way, and if he could send a truck with a mechanic . . ."

"Right-oh," said Andrew.

"Ever so grateful. Do you a good turn one day. Scout's honour."

The wink was in his voice, not his eyelid.

"What a peculiar man," said Cousin Brown, almost before the renewed hoof-beats could cover her strong voice. "A *spiv*, right out here in the country! No doubt he gets his petrol from his American friends — they seem to have such masses of everything. I think I told you in one of my letters that we now have American officers in the house, General Odway's staff, preparing for the invasion, if it ever takes place. May plays bridge with the General most evenings. Do you know, when they first arrived they brought their own drinking-water, in *tins*, shipped all the way from America, in case ours was not safe to drink! Think of the dreadful cost in the lives of our poor seamen! And we have had to move ourselves upstairs into the old nursery wing, though Father of course has retained his

72

study . . . Now, another problem with Prospero is to establish his *right* to behave as he does. His own dukedom has been usurped, but he is in definite sense also an usurper . . ."

Halfway down the drive to The Mimms the smooth tarred surface, laid to take the big American trucks, swung left. Cousin Brown flipped the reins as soon as Andrew had climbed down and the pony, brisker now with thoughts of home, took the trap scrunching down the unmended gravel of the lower part of the drive. The new road led out under arching holm oaks into what had been the park. At the point where it emerged into the open it was barred by a red and white pole which could be swung up to let traffic through. A soldier sat in a canvas booth beside the barrier reading a pulp magazine. He was chewing gum. His cap was pushed to the back of his head.

"Yeah," he said — as much a yawn as a word.

"I've got a message for Sergeant Stephens. In Supply."

"Right on up the track. Take a left at the crossroads. Second Quonset under the trees."

"Thanks."

"You're welcome," muttered the soldier, already reading again.

On his earlier visit Andrew had seen nothing of The Mimms by daylight. The road led across a shallow sloping valley. The house — red brick, red tiles, large white-painted windows, massive fluted chimney-stacks — stood on a platform of terraced gardens with woodland slanting away beyond and looking across the valley to the wood that crowned the opposite slope. The parkland between was dotted with coppices, whose shelter had been extended with screens of camouflage-netting to hide trucks, huts and tents. The main camp lay in the wood. It was from there that the tannoy sounded, loud despite the distance. It was playing "Is you is, or is you ain't, my baby?" now. A jeep came storming out of the wood and whipped down a side-road to one of the smaller collections of huts, but once there the driver merely climbed out and leaned against the mudguard, smoking. The scurry had nothing to do with urgency. That was how Yanks behaved. So was the waste of petrol.

A few yards before Andrew reached his turning a new object

73

came into sight, hidden till now by the alignment of the coppices. It was so odd that he actually stopped and looked. Well down towards the bottom of the valley, outside the fence that divided the camp from the ploughed field beyond, rose a squat, round flint tower, pierced with two rows of small holes. A dovecote, or something like that, plain and functional for its lower two storeys but crowned with a ridiculous top-knot like something out of a fairground with fancy pillars and bobbly bits and a green copper dome with a weathercock on top. More than anything it reminded Andrew of Mum slopping round the house in her slippers and apron but wearing one of her party hats to cheer herself up. It was a joke building, inviting you to laugh at it, just the way Mum used to when she was in one of those moods, so Andrew laughed and walked on.

His side-road took him up towards a coppice of sycamores which with their surrounding net hid half a dozen nissen huts. There seemed to be nobody about. Food smells floated on the breeze, unfamiliar and interesting, the oil they'd fried their evening meal in, mainly. It was nearly seven. Not much chance of finding this sergeant still in his store . . . But the door of the second hut was open, and light shone from inside. He tapped, heard a grunt and went in. It was a sort of office, a shadowy cave under the arching roof, lit by a pool of yellow light from a lamp on one of the three file-cluttered desks. A man was sitting at that desk reading his way through a document and making ticks on it as he compared it with another piece of paper. A black cheroot slanted up from the corner of his mouth.

"Yeah?" he said, not looking up.

"Sergeant Stephens?"

"Right."

"Mr Trinder asked me to tell you that his car has broken down about half a mile from the gate. If you could send a truck and a mechanic, he says."

"Jesus Christ! He figures we're over here for that!"

The sergeant spoke in a slow nasal monotone and went back to his figures. Andrew waited.

"You tell him . . ." said the sergeant.

"I'm not going back. They're expecting me down at the house."

"Uh. You visiting?"

74

"Yes. I'm here for three weeks."

"What's your name, sonny?"

"Andrew Wragge."

"That so? One of the family?"

"Sort of."

The sergeant made a note at the bottom of the sheet he had been checking and rose. He was extremely tall, about six four, but thin as a dangling skeleton, with a narrow muscular face, black brows and close-cropped grey-black hair.

"OK," he said. "Let's go."

He switched off his lamp and locked the door as they left. They climbed into a jeep and went bouncing down to the main track and then more smoothly off to the wood on the ridge. Here there were signposts with military initials, and whitepainted guide-ropes so that men could find their way around in the black-out. The camp seemed to spread endlessly off under the trees, but there were not many soldiers around. The tannoy was playing "Why don't you do right?" The cooking smells were strong, their foreignness making them seem to promise much more exciting tastes than British war-time food. The sergeant swung into an area of camouflaged trucks and braked beside one where a man's feet protruded behind the front wheel.

"Hey! Tony!" he said.

A grease-smeared face craned out below the running-board.

"Get a tool-box and tag along," said the sergeant.

"Look, I promised Captain Schwitters . . ."

"OK, OK, I'll fix the captain. You pack your tools."

The sergeant unfolded himself and loped away. His long, thin legs in their sharp-creased trousers ended in a pair of enormous boots, size fourteen at least, so his gait was that of a figure in an animated cartoon. The mechanic humped his toolbox into the back of the jeep and stood leaning against the side. He seemed to have no doubts about the fixability of Captain Schwitters.

"The officers, they figure they run the camp," he said. "Sergeant Stephens and the men, we know different."

His New-York-Italian lilt was very strong. A few minutes of him would be more useful than twenty gangster films.

"Are you from New York?" said Andrew.

75

"Brooklyn. You ever been in New York?"

"Not a chance yet."

"When you go, you never want to come away. This dump . . ."

His dark southern eyes looked out from under the trees. Across the valley the house was in shadow but the setting sun still lit the big chimney-stacks, whose smoke drifted into the pale spring sky.

"Does everyone feel like that?" said Andrew.

"It ain't home. You get pretty sick waiting. Eight months I been here, sitting on my ass. I got a girl . . ."

The movement of his hands accented his longing. He fell silent. To start him going again Andrew gazed around and said, "It seems a bit empty."

"Sure. Transit camp, ready for the invasion. When we start filling up you'll know it's gonna happen."

"There's a general and his staff moved into the house."

"Sure. It'll be this year. It gotta be. June, I heard a guy saying."

"What's your girl like?"

"She's great. She's . . ."

Tony's enthusiasm carried him on without further prompting until Sergeant Stephens came loping back. The engine seemed to start before the lean rump touched the driving seat. They went storming up to the camp gate with the horn blasting. The sentry slouched out of his booth to raise the pole.

"I'll get down here, please," said Andrew.

"Not coming for the ride?"

"No thanks. It's been fun, but I'm late already."

"Right. Say, you the kid who ran away from fifty million bucks?"

"Me? Oh, well, I didn't exactly run away. I got thrown out."

"But you're back to collect."

"I don't know about that. I don't even know if I want it."

"Jesus! Kids! Well, I guess it's your life."

"At least it isn't anyone else's. Thanks for the ride."

"You're welcome."

There was a sentry-box now inside the porch of The Mimms, with a military policeman — white helmet, clean uniform, gleaming boots, stiff pose, very different from Sergeant Stephens's casual lope and lounge.

"You Mister Wragge?" he said. "OK, pick up your pass at the front desk."

The hall had been turned into a kind of office with a telephone switchboard, desks, filing-cabinets, pin-boards. As Andrew waited for the WAC receptionist to find his pass he noticed another difference, in its way much more surprising.

"It's warm!" he said.

"I'm from Florida," said the WAC, "and I say it's cold."

"Last time I was here . . . I suppose they've got the central heating going."

"Just about stops the icicles forming," she said, cuddling herself sexily. She was not particularly pretty but wore a lot of make-up and looked as though she expected anyone who came through the door to make a pass at her. They probably did, too. It was almost part of their language, like the "You're welcomes".

The big radiator at the foot of the main stair was too hot to touch. How many tons of coke a week would that take? Three officers came down the stairs with files under their arms. They seemed to be working late.

"I'll chew his balls off," said one. "I've just been waiting for the chance."

"Better watch out or he'll chew right back," said another. "He's gotten himself a line through to GA3."

Their tone and attitudes expressed both urgency and frustration. They crossed into the Library from which came the rattle of typewriters. On the pretence of looking for the nursery wing Andrew moved on down the main corridor. The door of the Saloon was open so he peered in. The room was empty, the furniture not much changed, though moved to make room for a pool table. There were piles of *New Yorkers* and *Saturday Evening Posts* on a table near the door. The door of the Morning Room bore a sign saying GENERAL HIRAM D. ODWAY. A WAC officer came out carrying a wire tray full of files and talking angrily over her shoulder to someone in the room. She was decidedly pretty, with hair as yellow as butter — generals presumably could take their pick. In the Dining Room three orderlies were laying for the evening meal. The table had all its

77

leaves in but the cutlery was steel, not silver. There was iced water in jugs on the table, Coke bottles on the sideboard, thick coffee cups by each setting.

"For crying out loud," one of them was saying. "I tell him nineteen and he only sends seventeen!"

They fell silent at the movement of the door but as soon as Andrew backed out the furious mutters began again. The green baize door was hooked open and from down the stairs came the same smell of frying that Andrew had noticed in the camp. With it rose the bellow of male voices. Though he knew it was the wrong direction he ran silently down the stairs and along the lower corridor. The shouting came from the kitchen where four army cooks were getting the officers' meal ready. A man at the centre table was making most of the noise, bellowing his rage as he pounded great spreads of red meat with a rough-ended mallet. A second man yelled back as he sorted bits of vegetable on to salad plates. A third was scooping butter out of a half-gallon can on to another set of plates; whenever he tried to join in the argument he raised his scoop for emphasis, as if about to hurl its contents (a good week's ration) across the room. The fourth seemed to be trying to count portions of ham and pineapple, losing count at each fresh outburst of yelling, shrugging and starting again. Over all hung the blue haze of frying. It was a transfixing scene, the dreamlike mounds of unobtainable food, the furies who commanded them. It expressed something that Andrew had felt more diffusely upstairs, a sense of frustration, beyond boredom, of the huge weight of American energy and wealth bogged down, stuck, unable to get on with the job it had come to do.

"Outta the doorway will ya?" snarled a voice behind Andrew's shoulder. "Looking for someone?"

"I'm sorry. Where do the family . . ."

"They don't teach you Limeys to read, huh?"

The newcomer jerked his thumb along the corridor and hustled into the kitchen yelling at the disputants, louder than either of them, to lay off. Andrew moved off in the direction he had pointed. The rooms on his left, like the kitchen, had windows opening into daylight, now almost dusk; the ones on his right seemed to be coal-cellars and store-rooms, dark chambers running into the hill, their walls massively thick to

78

support the pile above. Halfway down the corridor stood a notice-board. "NO US PERSONNEL BEYOND THIS POINT. D. STERNHOLZ, LIEUT." Andrew sidled round it and went on.

The first door on his right disclosed a long vault with brick compartments either side. By the weak yellow bulb just inside he could see that it opened out into a great dark space. He paused for a moment to look, and as he did so Samuel Mkele came out of the darkness carrying a dusty bottle which he placed carefully on a shelf near the entrance. He had seen Andrew and turned.

"Supper pretty soon, Master Andrew," he said. "Do you want me calling you that? Or I jus' call you baas — you saying."

He had deliberately slipped his voice halfway through, from Hampshire to the nigger-talk he used with Uncle Vole. Andrew laughed.

"I don't mind," he said. "I suppose I'd get used to either. At least they're better than some of the things Caliban calls me. I say, congratulations on the way you played him. I didn't get a chance to tell you."

The old man was delighted but shook his head.

"Last time we had plenties good actors. Now it's just Miss Elspeth and you. The others . . ." He shrugged.

"And you," said Andrew. "Some of the others will get better, I expect."

Samuel shrugged without optimism and turned to another broad shelf which held a number of dishes protected by wire-mesh covers or pottery lids. Evidently this was now the family larder, the Americans having taken over the one which belonged to the main kitchen. A faint draught blew through from the wine-cellar beyond, smelling cool and earthy, making the vault feel like a natural cave, far older than the house; Samuel's solemn and dignified movements as he moved one of the dishes towards him and lifted its cover seemed like the preliminaries to a mystic rite he was about to perform in these depths, in order to keep the whole building above from melting into air, into thin air.

In fact all he was doing was dividing a half-pound slab of butter into four portions, using a schoolroom ruler to get the measurements exact.

"Did you ever play Othello?" said Andrew.

"Only learned the lines so I could understudy for Mr Howard, and rehearse till he came down. You'd laugh, the way we done it. I don't read, and Mary Jane, she reads just about good enough for cook books, so first she puzzles the words out and tells me, and I learn 'em, and then I go off and say 'em to Miss Elspeth and she tells me what it all means."

"You can't read at all? That's amazing."

"Baas Wragge, he never let me learn. He reckoned I knew more 'n enough about him, without that."

With his knife-point he lifted one of the sections of butter on to a brass letter-balance. The beam levelled exactly. Andrew watched, remembering the shock of excitement which had run through him down at the Institute, summoning him out of his hiding-place, forcing him to respond. There weren't a lot of parts for a darkie, but still it was a fearsome waste of a life, of powers and possibilities, come down to fiddling with butter-pats so that Cousin Blue shouldn't be able to complain. The old man seemed to guess his thought.

"Miss Elspeth, she talked a bit about me going on the stage," he said. "She knew it was only talk. Baas Wragge, he'd never let me. Mary Jane, too. You get only the one life. No point in crying."

He paused to concentrate on cramming his exact two ounces into a hole bored through a small block of greyish wood and then with a wooden disc of the same diameter as the hole pressing it out on to a silver butter-dish. The butter came out in a neat cylinder, its surface stamped with a capital A. He stood, looking dreamily not at the butter but at the disc which he held poised on his finger-tips. The knob on it was carved to represent the head of an old man, crude, but still recognizable.

"That's Sir Arnold!" said Andrew. "Did you make it?"

"And Miss Elspeth, and Miss May. D'you want I make you one?"

"Well . . ."

"And while I'm making it, you do something for me? You read me my old book?"

"What book?"

"*Nada*, it's called. Used to belong to Baas Charlie. Miss Elspeth, she give it me, 'cause of it being all about my own folk

80

back in Africa. She says how Mary Jane can read it for me, but Mary Jane don't read too good, so we never got beyond maybe a couple of chapters."

"OK, I'll give it a go if you like. When's a good time — it looks as if I may be doing farm-work in the mornings?"

"Right after luncheon. Nothing much doing then."

"Fine. I suppose I'd better go and find my room. How long till supper?"

Samuel took a gun-metal fob-watch from the pocket of his waistcoat.

"Six minutes before I ring the gong," he said.

TWO

"Down by the Africa statue at the end of Top Walk," Cousin Brown had said. "That brings you out at the Amphitheatre. You will know it when you see it. Such a shame we cannot use it this time. You will find a path going up through the plantation just to the right of the Green Room huts. Up there and over the stile and you are immediately below the farm-yard."

Top Walk was a terrace running for almost a hundred yards behind the house. Statues guarded either end, Europe first, wearing breeches, bushjacket and wide-brimmed hat and carrying a rifle under his arm while shading his eyes with his other hand and gazing towards the statue of Africa, a bare-breasted woman carrying a basket on her head. Between them the ground sloped away into a valley, wooded on the far side but on this side what once had been a huge sweep of mown lawn dotted with topiary but now was hummocky with brown winter-killed tussocks, though patched here and there with daffodils. Dead bramble stems arched out of the blocks of shrubs, and the yews had lost their shapes and become fuzzy mounds. It had rained in the night, and the air was full of the mixed smells of spring growth and winter left-overs.

Andrew did breathing exercises as he walked down the winding path that branched off at the Africa statue. He felt fully alive, fully himself. This was partly because it was a pleasant soft morning with lolloping white clouds, blue sky and sunshine, partly because he now knew he was committed to the production in August, but mainly because the decision had somehow been made while he slept that he was going to use the time between now and then to seduce Jean. Not "Have an affair with" or "Get off with". Not "Fuck" or "Lay" or anything like that. It was the actual process of getting there that mattered. That was going to be the test. It wasn't just a way of filling the next few months, taking his mind off call-up, and so on. It was a necessary and important proof of his hidden powers.

Too soon to make actual plans, though a farm should have a quiet hay-loft somewhere, breaks in the farm-work to do a bit of private rehearsal, not just the Prospero scene, Ferdinand's too, later . . . He was still brooding on possibilities when he reached the Amphitheatre.

Yes, he knew it when he saw it, but despite its name and the photographs in the albums it still surprised him. The stage was a paved oval, backed by a ten-foot yew-hedge pierced for entrances and with lichened statues of Greek gods at either end. Facing the stage was a semicircular back into which tiers of seating had been cut, slabs of paving laid stepwise up the slope with twin flights of real steps going down between them. Tussocks of grass now grew along the rows but someone had tried to keep the stage itself weed-free and had rough-clipped the openings in the hedge.

Andrew paused at the top of the seating, looking down, then walked down and climbed on to the stage itself. He stood and turned at its centre.

The lip of the bank hid the nearer ground, but the beech wood rose on his left and stretched away, curving gradually in to join the opposite slope. The whole valley was silent, empty, waiting for something. Not even a pigeon called. Andrew raised his arms in a gesture of blessing.

> "Ye elves of hills, brooks, standing lakes and groves,
> And ye that on the sand with printless foot
> Do chase the ebbing Neptune . . ."

He did the whole invocation. In the pauses he could hear the whisper of an echo, but he felt certain that however he lowered his voice the top row of seats would still hear every syllable, and be aware of the energies in the quiet words. Yes, you could do something here which people would remember for a long time. Such a pity, as Cousin Brown had said.

Behind the hedge he found a pair of what looked like small cricket pavilions, the Green Room huts, presumably, one for each sex. The path was obvious, slanting up through the trees, zig-zagging to take the steepest bits, but running in general towards the head of the valley. After a couple of hundred yards it crossed a ridge and dipped to a stile in a hedgerow, then rose through a cow-pat-mottled paddock to a muddy gate between two windowless flint-and-brick walls roofed with dull red tiles.

"Not a lot of you," said Mrs Althorp with a sniff. "Might as well go and help Jean muck out till cocoa. Carrie'll keep an eye on the pair of you."

Andrew answered with a smile, but Mrs Althorp was immune to charm, a severe, calculating woman who ran the farm because her husband had been killed, according to Cousin Brown, in a tractor accident last summer. Andrew believed himself to be pretty strong for his size, thanks to keeping himself fit with exercises. He found that mucking-out required a different kind of strength. It was back-breaking and blister-forming. He had to pick up forkfuls of dungy straw and sling them across the shed to the doorway, where Jean, working outside, picked up and slung them on to the muck-heap. There was little chance of conversation and in any case they were watched the whole time by one of Mrs Althorp's daughters, aged around nine. If Andrew rested for a moment she said, "Tired, mister?" in a half-jeering nag, copied no doubt from her mother.

At mid-morning they broke off for cocoa. As they crossed the yard towards the farmhouse Jean whispered with embarrassed urgency, "Don't ask about Dolly's husband."

Dolly turned out to be not Mrs Althorp but another woman, dull and floppy-limbed, part servant, part dependant, the mother of year-old twins who slept in a huge pram outside the kitchen door. Andrew perceived at once that Dolly didn't have a husband, and very soon guessed, from the snap of righteousness in Mrs Althorp's remarks and the seemingly submissive but also resistant tone of Dolly's replies, that the late Mr Althorp had been the twins' father.

The other cocoa-drinkers were the foreman, Dave, and his

83

grown-up but half-witted son, Brian. Brian was a sad creature. Andrew noted the forward thrust of the pallid face, the sticky down-dragging of the jaw as he attempted words, the barnyard cackle at a moment of excitement. Dave was also interesting, with a permanent dew-drop on his mottled nose, a gaze of stony aggression, and conversation interminably repetitious and so in the end comprehensible, despite the clotted accent.

As the holidays went by Andrew had plenty of time to study this pair, since Mrs Althorp divided operations into men's and women's work. She did this deliberately, and often at some inconvenience. At first Dave treated Andrew as a hostile intruder and spoke to him in a jeer. About anything else his tone was a whine of anger. Andrew had no problem coping with Dave's attacks — he let Adrian bear the brunt, listening with patient and respectful attention. On the fourth morning Dave became friendly. He showed Andrew how to do certain things, sharpen a sickle, use a hayprong to pick up a liftable load, and so on. His talk became more general. He confirmed with guffawing relish Andrew's guess about the twins' father, then explained how last autumn he had cornered Jean alone in an outlying shed, and described what he'd have done if she hadn't fought him off with a fence-pole. His account of the episode had the wrought and rhythmic quality of a recitation monologue. He evidently thought about it often, and told and retold it to his son when they were alone together. One of his ideas was that once he had broken Jean's resistance she would let poor Brian have his bit of fun too.

Jean had probably complained to Mrs Althorp, who had somehow persuaded her not to tell the Land Army supervisors who came round once a month — or perhaps Jean had been too shy. Mrs Althorp couldn't have run the farm without Dave, so since that time she had kept him away from Jean as much as she could, and when that wasn't possible had seen to it that one of her daughters was there too. The arrangement dominated the workings of the farm. Perhaps, Andrew thought, its real importance in Mrs Althorp's mind had little to do with protecting Jean, and was actually more of a sort of monument to the late Mr Althorp. At any rate, after that first morning she seemed to have decided that though there mightn't be a lot of

84

Andrew, what there was was still dangerous enough to be classified along with Dave and Brian, so he saw very little of Jean during his work at the farm. He didn't really mind. The test he had set himself ought to have practical difficulties, as well as psychological. It needed not only a dramatic shape — shifts and struggles and set-backs, leading to his eventual triumph — but also its own location, somewhere satisfying, right. Not the farm, with its dirt and smells and effort. Somewhere detached from the world. The Amphitheatre might be a possibility. When summer evenings came they could meet down there on the pretence of rehearsing. He might get a key to one of the huts. But that wasn't right either, somehow. Anyway, there was plenty of time.

There was another break at noon, for dinner. Andrew knocked off then and went back across the gardens to The Mimms for luncheon, as he had learnt to call it. Cousin Blue was very quick to pick on some of the things he said, always of course pretending to wish to help him, but really as part of her general sidelong attack on anything connected with Cousin Brown's activities, in this case the play. A typical snatch of conversation might go like this:

> Brown: I'll patch that shirt, Andrew, if you would bring it to me.
> Andrew: I'm afraid it's gone with the laundry.
> Blue: No, dear — gawn with the lahndry.
> Brown: Nonsense, May. We may say lahndry, but nobody under fifty does so. For Andrew it would be affected in the extreme.

Cousin Blue would then turn a sniff into a sigh and go back to her patience. Andrew, in fact, was grateful for these admonitions. The obvious ones, like not saying "marge", he simply adopted as sometimes socially useful — it would depend on who he was with. The more absurd he noted for the day when a part would need them.

Often he ate the mid-day meal alone. Uncle Vole had a tray in his study, and the Cousins' days were filled with little activities — not work, not play — which they felt had to be performed. Often these seemed to be little more than a defence against each other's intrusions. One or other of them sat on

85

various committees — the Village Institute, a home for the feeble-minded, the alms houses, comforts for the troops and so on. Cousin Brown was also a magistrate. Business of this kind took them at least to the village and sometimes as far as Petersfield, and then Mrs Mkele would pack them a luncheon basket to save them the slow journey home by pony-trap. After his meal Andrew went down to Mrs Mkele's cramped little parlour and read *Nada the Lily* aloud.

It was a challenge, he found. In fact the challenge was issued by the author on page four, in the clipped voice of an Englishman who has lost some cattle and been persuaded by his native servants to go to a local witch-doctor to see if he can help. While they wait for the cattle to be fetched the witch-doctor — a blind old man with a withered hand — tells the main story. Andrew had been put out — bored-in-advance, as it were — to see the size of the book he was going to have to plough through, day after day. But then he had come to the challenge:

> Neither has it been possible to render the full force of the Zulu idiom nor to convey a picture of the teller. For in truth, he acted rather than told his story. Was the death of a warrior in question, he stabbed with his stick, showing how the blow fell and where; did the story grow sorrowful, he groaned, or even wept. Moreover, he had many voices, one for each of the actors in his tale. This man, ancient and withered, seemed to live again in the far past. It was the past that spoke to his listeners, telling of deeds long forgotten, of deeds that are no more known.

Andrew found the old witch-doctor's voice with his very first breath and kept it throughout his readings, dry, quiet, not markedly different in weight and pitch from his own, and therefore capable of variations; not copied from anything he'd heard, Robeson or Samuel or the occasional darkie sailor who used to come wandering up from the docks, but right. Voices wouldn't always come like that, he knew. Often he would have to make them build themselves, slowly, trial by trial. But sometimes one would be there, speaking immediately from his inward cave, a spirit that had been waiting to be raised. Such times were important. They might seem like gifts, but then you had to give everything back, even when your audience was six

86

old dodderers in a country basement. Otherwise you betrayed the gift.

The dodderers, in fact, were a good audience. On the first afternoon it was only Samuel and Mrs Mkele, but from then on all the house servants came, and one or two from the cottages. They listened in rapt silence, apart from an occasional cluck of the tongue at some especially monstrous moment of savagery, the slaughter of the narrator's tribe or the trial scene when Chaka forces him to burn his right hand to the bone as a proof of his loyalty. The women knitted comforts for the forces, scarves, balaclavas and mittens. Samuel sat under the window, pecking with a knife-point at the block from which he was whittling Andrew's personal butter-mould, but for long intervals he would stop and sit motionless, apparently in one of his trances. He couldn't have been, because once Andrew came down and found him retelling the previous episode for the benefit of Jack's hunchback sister, who had missed it. He used all Andrew's voices and repeated the more striking passages almost word for word. At the end of the reading-hour he would join the polite clapping but not the clatter of comment. Only once, after the chapter about the murder of Balaka, he said something.

"You read pretty good, Master Andrew. I smell the blood in your voice."

The readings were satisfying in a way Andrew hadn't expected, nothing to do with his own performance. It was something about the audience themselves, their pleasantness with each other, their unity of outlook, the way they had managed to build themselves a satisfactory life in the spaces left to them by the family upstairs, a sort of unspoken conspiracy to be what they themselves chose while still fulfilling the demands of their masters. That may have been why they were so resentful of the presence in these spaces of the American cooks along the passage — much more so than the Cousins were of the officers who had taken over most of their normal living rooms. The feud this side of the green baize door was bitter and unforgiving, with poor Lieutenant Sternholz — young but shiny-bald and bespectacled, an embodiment of weak will, given to little gesticulations of impotence, fascinating to Andrew — trying to keep the peace. Reading to the servants

87

was very like reading to Mum, which Andrew had often done through winter evenings in Fawley Street, not that Mum could have knitted a mitten to save her life. And their content with themselves, their small certainties, were a bit like Mum too. Perhaps that was why Andrew felt so refreshed and encouraged by those after-luncheon hours — he could have a bit of his past without the wrench of going back.

The rest of the afternoon he had to himself. Cousin Brown had rescued for him from the Library, now occupied by General Odway's staff, a thirty-six-volume leather-bound collection of *British Dramatists*. Dutifully he started to read his way through, but the plays were dismal stuff, the jokes meaningless, the serious bits all wind and rant. If it wasn't raining he read an Act or two and then went out. The first few afternoons he mooned around the derelict gardens behind the house, did the Hamlet soliloquies in the Amphitheatre, staged imaginary duel-scenes. Then, by accident, he discovered an amusing hobby, climbing the house.

The latest move in the kitchen feud had been for the GI cooks to get an MP posted to guard the back door of the house, thus forcing the old servants to carry and show their passes each time they went in or out. Naturally the MPs regarded this as a boring chore, and did their best to get it stopped by enforcing the rules with unworkable rigour. Andrew had gone out, forgetting that he'd left his pass in the pocket of his farm-work trousers. The MP at the back door had told him to go round to the front and explain himself, and then someone would perhaps sign him through. In some moods Andrew would have enjoyed letting Adrian cope with that sort of confrontation, but not today. As he walked up the steep path between the woodland garden and the house he looked at the heavy façade with irritation. It was like a fortress, keeping him out . . . except that you could climb it. Yes, it was almost made to be climbed, with its ledges and nooks. If you could get up that first bit of drainpipe . . .

He wormed his way through the block of shrubs at the base of the wall and started. The drainpipe, it turned out, was the worst bit, because something the Americans had thrown down the sink in Samuel's old pantry had blocked the hopperhead, so that what they'd thrown down later had flowed on the outside. It wasn't very difficult, just filthy. There would have been an even easier way, he realized, if he could have climbed up to one of the windowsills of the big front rooms and edged along the ledge that joined them, running right across that façade, but that would have meant coming past the Morning Room, where General Odway sat stuffed with the secrets of the invasion. The appearance of a figure spread-eagled against the glass would have set off bells and sirens, and perhaps even bullets from the ebony-handled Colt which dangled against the General's taut-trousered rump. Not worth the risk.

The other risk, of falling, was small, but just enough to be exciting. There was a satisfaction too in the physical task, the balance and muscular control, the using of his hours of exercises. What he hadn't expected was the definite thrill he felt not only when he slid in through the open window he had spotted from the ground (it turned out to be Florrie's linenroom, with bath-towels airing) but while he was still climbing. Part of it was the simple childish pleasure of secrecy, of playacting spy or burglar, but part of it — though he only came to realize this slowly as he extended his routes and explorations on other afternoons — was subtler. It was a bit like the feeling he used to have walking the streets of Southampton after the panto, of being different, outside, free. Other people were trapped by the house. They had to stick to its rules, go up and down its stairs and along its corridors to get where they wanted to be. Andrew was not. He — at least in fantasy — could simply *appear* in any room he chose, act any role, vanish . . .

Tea was at four o'clock in the Schoolroom — fresh scones and jam, the tea itself much sighed over by Cousin Blue as she doled quarter teaspoons into the silver pot and then boiling water (again in indecisive dribblings) from the silver kettle that hummed beside her on its spirit-lamp. *The Times* crossword was done at tea, Cousin Brown reading the clues, starting with the quotations which she usually knew and then attempting the anagrams with the help of a set of ivory letters. Cousin Blue got most of the answers, without apparently thinking about them, and Cousin Brown put them grudgingly in, clearly hoping they would turn out to be wrong.

After tea on Mondays, Wednesdays and Fridays Jean came down to rehearse for an hour before milking. Andrew began to

89

see why Cousin Brown had insisted on the immense schedule of rehearsals she had arranged — in fact he said as much after the second session.

"That is a curiosity about such things," said Cousin Brown. "People make the mistake of thinking that one cannot imagine what it might be like to be able to do some difficult trick, when really it is harder for those who can do it to imagine what it is like not to be able to. I am not at all musical, but I can often perceive what my musical friends are driving at, while they remain exasperated by my inability to hear what they so easily hear. It is the same with you and acting. I am confident that we will get Jean there in the end, so far as her scenes with you are concerned. I am much more worried about the love scenes. I have not yet come across a remotely adequate Ferdinand in the neighbourhood, and we cannot keep one from a distance here all summer."

"What about me running through them with her?"

"Well, it's a possibility. At least she is used to you by now, and she is going to find those very difficult to start with."

This turned out an understatement. Cousin Brown was extraordinarily patient with Jean's numb stumblings but as the session closed she could not prevent a sigh.

"I'm terribly sorry, Miss Elspeth," said Jean. "I do wish you could find someone else."

"We mustn't give up," said Cousin Brown. "I'm sure you *can* do it. Your scene with Prospero is coming along quite promisingly."

"I suppose so. I just feel comfier with him."

"But they're both only me," said Andrew.

"Oh, no! Well, of course they are, but . . ."

"Shall I walk back with you? In case Brian's hanging around in the plantation?"

"Oh, all right. Thanks. I'll get my coat. Won't be a mo."

It was warm for April, so they had been rehearsing outdoors, under the cedar to the left of the terraces, with General Odway's staff jeeps bustling to and fro along the drive fifty yards away. Cousin Brown sighed again, this time with a genuinely despondent note, as Jean ran up to the bench on the terrace where she'd left her coat.

"Of course," she said, "Miranda might well be sufficiently

90

obsessed with her father . . . a middle-aged Ferdinand would certainly be easier to find, if your school-friends are unwilling . . . What do you think?"

"Well, he might be a bit older."

"A whole generation?"

"He says he's known a lot of women. But . . ."

"They are young lovers. The balance of the whole play . . . No, ridiculous!"

Walking with Jean down towards the Amphitheatre Andrew thought about it. Jean had not mentioned her father since that time in the Institute, but her yearning then had been obvious. Suppose he were to start by seeing if he could provide a substitute . . .

As she climbed the stile at the top of the plantation he said, "Going to the flicks tomorrow?"

"Yes. I told you. I always do on Saturdays."

"I'll come too."

"Oh. All right. Have you got a bike? It's eleven miles."

"There's one I can borrow."

He kept that tone of command throughout the expedition, paid for the tickets, sat well forward from the intertwined couples in the back rows, told her what to think about the films (the main feature was *Claudia* with McGuire and Young, story silly sentimental, acting deft enough to rescue it), refused to use her normal bun-shop afterwards and took her to a poky dark tearoom where middle-aged women in tweed hats talked in barking voices about WVS feuds. On the way home, as his legs tired (the bike belonged to Jack's sailor nephew and had a rack of a saddle and no gears) he put on a burlesque of age which made Jean laugh and encouraged her to join in by laying her hand against his shoulder to help him up a hill and then as they crossed the crest leaving it there for a few moments while they free-wheeled down.

On the Monday he played Ferdinand young and dashing, but let the mask slip at times to reassure her in Prospero's voice or tease her stumblings in that of his generalized dotard. A very faint improvement began, which Cousin Brown noticed and understood.

"Well done," she said afterwards. "A most ingenious ploy.

But you will need to be extremely sensitive how you proceed."

Andrew agreed.

Uncle Vole kept to his study all day, a book-lined den immediately below the Schoolroom, looking out over the back courtyard towards the plantation. Here, despite the dollar-funded heat in the radiators, he would heap logs on to his fire until the flames began to roar so loudly up the chimney that he became alarmed and doused them with a watering-can kept there for the purpose. He would then ring for Samuel to clear up the mess and rebuild the fire. The books on one wall were fakes, concealing doors — to his private WC, to a strong-room, to the electric lift, never used in peacetime by any other member of the household but now permitted to take meals up to the Schoolroom. Uncle Vole seemed even shakier than he had on Andrew's January visit, and sometimes stayed in bed all day. He never referred to that episode and showed no wish to talk after supper, so Andrew rose with the Cousins and left him to his port. He and Cousin Brown settled in what was called "Mother's Boudoir", a bright room cluttered with chintzy furniture and cabinets of Venetian glass, while Cousin Blue went downstairs to play bridge with General Odway. Cousin Brown had kept a diary of every theatrical production she had ever seen, running now into several volumes. She brought these out after supper and started to go through them with Andrew, expanding from memory on what she had written. Often neither the plays nor her own views were of much interest, but Andrew concentrated, knowing this was something he might not get many chances to listen to. Cousin Brown had seen Irving, of course, and Bernhardt — not only on the London visits, which she described as "ludicrous" — but in Paris too. She had seen all the Granville Barker Shakespeares. She had seen Terry and Campbell, Tree and du Maurier times beyond counting, and the débuts of Olivier and Gielgud and Evans, and almost everyone now working. She had seen Robeson's Othello. Though stage-struck she was not starstruck. She had absolutely no awe of reputations. Through she admired fine acting she was always more interested in the production than the performances, and had the knack of making both vivid enough for Andrew to recreate in his own imagination.

These sessions sometimes lasted a good three hours, and would have been impossible if her sister had been in the room, sighing and interrupting. Andrew got a glimpse of how Cousin Blue spent her evenings when he found a major on the stairs one morning, standing under the landing window and checking the money in his wallet, a sight that would have been unusual even in a GI. Andrew said good morning and the major looked up, half his mind still calculating.

"That your auntie who's been skinning us at bridge?" he said.

"My cousin, really. Has she been winning?"

"Has she! A dollar a hundred the General likes to play. Your cousin plays a mean hand."

"You mean she's been cheating?"

The major took the suggestion seriously for a moment.

"Don't think so," he said. "It takes two to cheat at bridge, you've got to work it out between partners, and we cut in. She's just one sharp little old lady — you bat an eyelid and she'll know which side of her the king's sitting. Three nights back she took ninety-eight dollars off the General — looked like he was going to bust a gut."

"I'm surprised she hasn't suggested you play for meat and butter and things."

The major's eyebrows rose towards his crew-cut.

"She's been dropping hints," he said. "We didn't take her seriously."

"I'm sure she'd rather have butter than dollars," said Andrew.

"Well, I guess . . . Anyway, thanks."

The effect on the rations in the Schoolroom was immediate. There were often second helpings of meat, and canned pineapple and peaches. There was maple syrup for the breakfast porridge, and other odd luxuries. But Cousin Blue took most of her winnings in butter. Andrew had expected her to keep her loot for herself, but she made a point of sharing it round, much enjoying the predicament in which this placed her sister. Cousin Brown responded in various ways. She made a point of complaining of the canned taste. She insisted that Samuel should continue to use the small moulds he had made — it really wouldn't do to sit down to one's meal with more than a week's ration in front of each place. She shrugged but did not try to

93

rebut Cousin Blue's arguments that bridge winnings didn't count as black market — they were really only a sort of present. She pointed out that Andrew was still growing and work at the farm was hard, so he certainly should take what was offered. And that being the case it would be a nuisance to the servants if she herself had to be treated differently.

In fact the new arrangements caused considerable trouble downstairs. The American cooks were outraged and set about making Lieutenant Sternholz's life yet more of a misery. The family servants too disapproved strongly. They had welcomed the democracy of rationing, which had even given them a certain power, since it was Mrs Mkele who supervised the details of the share-out. She told Andrew that in the early days of the war Cousin Blue had argued that the whole household's butter ration should come upstairs and the servants be content with margarine, which they were used to — "as if I'd ever of allowed the muck in my kitchen before that Hitler went and made a nuisance of himself! It's not that I enjoy sending up scraps and morsels. That's never what I became a cook for. But some people like to behave as if there wasn't a war on."

Cousin Blue of course paid no attention to these mutterings, though very likely she was aware of them. In fact the discontent probably added to her own purring pleasure over her success. Andrew had quickly become aware of her knack of spotting the weak sections in other people's defence-lines. What seemed to be hesitant, dreamy, half-irrelevant comments were deliberate probings. In any kind of daylight she wore mauve-tinted spectacles, concealing the sharpness of her glances. Life at The Mimms had for years been a three-cornered struggle, unending because in any contest between two of the players it had been in the third one's interest to see that neither triumphed, but now Uncle Vole was steadily weakening and an end was in sight, so the conflict between the sisters intensified. It was fought on all fronts, in committees and other charitable works, in orders and counter-orders to the servants, in the regime of Uncle Vole's sick-room (there was now talk of having a nurse permanently in the house), and so on. Since Cousin Brown had established a salient with her revival of the Mimms Players and the introduction of a new fourth member of the family, Cousin Blue set about weakening both, not of course by direct attack, but, for instance, by her helpful corrections of Andrew's accent and vocabulary, and references to dear Charles having gone to Eton.

Probably it was for some such motive that she brought up the idea of the tours. It happened one evening when they were halfway through supper — just the three of them, as Uncle Vole had stayed in bed all day.

"Andrew dear," she said, "I've been thinking — these poor Americans, so uncultured. Not that it is their fault. They have never had our opportunity to live among lovely things."

"Lieutenant Bryce tells me he is writing a doctoral thesis on Cyril Tourneur," said Cousin Brown.

"But he is an officer, dear. Those poor men in the camp, almost savages, listening to that frightful music all day. And the dreadful thing is that in eight weeks' time they will be in France, and most of them will be dead."

"Don't be absurd, May. Nobody knows when the invasion will take place."

"General Odway told me. Well, not in so many words, and I'm sure he did not realize. It was just two or three little things he said. Anyway, it is to be the first week in June."

"May! You must not tell anyone. You must never mention it again. Not that I believe you can be so sure."

"I know my duty quite as well as you do, Elspeth, thank you. Of course I shall have to tell Doctor Spurrier that we must postpone the National Savings committee. The roads will be quite impassable. They are bad enough already, with these dreadful motor-lorries and whatdyecallums."

"In that case you must think of a different reason for asking Doctor Spurrier to postpone the committee. I'm sure you will have very little difficulty in thinking of something plausible."

"If you insist, dear. What was I saying? I do so hate being interrupted. It muddles my poor old brain. Yes, Andrew, I think we should arrange for you to conduct some tours of the house and garden for those unfortunate men in the camp. General Odway says that we may take them into the Saloon and the Dining Room when his staff is not using them."

"Why do you insist on involving Andrew? If you think it a good idea you should undertake it yourself. Andrew knows next to nothing about this house."

95

"My poor chest . . . And Andrew has such a fine voice. It is beginning to sound almost gentlemanly. And I will tell him all about the house."

"I think it a thoroughly tiresome notion. Nor do I see why Andrew . . ."

"It is too late to back out now, dear. General Odway has already given the orders and it would place me in a very embarrassing position if we were to change our mind . . ."

Of course it turned out that the only orders General Odway had given had been to tell one of his staff to see that the Saloon and Dining Room were unoccupied between two and three on three afternoons next week. The camp was outside his sphere of command. But before they realized that no GIs might be available to come on the tours Cousin Brown had counter-attacked against Cousin Blue's manoeuvre by taking the project over, to the extent of spending an afternoon leading Andrew round and telling him the little there was to be said about the various rooms and objects — books nobody read, pictures by painters no one had heard of, furniture which Cousin Brown herself described as hideous.

"Of course you will be able to make something of the Sargent," she said, "although it is not thought to be one of his better works — in fact Rex Whistler described it to me as a pot-boiler. But it will give you a chance to recount the family history, and Father's adventures in the diamond-fields. Everybody seems to be fascinated by diamonds."

They were standing by one of the tall Saloon windows, looking back across the room towards the fireplace, above which hung the picture she was talking about. On Andrew's earlier visit the room had been lit by a few low lamps around the fireplace and the painting had been in shadow. Cousin Blue's only serious suggestion about the tours she had foisted on him had been that he could use the picture to help the poor Americans understand what they were fighting for, but she had left it to Cousin Brown to tell him about dates and things.

Pot-boiler or not, Andrew found the picture interesting. It showed the late Lady Wragge sitting on a sofa in that very room, though the furniture had been rearranged and the position of the door altered to make the composition work. She was about forty, with immense dark eyes and gaunt face (ill?

96

dying?). Her red-brown hair was piled high and she was wearing a pink silk tea-gown whose froth of lace was pinned with a focal diamond. May, about nine, already in blue, cuddled against her side staring straight at the artist, while Elspeth in russet velvet sat more stiffly at the opposite end of the sofa, her head twisted to greet her father and brother who seemed just to have arrived from somewhere outside with guns incongruously under their arms. In the shadowy background, barely discernible, a black servant was carrying a tea-tray into the room.

It was pure stage — a scene from a Pinero comedy. Everything said so, the lighting, the way the artist had moved the walls of the room as easily as if they'd been flats, and the characters displaying their features in one direction, all (except the nearly invisible Samuel) with that controlled exaggeration which actors adopt to make the audience grasp their inwardness. The artist had put that in, of course, not the sitters. He'd decided to paint Lady Wragge's anxious would-be beauty, May's self-centred appeal, Elspeth's earnest but frustrated eagerness, Sir Arnold's cynicism and aggression, and Charles's . . . Charles's what? The face was firmly enough drawn but was itself weak, with something of the mother's fret, something of the father's spite, but no real signposts about what sort of man the boy was going to become, as though the artist had actually guessed he wasn't going to become anything.

It was a very clever picture, Andrew thought. In a funny way it reminded him of the Dame's monologue the night Mum had been killed. The slave's contempt . . . the painter's contempt for his paymaster. The faces were likenesses, prettified or handsomized but not beyond recognition; the glamour of wealth was there, everything Sir Arnold had asked for. The contempt was hidden, for strangers to perceive.

"I suppose they might be interested to be told that Sargent also painted Rockefellers and Vanderbilts. We are, after all, as *nouveau* as people like that. If you were to inherit, you would be only the fourth generation."

"Sir Arnold told me . . ."

"You need pay no attention to that. It is possible that you are already named in his will — he has never told us anything about its provisions, except that we are to have Charles Street. I

97

should be perfectly contented with that, though I doubt if May would. I am sure that there is no question of Father leaving either of us this house. Perhaps it would have been different if one had married, but now, mercifully, we are past that possibility. I must say, Andrew, I most earnestly hope that you will be the beneficiary. It would smooth your path so enormously not to need to worry about money, to be able to take only those parts which are worthy of your talents."

"I want to do everything."

"Ah, no. There is so little time in life. You must concentrate only on the best. You have so much to give, Andrew. You must not waste it on second-rate things. All my life I have fought and fought not to waste my own small talent, and in spite of the difficulties I might have achieved something. If it had not been for this dreadful war. People were just beginning to take my productions seriously. I had such plans. We were going to run special trains to our 1940 season. Ah, well . . . I suppose we must get on. You might well conclude by taking them down through the woodland garden and showing them the dovecote."

She had turned as she was speaking and was now leaning against the folded shutter of the window with one hand on its sill in a pose of hopeless yearning, and gazing across the young barley of the lower park towards the woods beyond. On the right of the view, further down the slope, rose the curious tower with its primitive drum crowned by its fancy top-knot.

"Now that is genuinely old," said Cousin Brown. "The lower part was a working dovecote from the sixteenth century — the mechanism for harvesting the squabs is interesting, but you must try not to let anyone swing on the ladder. Young men find it a great temptation but it disturbs the doves. The owner of the old house added the gazebo in the eighteenth century, for reasons of his own. You can get the key from Samuel."

By the time he found there might be nobody coming on the tours Andrew had begun to look forward to them. He wanted to see whether he could hold an audience with the thin material he had to offer, so on impulse he went up to the camp. It was mid-afternoon and raining. The tannoy was playing "Oh what a beautiful morning" for the third time that day. A different

98

soldier was at the gate but reading what looked like the same magazine and chewing as if on the same gum. Sergeant Stephens was in his cave, but now a corporal was working at the second desk and at the third sat a blonde WAC, pretty in a big-featured busty way. The clatter of her typewriter competed with the rattle of rain on the hut roof.

"Jesus," said Sergeant Stephens. "Why come to me? I'm Supply."

"I thought you might tell me who to ask. I mean, is there an entertainments officer?"

"Sure. Lieutenant Dooley — Entertainments, Sport and Sanitation."

"Thanks. Over at the main camp?"

"Hold it. You won't get to first base with Dooley. He'd sooner be fighting you Brits than the Krauts."

"He might be interested in the plumbing. It's, well, lavish."

The sergeant took the joke for serious. His thin but mobile lips tilted his cigar back and up, a gesture expressing calculation. Andrew had seen it so often at the flicks that he was amused to find it in real life. He guessed the sergeant was sketching possible moves in the game he played against the officers, looking for small advantages.

"OK," he said. "Leave it to me. How many passengers will you want?"

"Oh . . . about twenty at a time? Fewer if you like."

"Right, three tours of twenty, fourteen hundred hours, Tuesday through Thursday."

"Thank you very much."

The tours went rather well. Anything was better than the boredom of the camp. The men brought cameras, and photographed everything with each other in front of it. Sergeant Stephens came on all three, thus adding point to the joke Andrew had prepared about the painter of the family portrait. The second time he brought a flash-gadget for his camera, so that he could do interiors, and Andrew was gratified to find himself talking without a blink or stumble through the brief astounding glare. Last of all they trooped down through the woodland garden, where windflowers and primroses were sprinkled under the first bright leaves, and then out along a

99

farm track to the dovecote. Sergeant Stephens marshalled the men into groups of six and sent them up the narrow spiral stair while Andrew held forth.

It was a drum inside as well as out. The nest-boxes covered the wall from shoulder-level almost to the ceiling. The only light came through two rows of flight-holes which ran all the way round above and below the boxes. The floor was a shallow funnel with a hole in the middle, the idea being that every couple of months somebody would come and shovel the bird droppings down the slope into the space below, where they rotted down to manure for the gardens, but because of the war nobody seemed to have done this for a year or more, and the centre of the floor was several inches deep in muck. The projecting nest-boxes left a narrow strip almost clear of drop-pings round the edge of the heap, so Andrew got his six hearers to crouch there while he showed them how the dovecote worked.

The principle was that you harvested the young doves just before they learnt to fly. To get at the nest-boxes you climbed a ladder which slanted up close beside them and was fastened top and bottom to a couple of beams which pivoted round a central pole, so that standing on the ladder you could push your way round, reaching into box after box and taking the birds out to see if they were big enough to eat. It still worked, though Cousin Brown said that the dovecote hadn't been used for meat since the Wragges had been there, even during the wars. Their menus were adjusted to pheasant, partridge, woodcock and quail. Pigeon, she said, were highly indigestible. But Lady Wragge had stocked the dovecote with white ornamental birds and until the war one of the young gardeners had gone regularly through the nests to take out and destroy any young cross-breds of wild birds, so the ladder had been kept in good repair. But it was so covered with droppings — Andrew had scraped the bottom few rungs clean for his demonstration — that there was no danger of the young men — in their best uniform for the tour through a rich folks' house and in any case a lot more fastidious than Tommies might have been — giving in to the temptation to swing on it and disturb the doves. The doves, in fact, were very little put out by these visits. By no means all the nest-boxes were full, but a few birds would be perching on sills

100

as Andrew appeared out of the stair door and these would either duck out of sight or flip across the gloom to a flight-hole and be gone. Their whiteness made the moment beautiful.

When the third tour ended and Andrew had bolted the ladder back into its fixed position with its foot close by the door he stayed for a moment to catch the doves' return. As usual his imagination started to shape a piece of theatre into the space. It would have to be film, of course. The camera looking up, as he was. A girl on the ladder — peasant dress, but lots of leg. Everything foreshortened. The white doves whirring past. Sunlight slanting through the flight-holes, making the roof invisible. The girl looking down, happy, excited, saying something, not noticing that up beyond something . . . a trapdoor, slowly opening . . .

It was as though his imaginative power had by its magic caused the thing to happen. Not that the trapdoor opened, but it was there, just discernible in the planking of the shadowed ceiling. Of course it would have to be, now he thought of it. You'd need to get into that silly structure on top, even if it was only there to be looked at from the house. Andrew picked up the piece of broken slate he had used to scrape the lower rungs and slowly climbed the ladder, cleaning the droppings off the rest. The trapdoor wasn't bolted so he pushed it up and climbed through.

From three large arched windows the spring light dazzled in to the bare space. It was an octagon with a rounded ceiling under the outer dome. The windows were very dirty. It was the peeling whitewash which made it seem so bright after the gloom of the dovecote. He looked at the view. Funny — you couldn't see the house from any of the windows, though there was what looked like a window in that direction on the outside. It must be false, behind the one blank wall. The other four walls had niches for statues. And the ceiling had been painted. You could see that, where the whitewash had peeled. There was a dove, with a thin-fingered hand reaching or pointing towards it. A foot, too, opposite the blank wall, standing on an odd curved something. Other bits, all as meaningless as scraps of jig-saw.

For all its brightness and its nearness to the house (you could see the dovecote from all the front rooms) the octagonal space

101

seemed extraordinarily secret and remote — an eyrie on a crystal cliff, waiting for its nest. Andrew looked slowly round.

Yes, he thought. We'll need something to lie on, of course.

O N E

Andrew's first thought was that it oughtn't to have happened that way. A chance for a moment of drama had been muffed. He should have been the first to meet the man — wheeling his bike up the drive on a Sunday evening on his way back to Southampton, and there would have been this stranger wandering down, shabby, battered, but with a soldier's spine, looking about him with wondering vague eyes. The questions, the leap of understanding . . .

Instead it had all happened while Andrew was off stage.

My dear boy,

You will be surprised to receive a letter from me, since we expect to be meeting again in so very few days, but I feel I must warn you that something decidedly startling has happened. As far as you are concerned it seems to me very bad news, though certain things you have said suggest that you may well have mixed feelings on the matter.

The fact is that a man claiming to be my brother Charles has returned to us, as it were from the dead. He — if it is indeed Charles, but though I have not yet made up my mind it is simplest to write on that assumption — is much altered since we knew him, but then he has lived a very hard life for more than twenty years, having lost his memory in the attack in which he was assumed to have been killed. He still remembers none of that, nor indeed anything much else in his life, either before or for some years after. Until recently his earliest memory was of waking on a park bench in the rain in some northern town and realizing that he did not know who he was. This was

103

some time around 1930, he believes, though he is vague on many matters that are supposedly within his recollection. Since then he has barely survived, doing numerous jobs, obtained one imagines by his being well-spoken and evidently a gentleman, and then lost again.

So he might have continued, had it not been for this war. He was in Hull in the winter of 1942 when he was caught in an air raid. A bomb landed on the shelter in which he had taken refuge, killing half the occupants and burying the rest alive. By the time he was dug out he was in a poor way and was taken to hospital. While there he began to have a series of what he calls visions. He is unable to explain how these differed from ordinary dreams, except in their vividness, and the way they remained with him after he woke. Nothing happened in the dreams, except that he saw certain objects — a stuffed stag behind a billiard-table, a round tower standing in a green field with a structure like a greenhouse on top, a picture of a negro carrying a silver tray into a room, besides two or three other things less remarkable to those who know this house. Both while having them and afterwards he was convinced of the reality of these "visions", and further-more he asserts that from the very first time one occurred he became aware of his own real name, Charles Arthur Wragge.

He made some attempt to interest his doctors and others in his "visions" but was unable to get them taken serious-ly. He simply wandered about, surviving by begging (he seems to have neither ration-book nor identity card). In some ways this is the hardest part of his story to credit — I do not remember seeing a tramp since the beginning of this war. Be that as it may, some two months back he entered a public library to keep warm, and so as not to be ejected pretended to be reading a newspaper. His eye happened to be caught by a name in a company report: Father's name.

It took him some weeks to discover where we lived and then to make his way here and nerve himself to face us. He came, he says, not for the money but to try to ascertain the truth about himself, and especially whether anything in this house coincided with the details of his "visions". The American sentry at the door sent him round to the kitchen entrance and Mary Jane came out and talked to him. Quite properly, she sent for me.

I was not at first much impressed, but having heard him out I took him by way of experiment up to Mother's Boudoir and stood him at the window. He was silent for some while, though he betrayed signs of considerable agitation. Then he said, speaking like a man in a trance, so low I could barely catch the words, "The ladder went round and round".

Now, when we were small girls Charles used to steal the key of the dovecote and make us climb the ladder, with him at the bottom, and set it spinning, fast as he could drive it, with the doves whirling out around us. I can remember his laughter and May's screams echoing together. Unfortunately I was not able to test this particular memory further, as May, who was in the room at the time, immediately blurted the story out. She, I may say, appears to have decided that there is no question but that the man is Charles. Father has been poorly and has refused to see him. I myself waver. Certain things that he says and does, such as the moment when he first saw the dovecote, seem utterly convincing, others less so. We have of course sent for the lawyers, but unfortunately the active partners in the Winchester firm are away fighting and our affairs are in the hands of old Mr Foley, who is somewhat past the responsibility.

We have also to consider the problem of Charles's wife, who is now as you know in Australia. Since she has remarried, and that marriage would become bigamous should this man indeed prove to be Charles, we have thought it kindest not to worry her until we stand on firmer ground.

I tell you all this, of course, so that you may give yourself time (wartime mail services permitting) to consider your own position before you see us on Friday. I need hardly tell you whose side *I* would be on, should it come to a contest. May I at least advise you not to commit yourself in any way (tho' as a minor you may not be legally free to do so) until you have yourself consulted solicitors. Mutton and Boot in Bargate are I believe a very good firm, if their office still stands after the bombs.

Yours affctntly,

Elspeth Wragge

Wartime mail services permitted, just. The letter had come by the Friday post and Andrew found it when he went back to his lodgings to change out of his school uniform and leave his books. He read it through twice, and then tried to do as Cousin Brown said and consider his position while he cycled the twenty-four miles out to The Mimms.

It was mid–May now, pasture and plough and woodland all green as salad, and the underwoods smoky or skyey where the sun dappled through on to the bluebells. Cousin Brown had drawn him a map of a route along bye-lanes, safer she thought than the main roads with their thundering convoys of tanks and lorries; but now, as if brought on by the same forces as the uprush of summer growth, the pressure of armies round the ports increased every day until it was more than the main roads could hold and it squeezed itself out into narrower and yet narrower lanes, clogging them with grumbling khaki monsters. The pressure was not just physical. The whole landscape was tense with it, vibrated with it, with the churn of big engines, the rattle of tank-tracks, the scurry of despatch-riders, the clank clank of a mechanic repairing a bren-gun-carrier in a farm gateway . . . the busy hammers closing rivets up . . .

June, the GI at the camp had said. The first week, General Odway had hinted to Cousin Blue. The tensions gathered not just to the focus of the ports but also to a point in time, a few days, less than a month. Their energies seemed to suck every-thing into that moment. Andrew, pumping his way up the hills, was a fleck, a straw, a gnat, battling against the whirl of the vortex. He almost felt, as you do in a nightmare, that at any moment the new bike would melt away and he would be plodding hopelessly towards ever-more-distant safety. When Cousin Brown had quoted the bit about the hammers last week-end he had of course pictured himself playing the king, musing alone and noble through his sleeping army. Now, with the real armies jostling round him, he couldn't get out of his

mind the image of Bardolph, rubbed out of the script unnoticed, hanged off-stage.

The nightmare made it impossible to think about Cousin
Brown's letter. He still believed that he didn't want The
Mimms, and its immense fortune, but in spite of what he had
always told himself he had found that he would prefer to miss
out on the noble poverty too. The comforts of his new
existence — the lodgings Cousin Brown had found for him, the
allowance she gave him, the good-as-new-bike with its five-
speed gear and drop handles — were well worth having, but it
wasn't just that. Money gave you a sort of psychic space around
you. You didn't have to spend your time jostling among the
sweaty and anxious. You moved on a larger stage. He would
like something out of Uncle Vole's will. Cousin Brown,
though, seemed to be asking him to choose between having
nothing and having everything. He couldn't make up his mind.

About six miles from The Mimms the lane dipped through
beechwoods, crossed a main road and began to climb the last
long hill before running along an undulating ridge and finally
dropping to the valley that held the house. An immense
ammunition dump filled the woods by the crossroads, long
stacks of shells and ammo-boxes stretching away out of sight
between the pale grey tree-trunks. Andrew had come to regard
this as a landmark, an almost-there point. Just this one more
hill. The main road was busy as anywhere, but beyond it the
pressure of armies dwindled and he could think. He pushed
both the nightmare and Cousin Brown's letter out of his mind
and thought instead about Jean.

Last Sunday he had kissed her for the first time, leaning
yokel-fashion across the stile below the farm, pretending to be
old-man-exhausted after the scamper up through the plantation, barring her way without seeming to; then moving on with
rehearsed naturalness to complain about having to ride all the
way back to Southampton . . .

"O, most dear mistress, the sun will set before I shall
discharge what I must strive to do."

That had been Adrian/Ferdinand, as he helped her across the
stile. A pause, looking into her eyes, still in the part, then
Adrian alone — quizzical, amused, professionally condescend-
ing.

"You'll have to practise a bit, you know."

She had waited, hypnotized, and let him put his arm round her shoulders and then break the spell by a brief brushing of lips, absolutely unfrightening. He had let go before she could push him away, laughing at the fun of play-acting the lover. She had begun to laugh too — with relief, mainly.

As Cousin Brown had said, he was going to have to be extremely sensitive how he proceeded. Keep the momentum up, but not hurry or scare her. More "practice" this week-end. At the stile again, but a bit longer? See what offered. Saturday after, if it was the right kind of flick, take her to the back rows. Then . . . Then it would be almost June. Amusing if he could beat the invasion to it. But not essential.

"This is Andrew," said Cousin Blue. "Andrew, this is your cousin Charles. My brother, you know."

"How do you do, sir?"

Andrew shook the trembling hand. The man frowned.

"Andrew?" he murmured.

His tweed jacket and grey flannels were slightly too small for him, though he was only a couple of inches taller than Andrew. Out of Uncle Vole's wardrobe, of course — he'd have sold or lost his clothing coupons, if he ever had any. Andrew had expected him to be bald, like Uncle Vole, but he wore his silvery hair brushed back over the ears. His face was mottled and veined, purple over the bridge of the thin nose, and his mouth stayed slightly open in repose, as though he were about to drag it down in a grimace like poor Brian's, but he spoke perfectly clearly, though in a tone of bewilderment.

"The other branch," said Cousin Blue. "Don't you remember about Father quarrelling with his brother Oswald before he went to South Africa? I told you again last evening. We found dear Andrew only this Christmas. He is here to help Elspeth put on her little play."

"Ah. The play. Yes. Of course. So we are long-lost cousins, Andrew. Though I have been lost longer, I suppose. What a rum story."

"Not a relation for a breakfast, sir," said Andrew.

The man blinked and shook his head. He looked at his sherry glass.

"But it is . . . ah . . . almost time for supper, is it not?"

His voice was baffled, as if he was in a waking dream, where without warning a meal can become a different meal. The headshake had been right too. But the involuntary blink before — had that been different, a response to another sort of ambush?

Cousin Blue laughed. Andrew had never seen her so lively.

"I expect it's a quotation from Tennyson or someone," she said. "You must not tease poor Charles, Andrew. His memory is coming back, but it is still rather patchy — isn't it, dear?"

"Comes and goes, comes and goes . . . ah, Elspeth, allow me to introduce your cousin . . . tsk . . ."

"Andrew and I are already well acquainted, thank you, Charles. I trust that the bicycle is still behaving."

"Going like a bird, thanks. Down hill, anyway. I'd have been earlier, but the lanes are crammed with convoys so you keep having to get off and climb into the hedge to let them past."

"Father is to have supper with us," said Cousin Brown.

"No!" said Cousin Blue. "Really he can be most trying. Do you know, Andrew, Father has been pretending to be ill and has refused to meet Charles, and now he is going to spring himself on the poor boy over supper."

"I . . . I shall be delighted to . . . er . . . see him again," said Charles. "I suppose he is much changed. Not that I remember him clearly. Just a presence I sometimes think I can recall."

"Now, Andrew," said Cousin Brown. "I want to talk to you about the rehearsal arrangements. I have the diary over here. If you will excuse us, Charles."

Andrew followed her to her desk by the further window of the Boudoir and joined in the pretence of looking at the rehearsal schedule. She kept her back to the room but signalled him round to stand sideways so that he could glance across to where the others were talking in front of the fireplace. Cousin May was whispering, her gestures ones of warning. The man reassured, made calming movements with his fingers. Andrew decided not to give him a private name yet. There could only be one Uncle Vole, but Charles might be one of any number of Charleses. He tried to recall the family portrait in the saloon. The face . . . hard to tell. It had the weakness, but it had been battered by time and poverty and (to judge by the mottlings)

109

drink. The boy's soft nose might have hardened into that beakiness. But the pose was spot on, with the right hand in the trouser pocket and the left holding the empty sherry glass in the exact hesitant gesture of the portrait.

"What do you think?" said Cousin Brown.

"Did he stand like that before he saw the picture?"

"You noticed? Yes. In here, when I first brought him up."

"I don't see how . . ."

"No more do I. We are presented with a few very striking details, but because of his loss of memory we have no way of testing them or anything else. I have only one straw to clutch at. I am convinced I have seen him somewhere."

"On the stage?"

"I have been racking my brains and going through the diaries. It would have been some very minor part. Chekhov? Or is it that he has become a Chekhov character now?"

"He could have acted a bit and still be your brother. I mean, he used to."

"Charles was an admirable Aguecheek. I have to admit to a bias. I do so much want *you* to be the one who inherits."

"Elspeth," called Cousin Blue. "Charles has just remembered . . . Hurrah! There's the gong! I must say all this excitement does wonders for the appetite. Dear Charles! So happy to have you back!"

It looked as if Cousin Blue must have started losing at bridge — at least butter seemed to be back on rations again. Cousin Brown and Uncle Vole each had about two-thirds of a cylinder left, Cousin Blue less than half that. Charles had an ounce-size cube in front of his place, but Andrew had a perfect cylinder, stamped with a small "a" what's more, to distinguish it from Uncle Vole's capital. Only the colour told him it was marge — quite fair, since his ration-book stayed in Southampton, but he'd become used to the luxurious crumbs from General Odway's table.

Cousin Blue did almost all the talking, mainly about the years before the First War, trilling and giggling as she sweetened every scene — Christmases in the sun above the spread vineyards of Constantia, Mediterranean dusks viewed from under the awnings of *Diamond*, tennis parties at The Mimms,

110

Fourths of June at Eton, Goodwood trips in the trio of Silver Ghosts — into panto-fairy prettiness. Cousin Brown's deep-voiced contradictions added an occasional demon-king note. Charles, between them at the bottom of the table, played a quavering Prince Charming — not a difficult part, but well done. Andrew began to see what Cousin Brown meant about the problem of disproving his story. You couldn't pin him down in a falsehood or contradiction, ask him about things Cousin May couldn't prompt him on — Eton, or his regiment, for instance. There were just one or two weak spots. You could go to Hull, find out if a shelter had been bombed that winter, check the hospital records . . . But here, even when he did admit to a memory, it was in a dreamy way, as if he couldn't be quite sure. He didn't make the mistake of remembering too much, either.

"You *can't* have forgotten tripping Canon Golightly into the perch-pond!" Cousin Blue cried. "It was one of the funniest things!"

"I'm afraid for the moment . . . perhaps it will come back."

"Very likely," said Cousin Brown.

Charles nodded, smiling, deaf to the tone of doubt. Andrew was not very well placed to watch him. Charles was at the far end of the table and Andrew was along the left-hand side, next to Uncle Vole. The noise of the old man's scrapings and gobblings drowned most of Charles's murmurs. Andrew hadn't seen his great-uncle for nearly three weeks now, and he looked a lot shakier than last time. The Schoolroom was almost too warm for comfort, but the trembling mottled hands seemed hardly able to hold the spoon and fork, and though Samuel only half-filled the glass it seldom reached the blue-lipped mouth without spilling. It took Andrew a little while to realize that though Uncle Vole's face was bent right down over his plate to eat, his eyes were rolled up under the bristling brows to peer along the table. The big silver ornament that usually stood in the middle was missing too.

About halfway through the meal Uncle Vole spoke for the first time. The wine was white, South African — it had been the cue for Cousin Blue's Constantia memories — and as Samuel floated silently up to fill Charles's glass for the third time Cousin Blue made a little ripple of tongue-clicks and shook her

111

index finger urgently, just above table level. Charles put out his hand to cover his glass.

"Fill it up," snarled Uncle Vole.

The glass was filled, but from then on remained untouched, though once when Charles reached absent-mindedly for it he snatched his hand back, clearly in response to a kick under the table. The glasses, Andrew now noticed were larger than usual. His own had only been filled once and there was a jug of water in his reach, but not in Charles's. Usually during suppers in the Schoolroom Samuel stood between the sideboard and the door to the lift, but this evening he had chosen a different place, rather awkward because the table was a bit too wide for the room, almost directly behind Cousin Blue's chair. He could see Charles's face from there.

Was Charles aware that he was performing to so intent an audience? If so, he gave no sign. When Cousin Elspeth finally pushed her chair back he instantly rose to help Cousin Blue with hers and then almost dashed to the door to open and hold it, courtier-fashion, clearly expecting to follow the Cousins and Andrew out.

There was a snorting bellow from the table.

"Hey! You two! Where you off to?"

"Don't be too long," trilled Cousin Blue from the doorway. She hissed a couple of words to Charles, who nodded, closed the door and came back to the chair which Samuel was holding for him on Uncle Vole's right. Samuel poured the first glasses of port, wheeled the dumb waiter with the used dishes into the lift and squeezed in beside it. The doors hissed shut and the lift whined down. There was nowhere for him to listen from up here, Andrew realized.

They sat in silence, Uncle Vole sucking and sluicing, Charles frowning as he sipped, apparently lost in a puzzling dream, but tense enough to spill when the old man spoke.

"Charles, uh?"

"Yes, sir. Pretty well sure of it now."

"More 'n I am, I can tell you. Know who this other little bugger is?"

"Er . . . Andrew . . . our cousin, May said?"

"Tell yer he hoped I was going to leave him the house till you turned up?"

"Good lord! No, I don't think she . . . My memory, you know."

"Drink up, man. Let's see what yer made of. I've told yer now. What d'yer think about it?"

"About . . .?"

"Andrew, yer fool! Not leaving the little bugger the house!"

"Oh . . . I suppose . . . but my dear Andrew, I can't say how sorry I am that things should have turned out like this."

Andrew let Adrian do the shrug and smile — our hero at life's gaming-table, losing his whole estate with a laugh.

"Not much money in acting, eh?" cackled Uncle Vole.

"It's a dog's life," said Charles.

"What yer know about it?"

"Well, ah . . ." said Charles, twisting his empty glass by the stem, frowning as though he wasn't aware of having drunk the wine.

"*He's* the one's going to be an actor," said Uncle Vole.

"Have you been on the stage, sir?" said Andrew.

"Me? Well . . . you know, I do seem to remember . . ."

"Jesus bloody Christ!" said Uncle Vole. "D'yer mean all I've got is a choice between a couple of fairies?"

Charles flicked a glance at Andrew, one eyebrow slightly raised. It was natural — Uncle Vole's line in theatre-criticism would have baffled any stranger — but was there, as well as the appeal for help, a momentary hint of collusion, as if from a colleague? Of course, all Charles might be vaguely remembering was his long-ago performances here at The Mimms, his Aguecheek, his Demetrius.

"Sir Arnold doesn't care for actors," said Andrew. "He says we're all queers. In fact the first time I came here he told me to go away because he said I was a bugger who wouldn't get drunk and couldn't talk women."

He spoke in a clinical voice as if telling a fellow-doctor the symptoms of a madness. The tone must have stung a bit.

"Little pansy runt," snarled Uncle Vole. "Fill yer glass, man. Not you, boy. You stick to water. Don't want to make you spew on the table."

Charles did as he was told and tilted his chair back, cradling his glass in his hand.

"Women," he murmured.

113

He took a gulp and nodded, as if having made up his mind. "They're all the same," said Uncle Vole.

"Ah, yes, but all different too," said Charles. "F'rinstance, I remember a French lass. Said she was French, that is, but she had a Chinese look. What was her name? Mimi? Fifi? Something like that. Did an act with a knife-thrower . . ."

Uncle Vole grabbed the decanter, sloshed himself some more port and huddled forward to listen. The story was obviously a recitation piece, similar in a much posher way to the Dame's saga about the siren, but Charles told it teasingly, falling into apparent reveries and having to be snarled awake, or rambling off on diversions about circus life. Though he said he had slept with the girl and described doing so he didn't claim to have played a part in the main incident, which concerned the anatomical reasons for her preference of a hunchback clown to the circus strong man.

Uncle Vole sat twitching and snuffling.

"Bitches are all the same," he said. "Seen it time and again, back in the Cape, white women getting on heat for a nigger boy. Why, me own cook here, simple country girl you'd have thought, she got it into her head she wanted to marry my Zulu boy. Everyone else said she was stark raving, not me. I knew what she was after. Provided it doesn't spoil her cooking, I said, having all that dark meat in her pot. Get it? All that dark meat in her pot."

Charles produced the guffaw demanded, finished his glass and refilled it. Uncle Vole sat cackling, then swung to Andrew.

"Learnt to talk better than milk-sop yet?"

"I could, but I'm not going to."

"Still not been with a woman?"

"I have."

"Tell us, then."

"No."

"Made a mess of it, of course."

"No."

"Don't want us to watch your maiden blushes?"

Of course Uncle Vole was pretending to set up a sort of competition with The Mimms as the prize, and Andrew could easily have talked about Lily in a way that would warm the old brute's blood for a minute or two, but he had no intention of

114

doing so, any more than he would have talked to anyone (except Mum, and she was dead) about what he was going to do and be as an actor. Both were gifts, powers he could command thanks to the mysterious daemon inside him, which must not be taken for granted by talking about them. It wasn't the physical ability to perform that mattered — everybody had that, almost. It was the power that had made Lily say yes, that had made Jean stand still and be kissed — and was also going to make the crammed tiers of a theatre stop their breathing at a gesture, their souls swaying all with one movement, reeds in his wind . . . There's a very extraordinary thing about Ariel, Cousin Brown had said. No other character in the play, not Miranda, not even Caliban, knows he exists. If they did then Prospero might lose his power over him. And it is Ariel who makes the whole plot happen. All the characters dance to his tunes, heard or unheard.

"I just don't talk about them," said Andrew.

"More'n one, hey?"

Andrew nodded to Charles, returning the flash of collusion, and rose.

"Siddown, you," said Uncle Vole.

"Thank you for supper, sir," said Andrew, and left.

Despite what she'd said on leaving the Schoolroom Andrew was surprised to find Cousin Blue in the Boudoir, looking through a leather-bound photograph album. She glanced up at his entrance, saw he was alone, and sighed.

"No bridge tonight, Cousin May?"

"Poor May's had a squabble with General Odway," said Cousin Brown.

"These Americans," said Cousin Blue. "Really, I think the Russians would be more considerate. They are much too fond of winning. If they lose, they seem to think that someone must be cheating them."

"He didn't!" said Andrew, all sympathetic shock.

"Let us not talk about it," said Cousin Blue. "Come and see what I have found. I was going to show them to Charles."

Cousin Brown was frowning her way through one of her diaries, still apparently hunting for a play in which she might have seen Charles act, so Andrew settled on the bungy sofa

115

beside Cousin Blue. She was wearing a lot of flowery girlish scent, he noticed.

It wasn't like an ordinary snapshot album. The pictures were brown and not shiny, but very clear. Each of them filled a whole page. The first showed a big white bungalow with a mountain behind it. Spiky and cactusy plants grew in the garden. You could guess how bright the sunlight was from the blackness beneath the heavy verandah. Under the photograph a clear round hand had written the words "South Mimms". The next picture was of children having tea on a rug in the same garden under the shadow of a leaning tree with deep-fissured bark. A white nursemaid supervised from a canvas chair. "M., C., Nanny Bounce, E." said the caption.

"That was us," said Cousin Blue. "I was only a baby, so of course I don't remember."

"Who took them?" asked Andrew.

"Mother did. It was her hobby. She was rather clever at it. She did all the messing about afterwards — what's it called? — too."

"Developing."

"Of course."

They leafed slowly on. Andrew looked at the photographs with interest. You never knew. Just possibly some time he might come across a part which needed a feel for that particular way of life, and the album seemed to hold it trapped in its own time, not just the moustaches and the women's hats and the glittering carriages and the sporting guns, but the whole feel of a society in its landscape. It was something about the sky, perhaps. You could feel the country going endlessly on and on. Andrew could even imagine, far away up north, a white man who might actually have come to one of the parties, sitting in a native hut and listening to an old blind witch-doctor telling him the story of Nada. In fact there were very few darkies in any of the pictures. Sometimes a servant with a tray of drinks. Once a line of men and women doing something in a vineyard. It was almost a shock when Cousin Blue turned a page and twisted the album round because the photograph was higher than it was wide and had been pasted in sideways.

Two figures stood in the foreground. Their stunted shadows showed it must be almost noon. One was a white boy, about

116

six, the other a black adult. The darkie was wearing the servants' clothes Andrew had seen in earlier photographs, bare feet, white trousers, a thigh-length white jacket. The white child was wearing nothing except a solar topi. "Master and Man!" said the caption.

The exclamation mark was justified. The picture was startling, only partly because in all the other pictures the children had been rather over-dressed. The standard throughout the album was high ("Mother used to throw hundreds away," Cousin Blue had said) but this one was special. It had energy, presence. It was a whole play stilled into an instant. The black man stared at the camera with a clear, calm gaze. The white boy's face was invisible in the shadow of his hat with the result that the focal point of his figure became the little dangling penis. The background was out of focus but the figures were sharp, with every wrinkle of flesh and fold of cloth exact.

"That's Charlie and Samuel, of course," said Cousin Blue. "That's the one I'm longing to show him. Isn't it quaint? It was a bit naughty of Mother to take him like that — we were never let run around without any clothes, like children used to after the war. But Mother said it was Art, so it didn't count. I do wish he would come!"

She rose with a sigh and left the room. Cousin Brown at once looked up from her diary.

"Of course," she said, "what happened was that May decided she would rather be with Charles in the evenings. They are like young lovers, Ferdinand and Miranda, almost, too ridiculous. Be that as may be, she chose to take umbrage at one of General Odway's jocularities — his style of badinage is decidedly heavy-handed. I have no doubt that May is a better player than he, but she took the opportunity to suggest to him in front of his officers that that was the case, and the upshot, among other things is that she can no longer gorge herself on tinned American butter. The arrangement has caused endless friction below stairs, and everyone but May is delighted that it should cease. She is far from unintelligent, but she has never been able to imagine that an action may have other results, besides the one she is set on. Tell me quickly, what do you make of Charles?"

"He good as let on he'd been an actor."

"Did he now?"

"But he might have been thinking about your plays here. You said he did a good Aguecheek."

"And an excellent Lucius O'Trigger. Do you know . . ."

She paused. A mischievous look, a sudden likeness to her sister, came into her face.

"Antonio has dropped out," she said. "I had guessed she might."

"It's quite a big part."

"Ah, but Alonso — Mrs Ferris, you know — has come along out of all recognition. I was regretting that I had not given her more. Suppose she were to take Sebastian, then I might persuade Charles to attempt Antonio, which is only some thirty lines."

"And all 'Prithee, peace' until that last scene."

"May will not like it, of course, but . . . Well, dear, are the gentlemen still enjoying themselves?"

Cousin Blue ignored the sprightly malice of the question, sighed, and put the album away. Andrew had risen as she came in and was waiting for her to sit down, but she did not return to the sofa. Instead she drew a chair up to a three-legged table, cleared the knick-knacks to one side and started to lay out a game of patience. After a couple of minutes she looked up.

"Andrew, dear, I'm afraid I must ask you to help Samuel put my brother to bed. You know, Father can be a brute, a real brute. No, not yet — they are still talking. It is enough to make one weep."

Charles sat slumped with his head on his arms across the Schoolroom table, snorting.

"I think I can manage the shoulders," said Andrew. "He can't weigh much."

"Easier each take one arm," said Samuel. "Like this, look. He won't feel nothing."

"What about Sir Arnold?"

"I just walked him to bed. Tomorrow he'll feel pretty bad. Stay in bed, maybe. He's not been too well. Just made the effort for tonight. Wanted to see the pair of you together."

"I'm afraid I refused to play."

"You did right. He'll respect you better for that."

Moving as though they had rehearsed the routine for days

118

they eased the inert torso up and twisted the body sideways on the chair. Andrew supported the shoulders while Samuel knelt and removed the shoes. With an elbow under each armpit they hauled the body out into the corridor. The heels slithered, made a ghostly thumping on the half-flight of stairs up to the family bedrooms, then returned to their slither along the soft carpet. In what thirty years ago had been Charles's bedroom they sat the body on an upright chair.

"If you'll hold his shoulders again, please," said Samuel.

He went to the mahogany wash-stand and fetched a face-towel and a large piss pot, decorated with Chinese figures.

"Now pull him up, high as you can. Let go when I say. Higher . . ."

Holding the piss-pot in his left hand he swung his clenched fist into the extended diaphragm. Andrew let go as the vomit came, then helped guide the body forward and down until it was on its knees in front of the chair, retching into the pot. Samuel caught the whole mess, put the pot to one side, rolled the body over and wiped the grey and sweating face with the towel.

"Learnt that trick from an English footman way back," he said. "Saves a lot of mess in the night. Baas Wragge always liked to get 'em drunk — 'See what you're made of,' he'd say."

He did Uncle Vole's voice spot on.

Florrie had already turned the bed-clothes back, going round the rooms during family supper. They heaved the body on to the mattress and covered it with the blankets. Samuel stood gazing at the life worn face, strangely blank, emptied of character, like a saint in ecstasy.

"What do you think?" said Andrew.

"Tisn't him. Baas Charlie could hold his liquor. Weren't good for much else, but he could do that."

"He's had a rough life . . . What will Sir Arnold do?"

"Let him stay, I reckon."

"Because he thinks he might be his son?"

"Don't matter. Provided there's a fight between Miss May and Miss Elspeth. Course, he'd like it to be Baas Charlie come back. Don't like to think of himself going off into the dark leaving nothing behind. So I reckon he isn't going to make up his mind for a while. 'Nother thing — suppose he goes and decides it *is* Baas Charlie. Always hated doing anything about changing his will, because of it reminding him of dying. Last will he made was after he lost his case to make Master Nicholas — that's Baas Charlie's son — a ward of court. He went raging along to the lawyers about it."

"What does it say?"

"Don't know. All I know is Mr Foley didn't like it — said it wasn't right law somehow — but Baas Wragge he put his foot down and made 'em say what he wanted. Mr Foley, he's been at him time and again to change it, but Baas Wragge he wouldn't listen, not till he suddenly went and sent for you. I reckon till this fellow turned up, he was still thinking about putting you in . . ."

He gazed at the figure on the bed, shaking his head slowly from side to side in one of his strange half-trances. His fingers felt in a pocket of his striped waistcoat. He turned and showed Andrew on the palm of his hand a disc of lightish-coloured wood with a knob the size of a hazel nut in the middle. Andrew picked it up and looked at the image of himself.

"I guessed from my bit of marge that you must have finished," he said. (The tours Cousin Blue had arranged had meant the cancelling of three *Nada* readings, so he hadn't got right through the book in the hols. Week-ends were no good: Saturday afternoon was spent at the flicks with Jean, Sunday afternoon most of the servants went out.)

"Third one I made," said Samuel. "First two not right. Not going to bother making one for this feller."

The sudden side-slip into nigger-talk was extraordinarily contemptuous.

Andrew peered at the tiny head. It was very odd. Just a knob. Knife-pecks for eyes and mouth, a ridge for a nose. It could have been anyone, but it was him. Not Adrian, Andrew. He was glad to hand it back.

"It's going to be tricky to prove he isn't Charles," he said. "I suppose you could go to Hull and try and find out if a shelter was bombed, see if anyone remembers him at the hospital. Even if you found out what he was calling himself before that it mightn't help. I mean the real Charles would have had to call himself something. You'd have to find the name and then trace it back to before 1917, wouldn't you?"

120

"Just have to do best we can," said Samuel. "Listen to everything he does and says. Maybe we'll catch him out. All I know is, if he isn't Baas Charlie then it isn't right he should inherit."

On Saturdays Andrew rose at seven, breakfasted in the kitchen and walked across to the farm to help Jean get through her morning's work. Mrs Althorp couldn't object as Cousin Brown had arranged this specifically to release Jean by eleven. Jean would then bicycle round, bringing a packed lunch, while Andrew walked back. They would rehearse for an hour, and after that bicycle off to the flicks at Petersfield.

"You are being admirably patient," said Cousin Brown, "but I am afraid it is the only way with a child like Jean. I have to drill her and drill her. With only one rehearsal a week and then six days to forget . . ."

"It's interesting," said Andrew. "Specially the love scenes. Like coaxing a bird to eat out of your hand."

(Before the war there used to be an old one-eyed sailor who did that with sparrows — first the darting snatch and flurry to safety; then, still trembling with the terror of nearness, perching on a finger to peck at crumbs in the palm; fear shading into trust, the spread fingers imperceptibly rising at each visit, upright round the cupped palm, the bird in the middle, got you! Usually the old boy held the sparrow a few seconds, peering with his short-sighted eye at the pattern of head-feathers; but sometimes, if the right child was watching, he would gape with broken orange fangs and pretend to bite the head off.)

That Saturday was sheeting wet. They both had capes, but on their way back from the flicks the rain densened till it was like a waterfall and they were forced to stop for shelter under a railway bridge. The downpour made pearly curtains over both arches. They talked about the film, a silly thriller, and the trailer for next week's war-film. Jean didn't care for war-films. The rain drenched on. Chill breathed from the slimy bricks. She shivered.

"Practise a bit?" he suggested.

She blushed — she knew at once what he meant.

"Might warm us up," he said.

"Oh, all right."

He undid the buttons of his cape. When he moved to do hers she edged back.

"We don't want to squelch squelch," he said. "Now, for Pose A — this is the one right at the end of the flick. You know, sunset, palms, two dozen violins. It's in profile. I ought to have something to stand on so you can tilt your head up — I'll have to do it tip-toe and you bend your knees. Fine. Arm there and arm there. Don't giggle . . ."

He clowned it lightly, helping her do the same. As soon as he felt her hand moving on his shoulder-blade he broke off, laughing. A train crossed the bridge, filling the cave below with its dull thunder.

"Pose B is your sort of thing — costume, duels, elopements. Let's say your guardian's taking you to the brutal viscount he's making you marry, and I'm the highwayman who's held you up. Your dowry's in the coach, but I've been a gallant idiot and said I'll let you go in exchange for a kiss. You're dead against it, but your guardian says what about the dowry? So down you come from your coach. Long sweeping dress, high heels, utter disdain. This is my cloak, OK? I'll lead, you follow. Just think about your guardian peering out of the coach, getting more and more pop-eyed. OK, off we go."

She was heavy enough to make Pose B a strain in its later stages. Beyond the blurred curve of her cheek he could see the crinkled stream of water slithering over the road-surface towards its drain. The guardian's eyes would be popping all right, he thought. Promising. The slosh of falling water drowned the noise of the approaching motor almost until it reached the arch. He lugged her upright with a second to spare.

"Lorry coming," he gasped.

A bulging khaki bonnet barged through the curtain. They pressed against the wall to let it pass, but before it reached the further arch it braked. A head, unrecognizable in silhouette, craned out.

"Want a ride, Mr Wragge?" called Sergeant Stephens.

Andrew glanced at Jean. Discontent? Yes. But the bridge was no use for anything beyond clowning, and anyway his strategy demanded that he should override her wishes, the way a parent might a child's.

"Thanks," he called.

Sergeant Stephens climbed down, lowered the tailgate and lifted the bikes for Andrew to stow in the lorry, which was empty except for a pile of loose boots in the far right corner.

"Room for the young lady up front," he said.

"We'll be OK in the back, thanks," said Andrew, letting the eyelid Jean couldn't see droop for an instant.

"You're welcome," said the sergeant, and before Jean could move he took her under the arms and heaved her bodily up. She produced a curious sound, between a squeak of surprise and a shriek of outrage. He didn't even smile. The tailgate banged up.

"It'll be a bumpy ride," said Andrew. "You know how Yanks drive."

They settled next door to the pile of boots with their backs to the cab.

"It smells like a pub," said Jean.

It did, too, and as the lorry lurched off Andrew put his palm on the floor to steady himself. The floor was wet — not surprising in this weather, but when he sniffed his hand he smelt whisky. Spilt not long back, either. A broken bottle — but no glass splinters. A whole case then, one bottle broken, taken into Southampton hidden under the pile of boots. The rest of the stores unloaded, but the boots brought back for next time. Mr Trinder? He'd been driving out to meet the sergeant back in March . . .

The Yank driver was true to form — any more "practice" would have meant broken front teeth. They pressed their bodies against each other for support. A pleasant pocket of warmth grew between them. No chance of talk through the drum of the downpour on the canvas roof, and the clatter of the bodywork and the roar of the engine, but on the last smooth swoop down the new tarmac inside the lodge gates Jean put her mouth to his ear.

"Sweet Lord, you play me false," she whispered.

In the near dark under the canvas he stared into her eyes, letting the tension rise. The growl of gears as the lorry took the turn into the camp entrance drowned his answering line, but she must have heard the sincerity throbbing in his voice. He'd been expecting the lorry to brake and let them down there, but it bounced on across the park, turned left again and stopped by the sergeant's store-huts. The moment it was still Andrew put

123

his arm round her and kissed her as if he meant it. The rain thundered down.

A hand appeared at the rim of the tailgate. Andrew was on his feet and lifting Jean's bike to pass it down by the time the tailgate fell, but instead of waiting to receive the bike Sergeant Stephens climbed up into the shelter of the canvas.

"Jesus!" he said. "You call this summer! Been wanting to talk with you, Mr Wragge. It's my folks back home. I wrote them about you maybe being the heir and all — it ain't easy to know what to put in a letter — and that's got them all worked up. They think Britain's full of barons and duchesses and they can't see why I ain't meeting any, so when I tell them about Sir somebody and his long-lost heir they gotta know more. So if you'll pardon me asking, how's it going?"

Andrew laughed. He didn't believe the sergeant's excuse, and wasn't even certain the sergeant expected him to. It was a sort of clumsy politeness pretending he wasn't himself being inquisitive, excited by the notion of all that money . . . but Andrew owed him for the ride, especially the last few seconds.

"There's a new chapter in the drama," he said. "D'you remember the picture in the Saloon, the family one?"

"Sure."

"There's a boy in it with a gun under his arm — Charles, Sir Arnold's only son. He was missing presumed killed in the First War, but now a man's turned up saying he's him."

"Jesus! And is it him?"

"My Cousin May says so. My Cousin Elspeth isn't sure. Sir Arnold won't say. Some of the servants knew the real Charles, and they aren't sure either."

"Somebody's on your side?"

"I haven't got a side — I'm just an interested spectator."

"Crap. You gotta fight it. You tell me anything you need."

"Only if you know a good cheap private detective."

"I got the man right here in the kitchen. Used to be a private eye in Albuquerque."

Andrew hesitated. He didn't want to stand around arguing. He had asked about the detective as a joke, a quick dismissive impossibility to get the conversation over, so that he could go off alone through the rain with Jean.

"I can fix him for furlough," said the sergeant.

"But . . ."

"Money? Listen here. I got a proposition for you. You a betting man? What odds'll you give me against you being the one who inherits?"

"Oh . . . fifty to one?"

"Hell, I'll give you better than that. Twenty to one, how's that sound? So I lay five hundred bucks on you at twenty to one — OK? That's for Phil's travel and expenses. If he can't dig up nothing useful, then that's my five hundred bucks gone, and you ain't out a dime. But if your number comes up and you inherit the whole thing, then you pay me ten thousand bucks. What do you say?"

"Can I think about it?"

"Sure. Come up here tomorrow and meet Phil. What time?"

"All right. It'll have to be about half past nine, because of getting off to church. Can I bring someone with me — one of the servants? He's very interested. He might be able to help."

"Sure."

"What was that about? You never told me," said Jean as they walked their bikes back across the valley with the rain buffeting down on to their capes and sou'westers. Andrew had kept quiet about the inheritance business. It wasn't part of his strategy — long-lost heirs are supposed to be young and a bit unreliable — though the hard luck of losing it all to Charles might have come in useful later. Besides, all that concerned Andrew. It was Adrian who was supposed to be playing his game with Jean.

"It's a bit of a story," he said.

"Do tell me."

They squelched on. He was conscious of the dovecote, down to their left, coming and vanishing as the rain-veils parted and closed. Too soon. Besides, he hadn't got it ready.

"I wish we had somewhere to go," he said.

"Dolly says it's going to clear up after milking. She's usually right."

"Can you get out?"

"Well . . ."

"Look. Let your back tyre down before you get home. Say you've got a puncture. Put it in a shed Mrs Althorp can't see from the kitchen. I'll meet you at the stile."

125

"What'll you say?"

"It's cleared up and I feel like a walk."

"Oh, I wish I was a man!"

"No you don't."

Her cheeks, freckled, tanned, streaming with rain despite the sou'wester, reddened appetizingly.

It was hard to imagine Phil leaning in a doorway with a fedora tipped back on his head and a smoking automatic in his hand. He was round and rubbery with a high bald brow and doggy eyes, but he took notes on a pad and asked what sounded like the right questions. Samuel answered most of these, usually with a shake of the head. Now that the family was living up in the nursery wing he had fewer opportunities for listening to their talk, and in any case Charles, thanks to his memory-loss, real or phoney, had given very little away. There was only the air-raid on Hull, plus a few laundry-marks on the ragged clothes he had arrived in. Cousin Blue had given Samuel these to burn, but he had kept them. The laundry-marks were all different, probably because the clothes had been begged at doors. Even if Phil found the donors it wouldn't prove much.

From the moment Andrew had suggested it Samuel had taken the inquiry completely seriously. He wasn't happy about the bet with Sergeant Stephens, and offered to pay the costs himself — he had a little money saved up, he said — but Andrew had refused, not really believing the inquiry was worth spending money on. Only if a Yank chose to chuck his dollars around, well, that was his look-out. In fact, left to himself Andrew would probably have told the sergeant he'd decided against the idea. His whole instinct was to stay as neutral as possible, to do nothing whatever to make himself Uncle Vole's heir. Then, if it happened, he would still be free. Anything else, and The Mimms and its fortune would become a huge trailing weed on his smooth hull. So now he let Samuel take the responsibility both of deciding to send Phil off to Hull and of answering his questions while he, Andrew, stood back and watched. While Phil looked shruggingly at the laundry-marks Sergeant Stephens came over and edged Andrew yet further aside.

"You didn't say he was a nigger," he muttered.

Andrew had in fact noticed the change in the two Americans' looks when he had brought Samuel into the hut, but had put it down simply to surprise at seeing a darkie in butler's uniform in the middle of green England.

"I'm sorry," he said. "Does it matter?"

"Sure does. You wouldn't understand. Me, I'll do a deal with any colour. But you just tell your pal not to come wandering into the camp looking for me. Specially after dark. The guys here — they're bored, they're frustrated, they're a long way from home, they don't care a whole lot about your British laws. Next few weeks some real rough guys'll be coming through. I tell you, there's guys homesick for a good lynching. I can see your friend's got his heart set on proving you're the real thing, much more'n you do, Mr Wragge. He'll be after me for news. That's OK, but you tell him he's gotta phone me first, and I'll arrange a place to meet him. Look, I'm taking a risk, fixing Phil's furlough. I don't want nobody asking questions. So you tell your pal to lay off, take it easy, phone me first if he wants to talk. OK?"

"We could just forget the whole thing if you like."

"Jesus, no. I'm interested. Just that it's gotta be done my way."

"OK, I'll tell him."

The discussion about the laundry-marks seemed to have ended. Phil looked up.

"I'll need mug shots," he said.

"I better lend you my camera," said Sergeant Stephens.

"It may be a bit tricky persuading him, specially if he's a phoney. I'll have to get my Cousin May to coax him somehow. I can tell her you want the picture to send to your folks back home, but . . . Tell you what — she's quarrelled with General Odway."

"She and who else?"

"The point is the General used to let her have extra butter and now he's stopped it. I don't suppose you could . . ."

"No problem."

Though he was later than he'd said, Andrew climbed the plantation path slowly. His legs were still rubbery tired after the ride from Southampton. No harm in keeping her waiting — and when he got there, still no hurry. She'd had five days to brood since Sunday's farewells. Things had gone with a rush after the Saturday evening tryst at the stile among the still-dripping beeches. She might easily have become frightened again. So just chat to begin with, perhaps about the rather amusing business of watching Cousin Blue cajole Charles into joining a family photograph — picture to be taken tomorrow morning — to send to Sergeant Stephens's folks back home. (Equally amusing, though he could not tell Jean this, had been Cousin Blue's delight at being allowed an entry into the mysterious world of the Black Market. The Sergeant's butter wasn't a gift. She was paying for it, at real black-market prices. Thrilling!) Then, perhaps, ask about the farm gossip . . .

A cry in the still woods — a sort of squawk, cut short. A throaty growl continuing. A mad high cackle. That was Brian. Before that Dave's snarl. The squawk had been human too — when Sergeant Stephens had hoisted Jean into his lorry she . . .

Andrew ran up the slanting path. Rage made him stupid, those two repulsive louts barging in and ruining everything — but in a few strides he slowed. The imagined scene cleared in his mind, Jean threshing in Dave's grasp, Brian standing by with his father's blackthorn stick, thick as a cudgel, himself rushing into the dell. Dave was far stronger than he was. Brian too.

He slowed to a fast stride, still trembling with fury. Brian's mad laugh filled the underwoods. Andrew picked up a fallen branch and drew a deep breath.

"This way, men!" he yelled. "Up here!"

"Coming, Sarge!"

He thrashed the branch against a holly as he passed.

"Get moving! Set the dogs on 'em!"

He barked, yaps, mixed in with deeper baying, inarticulate human shouts. He thrashed at the bushes. Brian's laughter had stopped. Where the path levelled Andrew forked to one side,

128

still yelling and baying and threshing his feet through the leaf-litter. Between the tree-trunks he saw Brian scampering ape-like up the paddock towards the cow-sheds, but the dell with the stile was empty.

A muffled movement under the hedge hazels. He ran into the open shouting in his own voice.

"Over here! Sergeant! There they are!"

Dave broke from a hollow under the hedge and scurried away up to the right. Andrew ran a few paces after him shouting in three voices and thrashing his branch around, then, still yelling and barking, turned and made urgent signals to Jean, who was climbing to her feet with her fists clutched at the waistband of her riding-breeches.

"Thataway!" he shouted. "Up by the hedge!"

"You OK, lady?"

She pulled herself together and ran for the path, up over the ridge. He loosed one more flurry of baying and trampled around, calling to himself, losing the trail, then followed her at a wallowing run all the way down to the Amphitheatre, catching her just beyond the Green Room huts. As he touched her shoulder she swung round, snarling, her fingers griped into talons. He caught her wrist before she could claw his face.

"It's me, darling. Andrew. You're all right. You're all right."

Calm, assurance, power.

Her face went white and her mouth gaped like a hen's. He thought she was going to faint, but she fell conscious into his arms. He soothed her back with gentle strokes as she sobbed.

"Did he hurt you?"

"No . . . not really . . . only . . ."

He kept his eyes on a slant of path he could see between the tree-trunks, just in case Dave realized what had happened and came after them. At last Jean raised her head and looked dumbly round.

"Where . . . Where are the others? The dogs?"

"Only me."

"No. No. The others. The wood was full of them."

"The noise of hunters heard. Enter divers spirits in the shape of dogs. Ariel setting them on."

"All . . . you?"

He nodded. The conceit was real. The power was there. If a

129

dozen yokels had broken from the wood with cudgels and hayprongs he would have faced and cowed them. Adrian — the secret spirit whom nobody else in the play was aware of — could do it. The whole arena between the sunlit wood and the shadowed slope of derelict lawns was filled with his private magic, so strong that it changed the physical shape of things — she was staring *up* at him, her green eyes and ginger lashes wet, her lips parted, her whole face trembling. He saw that from now on he could make her do whatever he wanted. He kissed her gently and let go.

"You mustn't sleep at the farm tonight."

"No. Oh, no."

"We'll go and talk to Cousin Elspeth. She'll know what to do. She's a magistrate, anyway. Don't worry. I'll do the talking."

"The difficulty," said Cousin Brown, "is that Mrs Althorp cannot run the farm without the men. Our local Land Army officials are not really up to the job — in fact they are thoroughly spineless. We have had several cases of this kind, and I am sorry to say my male colleagues on the bench tend not to take them seriously. They regard the war effort as more important than what they see as a minor misfortune for the poor girl. Anyway, clearly Jean will have to transfer . . ."

"Oh . . ." said Jean. "But . . . I mean . . ."

She managed not to look at Andrew.

"What about the play?" she said.

"My dear Jean, how very considerate of you to think of it. Certainly it would be a great blow should you have to leave us, but I think it very unlikely that we can find you another billet close by."

"I don't mind working at the farm. Mrs Althorp will look after me. It's living there, so I can't go out in the evenings or anything."

"What about West Lodge?" said Andrew.

The power was still there. He was in complete control. He need only make the smallest moves, just a nudge or a pause, and the whole flow of events would run along the channel he chose. The idea of West Lodge — a cottage at the top of the drive which seemed to have been built as an excuse to display one

130

monstrous Jacobean chimney — had come to him just at that moment.

"Now, that is a distinct possibility," said Cousin Brown. "Do you know old Mrs Oliphant, Jean?"

"Only what she looks like."

"And sounds like, I dare say. Deaf as a post but cannot stop talking. She keeps a room for her grandson, but he is fighting in India. You would have a cycle ride along Abb's Lane from the farm. Let me see. I will telephone Mrs Althorp and tell her that you will be spending the night here, and that I wish to speak to both Brundells tomorrow morning. I will make arrangements with Mrs Oliphant on the way. Andrew, dear, will you go and ask Florrie to put the Ivory Room in order for Jean?"

Some time after midnight Andrew woke and saw through his open curtains a starry sky and the sheen of a waning moon on the cedar branches close outside. He pictured Jean dreaming in the white four-poster three doors along the passage. The moonlight would seem stronger in there, with the creamy hangings, and fairy-tale white furniture. Her hair would be a dark cloud on the pillow. There was nothing to stop him. If anyone heard a footstep they would think it was one of the Americans moving around on the floor above — they did a good deal of that. Almost he could send out his invisible messenger to whisper through Jean's dream and she would slide from her sheets and come drifting to his summons . . . No. He needed no effort of will to turn on his side and close his eyes. The Ivory Room was pretty, but it was not the set he had designed. He wanted the eyrie above the dovecote, the sideways light of a summer dusk, so that he could watch the come-and-go of blood beneath the freckled skin. And she must come because she chose, not in the after-shock of Dave's attack. No tricks, no traps. He would tell her to come, and he would wait there. She would climb the ladder pretending not to know, but knowing all the same, what was going to happen. She must obey — his Art was of such pow'r.

Sergeant Stephens's camera, like all props and gadgets, refused to function for Andrew.

"Let me try," said Cousin Brown. "I took the pictures for

my plays whenever that was possible. Look, you have forgotten to set the shutter. Charles, please take off that hat and those sun-glasses. They make you look like an Argentinian gambler."

"Just like!" trilled Cousin Blue. "Oh, don't you remember that dago who hoped Father might invest in his patent trams? Take them off, Charles. We must keep faith with our allies."

"But my eyes . . ." said Charles.

"Nonsense," said Cousin Brown. "The light is not as strong as all that."

Since last week-end, Andrew noticed, the relationships had shifted. Cousin Brown's absurd-seeming idea of involving Charles in the play was now seriously being discussed. Part of her motive, only half-unconscious, may have been to detach him to some extent from Cousin Blue's influence, but the play itself might become a hostage if she could not afford to have Charles proved a phoney at least till August. Indeed everybody except Samuel seemed to be settling down to a wary and provisional acceptance of the new order, and Cousin Brown was emphasizing this by bossing Charles around. Perhaps the sisters were so used to a three-cornered relationship that with Uncle Vole increasingly withdrawn to his sick-bed they were beginning to build a new triangle, an inversion of the old one, with poor Charles at the bottom point. It was all very interesting to watch, expressing itself hardly at all in words, but in attitudes, gestures, tones.

Cousin Brown did not relinquish the camera.

"Andrew," she said, "if you were to lean against the sundial that would balance the composition. Less of the Gielgud look, I think. You must be your own man. Capital. Try not to simper, May. Stand still, Charles. And again. One more. There. You may put your disguise back on, Charles."

She laid the camera on the sundial and nodded to Andrew to move aside with her.

"Did you see Mrs Oliphant?" he asked. He had breakfasted in the kitchen with Jean and walked back with her through the plantation to the farm. They had found Mrs Althorp juddering with exasperation, mainly at Jean for sneaking out in the dusk and letting herself get caught by Dave and Brian. She made it clear too that she thought it no kind of coincidence that Andrew should be coming up through the wood at that moment. No

132

doubt she had said the same to Cousin Brown. At any rate, while Jean had gone to help Dolly finish the milking, Andrew had been sent with Carrie to move a batch of heifers into a fresh field and then to attempt to repair a gap in a hedge through which they had been breaking out into a barley-field — work which would normally have been done by Dave and Brian, but they had to stay up at the farm for Cousin Brown to talk to. Andrew had only got back to The Mimms just in time for the camera session, with no knowledge of what else had been happening, but he was not in the least worried — he knew it was all destined to go as he wanted.

"She is delighted," said Cousin Brown. "It will be somebody to talk to, she says."

"Great. I thought I'd help Jean ferry her stuff across this afternoon, instead of going to the flicks."

Cousin Brown glanced to where her sister and Charles were chatting by the sundial and lowered her voice.

"Andrew, dear, you may think it none of my business, but perhaps we should have a word about Jean. Of course she is some years older than you, but in other ways she is a child by comparison."

Andrew let Adrian smile, unembarrassed, open, trust-worthy.

"It's all right," he said. "She just needs a bit of company. It's not much fun at the farm. You were quite right about her father — he sounds a pretty good tyrant."

This was true, though not perhaps in the way Cousin Brown took it. Mr Arthur was not much like Uncle Vole, just the sort of dad who doesn't want his little girl ever to get beyond twelve. The mum running off must have made it worse.

"You do want a happy Miranda, don't you?" he said.

She smiled, abandoning the attempt at reproof.

"I suggested she might prefer not to rehearse this morning," she said. "But she seemed determined to. I never supposed I should find her such a committed actress . . . you will be careful, Andrew?"

"Yes, of course. What did Dave say?"

"Old Brundell? No sign of shame, but I hope I managed to frighten him sufficiently. I explained the maximum sentences for crimes of this nature. Of course, there is nothing one can say

133

to his poor wretched son . . . Charles! Put that camera down!
Really, if you have let the light in . . .!"

Like Dave, Mrs Oliphant had her recitation-piece, an account of
her husband's slow and agonizing death, told in identical detail
to every fresh face and now having become by repetition a
one-woman folk-drama, giving her deep satisfaction no longer
connected with her loss, or anything except the performance
itself. While Jean unpacked upstairs Andrew listened and
watched, mouthing the ritual replies for her to lipread. Her
deafness, he discovered, was absolute. The lodge had been built
to the same standards as the main house — nothing would
quiver at a footstep. There was a latch to the parlour window
Jean could sneak down and undo.
    "How can you bear it?" said Jean, as they walked down the
drive. "It was all so dreadful."
    "She's made it not-dreadful by the way she tells it. Purging
pity and terror, you know. Anyway, I had to listen. I want her
to think of me as a nice young chap, so that she doesn't sling me
out when I come calling on her lodger."
    "What are we going to do?"
    "I've begged a picnic off Mrs Mkele. We'll find a nice flat
private place somewhere . . . and do another run-through."
    "Oh."
    "Remember you've got your real Ferdinand coming out next
week-end."
    "What's he like?"
    "All right, except that he's under the impression he can act.
His name's Pete Boller. He's five foot eleven, so you won't
have to bend your knees."
    "I'm not going to kiss him!"
    "You're going to kiss anyone the producer tells you to,
including my new Cousin Charles who looks like becoming
your father-in-law."
    "My . . . oh, in the *play*, you mean."
    "If it's any comfort I don't think my Cousin Elspeth is the
kissing kind of producer. She hasn't suggested it so far."
    "But we've only been saying the words. Anyway, you
said . . ."
    "I had to break the ice somehow."

134

She looked at him sideways for several paces.

"You were right in Sergeant Stephens's lorry," he said. "I played you false. Do you want to go back and pretend none of it happened?"

They were passing the camp entrance as he spoke. A couple of lorries came swinging out, their canvas covers down, crammed with GIs. Jean tossed her head and blushed, trying to look as though she thought the whistles meaningless as bird-song. Just what you would have expected, but different some-how. She had changed. You couldn't even say she was prettier, but there was something new there. Not exactly new, but hidden before, a liveliness, energies of her own, sensed behind her defences at their first meeting, an interestingness as a person . . . Watch it, he thought. You don't want to get too involved with her.

As the lorries climbed out of sight she felt for his hand. He let her fingers twine into his for a moment but then eased them free.

"Let's go on play-acting," he said. "When anyone might be watching."

"Mrs Althorp suspects the worst."

"Yes. And she told my Cousin Elspeth."

"What did you say?"

"You're a bit lonely. I wanted her to have a happy Miranda."

"Really?"

"I want that too. But in public we're not serious. OK?"

"What about in private?"

"You'll have to work it out for yourself."

THREE

"I forget," read Peter. "But these sweet thoughts do even refresh my labours, most busiest when idlest."

"Oh, dear, you have a different text," said Cousin Brown. "Never mind, since you have not learnt it it will be simple to change. Now, enter Miranda. Prospero at a distance, unseen."

Standing to one side, wrapped in his cloak of invisibility, Andrew watched the lovers rehearse. Peter had of course promised to be word-perfect when Cousin Brown had come to

135

audition him in Southampton three weeks back, though Andrew had warned her he wouldn't be. It was a pity there was no one else. On the other hand it was part of the whole experience, performing with somebody you detested. Andrew knew Peter only too well. He had been Rosalind to Peter's Orlando, Viola to his Duke, Titania to his Oberon. He had the looks for Ferdinand, the hidalgo stance and the passionate glance under strong black brows, but working with him was going to be hell. Though Cousin Brown was actually treating him as a pro, and paying him — not much, but something — he would somehow not manage to make half the handful of rehearsals he'd agreed on; he would barely know his lines by the opening night; he would treat the rest of the cast as though they were privileged to be on stage with him; and regard the scenes when he wasn't on as a boring waste of time. Years ago Andrew had realized that he couldn't afford love or hate. Mild liking, slight antipathy had got to be his limits — anything more would be an involvement — but somehow he couldn't help it with Peter. Others, however repellent — Uncle Vole, Dave Brundell, playground thugs long ago — were outside the castle. He could send Adrian out to fight or parley. Peter, by his pretensions to be an actor, his announcement that that was going to be his career, had a spy in the keep. They were almost twins. They had been born two days apart, lived in the same town, been taught in the same classes, acted in the same plays under Mr Dingle's frenzied direction. Their call-up papers were due the same week. Suppose they both survived (suppose, suppose . . .) a vista of twin careers stretched ahead — Peter would get a start on his looks and self-confidence. But one day, one day, Andrew thought, I am going to boot you off the stage in such a way that you won't ever come back. And you won't ever know why, either. I shall look forward to that.

At Ferdinand's first entrance Jean had frozen into a mumble and glanced in despair at Andrew. He had replied with an Uncle-Vole glare, and she had pulled herself together enough to make Cousin Brown clap her hands at the finish of the log-carrying scene.

"Capital, really capital! Jean, you have come on, Now, Peter, there are just two or three little things . . ."

Jean sidled over to Andrew.

136

"You said he was nice!" she whispered.

"I said he was all right."

"I think he's perfectly horrible!"

"Good."

"What do you mean good? It isn't good at all!"

"I mean that when you're saying you think he's the tops I'll know you're acting, which is what you're supposed to be doing."

"Why can't you be Ferdinand and him Prospero?"

"Because then you wouldn't have to act."

"Big-head."

"Now, listen. I thought he was going home this afternoon, but when he saw how posh the place was he decided to stay on. Cousin Elspeth's going to ask you if you can do another rehearsal tomorrow, after luncheon."

"But that means we're stuck with him all week-end!"

"'Fraid so. You'll have to go to the flicks alone."

"What are you going to do?"

"Make him help me clean out the dovecote."

"I'll come too."

"Not if you want a change from mucking-out."

"I want to be with you."

Peter, as Andrew had foreseen, was not much interested in the dovecote. For a while he sat on the ladder watching the other two shovel and sweep the encrusted bird-droppings down the central chute, but then decided that the smell was bringing on his asthma and left. When they'd finished clearing the floor Andrew made Jean climb the ladder, unbolted it and swung it round its circle. The effect was disappointing. Only a couple of doves came and went, instead of the storm of blurred white flutterings he'd imagined. The light was wrong, too — you needed horizontal bars through the flight-holes — and Jean should have been wearing a long cotton skirt, not breeches. He bolted the ladder firm.

"Go on up," he said. "There's a trap-door at the top. It isn't fastened."

As soon as she was off the ladder he followed her up into the empty whiteness of the eyrie. She was standing at a window, looking towards the camp. Over her shoulder he saw Peter chatting with a GI by the fence. Peter was enthralled by anything American — he'd probably end up in Hollywood playing smooth Brit cads in B movies. Something was happening in the camp. A line of lorries waited, right across the park, crammed with soldiers. The head of the line crawled into the trees and the rest moved up.

"Hello," he said. "The camp's filling up. That's a sentry Pete's talking to. Look, there's another one. You know what that means?"

She wasn't interested, but turned and put her arms round his waist.

"Can't you get rid of him?" she said.

He kissed her for a little and broke off.

"I've had an idea," he said. "What time does Mrs O go to bed?"

"I listen to the nine o'clock news and yell at her what's happening and then she goes off."

"Right. Tomorrow evening I'll start off back with Pete but I'll fix my gears to pack in, something I can't mend, I'll say — *he* won't bother to check — and I'll tell him to go on alone. I'll ask him to take a message to my digs. I'll come back. Soon as Mrs O's gone off you sneak down and climb out of her parlour window. I'll wait for you under the copper beech just down the drive. We'll go and count the stars coming out."

"All right. Lovely. But what about you — after, I mean?"

"I can bike in to school early next morning."

"You'll have to sleep somewhere."

"Here. This is my magic tower. I can make it pretty cosy."

"Cosy!"

"It'll be fine."

As you will find out, the Sunday after, he thought.

FOUR

On Friday morning Andrew found Mr Trinder leaning against the static-water tank ten yards beyond the school gate, seeming even more out of place in the blustery morning than he had done in the spring sunlight at the roadside six weeks ago. There he'd had a role — broken-down motorist — to account for his

138

presence. Here he was a character strayed in from the wrong play, a beast of the adult night beside the morning tide of boys. He must have been watching them though his hat was tipped forward over his eyes and he seemed absorbed in yesterday's racing results, because as soon as Andrew freewheeled round the corner he raised his hand and flicked a forefinger. Andrew scooted the bike across.

"Morning, Mr Trinder."

"Not much of one, if you ask me. Going to have to put off this invasion of theirs."

"When's it supposed to be?"

"Monday, they're saying, only not if the sea's bad. Stupid little landing-craft won't take the waves. Catch me in one of them contraptions."

"Can't they put it off?"

"Not beyond Tuesday — after then it's bleeding weeks. Something about the tides. How've you been keeping? Nice bike — present from someone?"

"It's so I can bike out and help one of my cousins put on a play."

"Nine to four it'll be the old bard."

"*The Tempest.*"

"Juvenile lead? Course you'd need platforms for that."

No, thought Andrew. I would make them see me those inches taller. He didn't mind Mr Trinder's remark, the way he resented it when Peter Boller patronized him about his missing inches. Mr Trinder was objective, but interested. Interested in anything, knowing a bit about everything — the invasion, the theatre. It must have been how he worked. He was a sort of sea anemone, floating out soft tentacles of inquiry all round him, dragging back the scraps with money in them.

"Character," said Andrew. "The heroine's dad, but it's the lead role."

"Good for you. How's everything else out there? Didn't I hear as some chappie turned up saying as he was the old bugger's son, one went missing?"

"That's right. Charles."

"And is he?"

"Nobody knows. He's lost his memory, but from the start he got a few things right which it looks as if only one of the family

139

could've known. One of my cousins is sure he's Charles and the other can't make up her mind."

"It's all down to the old bugger, innit?"

"He's been pretty feeble. I haven't seen him for a while. He stays in his room and they've got a nurse in."

"Sounds like he better make up his mind bloody soon. And what about you, young feller? What's your line?"

Andrew shrugged.

"Come off it," said Mr Trinder. "Money's money. Don't tell me you ain't changed your tune, now you've had a smell of it. Nice bike, that. Nice shoes — pair of Sir Arnold's? You don't see leather like that, not wartime, and they'd've set you back eighteen guineas before."

The bell had started to clank as he spoke.

"I've got to go," said Andrew.

"Hang on — something you can do for me. Going out to visit your cousins soon?"

"This evening."

Mr Trinder had moved slightly away from the tank and half turned towards it. In the angle between his body and the grey metal he slid a brown octavo envelope out of his newspaper, folded it and slipped it into the side pocket of Andrew's blazer.

"That's for Abe Stephens," he said. "Urgent. I'd run it out myself, but this bleeding invasion's made that a bit dicey. I'm not in a position where I want to answer a lot of silly-bugger questions every half-mile. Shove it in among your books, eh? Lad on a bike won't notice."

"OK. I've got a pass to let me into The Mimms. It seems to work at the road-blocks too."

"Just the job. Tell you what — I wouldn't mind the loan of that one day for a couple of hours."

"Well . . ."

"Make it worth your while."

"I've got to go. If we're late they keep us at school, and then I don't get out to The Mimms by supper."

"Feeding you OK?"

"Mrs Mkele's a terrific cook."

"Lashings of butter, that sort's used to. Be good."

Now there were road-blocks in the smallest lanes, manned by

stodgy bobbies or eager-beaver Home Guards. It was a dour evening for June, grey, with gusty showers and the odd glimmer of sun. You could tell the Channel would be rough. By now Andrew was used to biking out through a landscape crammed with armies, but this Friday he felt that the nature of the pressure had changed. The vessel was pumped full. It was ready, waiting. It couldn't hold like that — it must either subside or burst. There wasn't a cranny that didn't conceal troops or weapons. A few last bluebells still glimmered in the hedgerows but under the woods and copses they had all been mashed flat. The gusts reeked not of green summer, but of frying from field kitchens, urine from latrines, exhaust fumes, hot metal, the oil of weapons, the acid of charging batteries, war.

At the second road-block a corporal flipped briefly through Andrew's satchel, but the envelope was clipped to his handlebar with his route sketched on the back. As an exercise in not thinking about Jean (he was determined not to stale the performance by over-rehearsal — Sunday had to be a real first night, the risks essential to the triumph) he considered while he biked on what it might hold.

It was too thin to contain money. Mr Trinder wouldn't put anything on paper — not if he could help it — so it wasn't anything like a cheque or a receipt of an order for more whisky. He'd order by phone and pay in old notes. So it was something which had to be on paper. Something forged? The ration-books in the tea-pot might have been forged, not stolen — Andrew should have checked whether their numbers were different. And that's why Mr Trinder had wanted the pass — to copy. He must have a tame printer somewhere. Anyway, he'd kept in touch with Sergeant Stephens. He knew what was happening in the house. You could tell, from the way he'd asked his questions — just that shade too off-hand. Same as last time, in the café on the docks. He knew the answers already. Couldn't help hinting. That last pointless remark about the butter. Yes, it had to be Sergeant Stephens who'd told him. No one else knew that. But about Uncle Vole being worse? Well, Samuel might have said something to the sergeant — had Phil found anything out? It was getting urgent — anyway, what was in the envelope wouldn't have anything to do with that. A forged US Army form the sergeant wasn't supposed to use, but needed to order more black-market supplies? In that case, was it a risk even to carry it out? Was that why Mr Trinder hadn't wanted to take it himself? Wouldn't it be best to stop and stuff it down a rabbit-hole? Or at least open it and see — he could tell the sergeant someone had done that at a road-block? No. Either of those would get him deeper involved. Ignorant messenger was least worst, though it was bad enough. It certainly cleared all debts to Mr Trinder. No question of lending the pass.

There was a brass band on the tannoy, a Sousa march or something. At the camp gate, instead of the usual gum-chewing sentry, there was now a smart MP. Andrew explained his business.

"Hey! Corp!" called the MP.

A group of MPs stood just beyond the gate. An officer was looking at his wrist-watch. A line of lorries, their engines running, stretched all the way to the far wood. A corporal came striding over at the MP's call. Andrew explained again. Sergeant Stephens's name worked no magic.

"Forget it, son," said the corporal. "This is a military establishment. We have four thousand troops in here. We can't allow citizens come assing around among then. You give it me, and I'll despatch it up to Supply. OK, out of the gate, now."

A whistle blew and the first lorry crashed its gears and came churning on. The MP had waved Andrew to the wrong side of the entrance, so he was trapped and had to wait. The lorries had the sides of their canvas covers rolled up, so that the troops in them could look out, thirty or so GIs in full battle gear, steel helmets, rifles, huge back-packs. It could have been another exercise, but it wasn't. You could tell from the men's behaviour — some whooped, some chattered, some sat silent, but they all had a tension about them. The major at the gate saluted each truck as it passed. They were heroes, so he saluted them as he sent them off to die. How many? Which ones? You and you and you there, tugging at your chin-strap. The individual faces became blanks, pale oval targets propped there jiggling to the lurch of the lorry as they waited to be splattered into blood and bone and brain. Wasn't that Phil? Andrew stared. The man stared back, the lorry swung out of sight and the dreadful anonymous parade continued, hypnotic, seeming to carry a magic beyond anything Andrew could command or control. It was as though his own soul sat invisible in every truck and was roared away, naked and helpless to the battle, leaving behind only a dissolving wrack of might-have-beens.

A whistle blew again. The next truck halted at the gate, leaving a gap. Andrew shook himself out of his horror, rushed through, and escaped. As he went jolting down the pocked gravel of the unmended drive he realized that the man couldn't have been Phil. The GIs in the lorries were assault troops who'd only come in the week before. Phil was one of the permanent camp staff, a cook, not an infantryman. Anyway, he was in Hull.

"Wretched weather for their invasion, poor things," said Cousin Blue, smearing a thick layer of butter into her open roll.

"It is no more than a rumour," said Cousin Brown. She always cut her roll into precise halves, whereas Cousin Blue grappled hers apart, but it was noticeable that she too had a full round of butter in front of her place and though less lavish than her sister was not expecting it to have to last a full week.

"Nonsense," said Cousin Blue. "They stopped all leave in the camp since Monday. General Odway has sent that frightful dog to kennels. The Library is full of packing cases. They are playing nice war-music up in the wood. I heard a lot of motor-lorries start up while I was dressing — oh, it's all too exciting! Don't you wish, Andrew, you were old enough to be going?"

Like the men in the lorries? A crammed ship churning the dark sea? Dawn, and a landing-craft wallowing towards the shingle. Lines of shell-bursts whipping into the waves, nearer, nearer? A scream beside you?

He forced Adrian into existence to speak and smile for him.

"I'd be too sea-sick to enjoy it properly."

"Of course, dear Charles has been through . . . Samuel, is that the telephone?"

"Going, miss."

Silence fell. Andrew was aware of something new, different from other week-ends, a tension, a sense of nervy waiting. The invasion? No. Anywhere else in England it might have been, but for all Cousin Blue's excited prattle it wasn't here. Here

143

they lived on their dream island, with the war just something to talk about, a storm beyond their shores. It must be something else.

Thanks to the road-blocks and the convoy at the camp gate Andrew had been only just in time to clean himself up for supper after his ride, so had had no chance to talk to Cousin Brown alone. He had to guess. Charles had perhaps changed a little, was surer of himself in certain ways, not so ready to play lovey-dovey with Cousin Blue the whole time. But he was very jumpy still. He looked a bit pinker in his cheeks, and that made the mottling of his nose less obvious. Uncle Vole had stayed in his room, so there was only one decanter of wine, not even full, just one glass each and after that water. Heavy drinkers get the jumps if they're taken off, of course. It was hard to tell.

Cousin Blue had talked more than usual, sighed less, tried to drag Charles in to every little bit of talk. Cousin Brown was very silent, almost morose, emitting little clicks of exasperation sometimes at her sister's remarks. But now nobody spoke while Samuel was out of the room, and as he came back all four heads turned towards him.

For an instant as he stood in the doorway he seemed to share the tension, to embody it, but then he spread his hands and smiled.

"Just a wrong number," he said.

Silence again, and the ebb of let-down.

"Charles *is* going to help in your play," said Cousin Blue. "Isn't that fun? He's going to be the King of . . . of . . . somewhere in Italy."

"Naples," said Andrew. Cousin Brown had made no effort to help.

"Yes, of course. It will be quite like old times — it was the dressing up I liked best. Do you have a good leg, Charles? Hose can be so revealing. I almost wish there were a part still for me, only I fear I should forget my lines."

"Which would make it even more like old times," said Cousin Brown.

"Try not to be catty, dear."

Silence again. The tension beginning to return. Andrew almost missed Uncle Vole's slurpings and suckings.

"How is Sir Arnold?" he asked.

144

Instantly he knew that this was it.

"Not very well," said Cousin Brown.

"It is too dreadful," said Cousin Blue. "And he has been so good to us over the years. Samuel, is there any more of that sauce?"

"Coming, Miss May."

Now Andrew could hear the news even in Samuel's voice. Uncle Vole must be definitely dying. Any day now. No wonder they were all so jumpy, Charles especially. If Uncle Vole died without acknowledging him, that mightn't be too bad. But if he were to repudiate him in these last few days . . .

"It is such bad luck," said Cousin May. "I do wish he had had a little longer to get to know dear Charles again."

"Will you be making your usual jaunt to the cinema, Andrew?" said Cousin Brown.

"As far as I know. There's not much on, though."

"I wonder whether that is wise in the circumstances. Perhaps if you were to . . ."

"Oh, it hardly affects dear Andrew, does it, Charles?" said Cousin Blue.

"Of course it does," said Cousin Brown.

"Perhaps we had better talk about something else," said Charles, very firmly, for him.

No, thought Andrew, it doesn't affect me at all. I will not lift a finger or breathe a breath, one way or the other. All that matters is that Uncle Vole shouldn't go and muck up Sunday night for me by dying at the wrong moment.

After supper, by a further exercise of her remarkably strong will, Cousin May made them all play cards, a nursery game called Dunces. Apparently the three Wragge children had been taught it by their mother, almost fifty years ago, and Cousin Blue said it might help bring things back to dear Charles, and besides, if Andrew was a proper Wragge he *had* to know how to play Dunces. Surprisingly Cousin Brown made only a token resistance to the idea, and then played the game with serious attention. Andrew was the dunce in all three games; cards meant nothing to him. Charles made more sense of the game than you'd have expected and had the odd small triumph. The battle for scholar was very close. Cousin Blue won the first

145

game by a few marks. She started with a rush on the second, but Cousin Brown grimly whittled her lead away until they were level on the last hand.

"There!" said Cousin Blue, laying down three nines. "Done you again!"

"But I have honours," said Cousin Brown, and showed her hand, which was all court cards.

"You can't do that," said Cousin Blue. "I had already claimed."

"Of course I can, if it is honours," said Cousin Brown.

"No you can't. Where are the rules?"

"They are in the bottom right-hand drawer of the long-boy in the Library, of course," said Cousin Brown. "I doubt if we can find them now, with all the Americans' equipment in there."

"Really, I will be so happy when they have gone," said Cousin Blue. "One cannot lay one's hand on anything. Mother's photograph album — do you remember, Andrew, I was showing you only the other day, with all those lovely pictures of South Africa — that has simply vanished. Colonel Ganz has taken it as a souvenir, no doubt. He is always picking up little things. He boasts about them quite openly, but I had supposed that at least he paid for them."

"Nonsense, May," said Cousin Brown. "Mabel has simply tidied it. It will turn up."

"I have already asked Mabel."

"You know," said Charles, "I think you *can* declare honours after someone's claimed. Elspeth is right."

Cousin Blue stared, her mouth half open.

"Thank you, Charles," said Cousin Brown, and gathered up the cards.

Perhaps it was his intervention on the wrong side that made the final game so tense. It was close enough, anyway, level-pegging all the way between the sisters, with the other two miles behind. Even Andrew became involved. He couldn't share the interest in the cards, but the behaviour of the players was absorbing — you'd never get through a career without playing the occasional poker-shark or gambling dandy. Cousin Brown played her cards slowly and kept her voice even, but a muscle to the left of her jaw began to twitch as the finish neared.

146

Cousin Blue sighed and giggled, double and triple bluffing, but it was actually harder to guess what sort of hand she might hold. Each accused the other of cheating several times. There were frequent squabbles about the rules, with appeals to Charles, but his memory appeared to have clouded again.

Andrew picked up the last card, the five of clubs. He had two other fives, so he took the two of hearts out and put it on the dump. They'd said something about the two of hearts, but he couldn't remember what. There was an instant of shock, then a slap as the sisters grabbed together . The dump scattered across the table.

"Mine!" shrieked Cousin Blue, but Cousin Brown kept her grip.

The card tore in half.

You'd have to tear the card first and paste it, Andrew thought, and rehearse and rehearse to get the timing right, and even then you mightn't achieve the sudden tiny intensity. Both Cousins stared at their half cards.

"It *was* mine," said Cousin Blue.

"Now we'll have to throw the pack away," said Cousin Brown, and tore her section in half again.

"We have missed the news," she said.

"They won't have said anything about the invasion," said Cousin Blue. "Isn't it fun, only us knowing? I won, didn't I?"

"Let's go to bed," said Charles.

"I shall go and talk to Nurse first," said Cousin Brown.

"Oh, listen to the bombers!" said Cousin Blue "Do you know what they remind me of? Lying in bed and listening to the sea on the rocks at Plettenburg Bay Hotel."

The dusk was still throbbing with engines as Andrew slid up the window of the linen-room, but then a gust of wind whipped through the woodland and drowned them.

He was a bit later than he'd meant. He'd been lying on his bed, getting his homework done while he waited for the movements in the corridor to cease, when Cousin Brown had tapped on his door.

"May has been deliberately attempting to prevent me from talking to you alone," she said. "Father, you realize, is dying."

"I'm sorry."

"I wish I could say I was, but unlike May I cannot act the part. My chief wish is that before he dies he should be persuaded to make some provision for you in his will."

"What about Charles?"

"Father has said nothing to me about Charles, but I would not expect him to. As far as I know he has seen him only once."

"At supper three weeks ago?"

"He should not have made the effort. It was that, I believe, that gave him this final push, though his decline in the past week has been rather rapid. He may even have forgotten that Charles is in the house."

"Won't Cousin May . . ."

"I think not. I have still not been able to make up my mind whether Charles is who he claims to be, but in any case the longer he stays without challenge the more May will be able to remind him about past events, and hence the more convincingly he will be able to play his part. It needs only one small thing to tip the balance either way."

"Would you mind?"

"Should Charles inherit? No, I think not. As a man I rather like him. He has manners and style, and but for his unfortunate addiction . . . but oh, Andrew, it is you and your future that truly concern me!"

"You needn't worry."

"The stage is such a chancy career. What I have come to say is that whether or no Father makes provision for you, he will not leave me penniless, and I shall make it my business to look after you."

"Oh . . . I don't know what to say . . . er . . . I hope I won't need it, but thank you very much."

"Not at all, my dear boy. I am being thoroughly selfish. You, I believe, are going to have the stage career I should have had, so naturally I wish it to be a success. For me it will be my career too."

Adrian had continued to stammer gratitude, but inside him Andrew had sat cold and angry. A lot of people were going to try this, he thought. None of them was going to succeed, ever. If they looked like being useful he would use them. When they had ceased to be useful he would let them drop. If that was what Cousin Brown wanted, he owed her nothing at all. It was better

148

that way. No entanglements.

He changed the subject.

"If . . . I mean if Sir Arnold . . ."

"Dies?"

"Yes. What about the play?"

"Oh, I shall continue with that, unless I am somehow prevented. We will have to cancel a few rehearsals, for decency's sake, but I see no reason why we should not pick up the strands again in a week or two. My mind has been greatly eased by the improvement you have managed to effect in Jean's performance . . ."

He had had to let her talk on. She was, he realized, far more tense than she was trying to make out. An age was ending for her, a god dying. The muscle in her cheek still twitched when she fell silent. It had been another half-hour before she'd left.

He climbed carefully down, reminding fingers and toes of the route. They knew it well already, but he was going to have to climb back up in the dark, which he'd never tried before. The mess on the pantry drainpipe was worse than ever. If General Odway was really leaving there'd soon be no guards on the front and back doors and he could take a key off Samuel's board and go in and out the easy way — but he probably wouldn't, he thought. Burgling made the whole adventure more private, more interesting.

Not being sure where other GI sentries might be posted he started on the long way round below the terraces, moving casually as if out for an evening stroll, but as he crossed the path leading down into the woodland garden he stopped. A movement had caught his eye under the trees, an echo of his own, not furtive, not particularly wishing to be seen. He stood, half-hidden by a shrub, pretending to look at his watch, but peering sidelong down the slope.

The man beckoned. The energy and clarity of the gesture told him at once who it was — Samuel, but not the gentle quiet-moving old man who served the Wragges. No, it was that other Samuel, the embodiment of earth, Prospero's slave. Hell, thought Andrew. He's het up about something. Can't be helped. She'll just have to wait a bit longer. He strolled down the woodland path as though his check on his watch had told him he had time for a detour. As he approached Samuel darted

149

towards him and with another Caliban gesture thrust a piece of
paper under his nose.

"You read this for me."

It was a sheet torn from a note-book with a short newspaper
cutting pinned to the top left corner. Beneath the cutting, in a
slant American script, was written "Hull Advertiser, Jan 12,
1943."

"Do you know this man?" Andrew read. "The authorities
are attempting to trace the identity of a man currently in the
Royal Infirmary. He is aged about sixty, 5ft 4in, slim build,
grey hair, blue eyes, clean shaven. He appears to have lost his
memory following recent enemy action, and does not know his
own name. At times he believes he may be called Charles
Arnold Wragge. If you can help identify him, please contact
Hull Royal Infirmary."

Andrew folded the cutting back. There was a bit of photograph on the other side, typical local-paper stuff, part of a man's
leg, a silver trophy-cup, the blimp-like end of a monster
marrow.

"Well," he said. "That looks as if it's that."

Samuel shook his head, dazed with disappointment.

"Where did you get it?"

"Phil just sent it. Sergeant Stephens, he rung during supper."

"When you said it was a wrong number?"

"Didn't want to tell anyone till I seen it. Any case, I got to
show Baas Wragge first. Just been to fetch it off of the
sergeant."

"Is that all right? I mean, you remember what the sergeant
said about . . ."

"Sure I remember. Bit after you told me that, I was going up
the drive — sergeant had got me some butter for Miss May —
when I run into a couple of Yanks. Started asking me questions
— where was I going? — and then calling me names. I didn't
say nothing, and it looked like they might get to knocking me
around when the sergeant happened down and they run off."

"You didn't tell anyone?"

"Didn't want Mary Jane worriting. Sergeant said me being a
nigger he'd not get the officers to take it serious. After that we
fixed a place — that old fell tree top of Five-acre — so he can
leave Miss May's butter when it's easy for him to get down

150

there, and I fetch it and leave the money in the morning, when they're all busy soldiering. I only come out now cause he rung me, saying he'd got something from Phil. I'd asked him, couple of days back, telling him it's getting urgent — can't tell you why. Thought he might've found something the other way."

He took the cutting back and stared at it, shaking his head.

"He still isn't Baas Charlie," he said.

"I suppose it doesn't absolutely prove it. But it does show he's telling the truth about losing his memory and so on. He can't have started making his story up that long ago and not done anything about it till now."

Samuel shook his head again and gave a grunting sigh.

"Better be getting long back in," he said.

"I'm going to wander round a bit longer."

"Guards don't like it, not if you're after dark."

"They don't know I'm out."

Samuel nodded and grinned, though his brow stayed frowning.

"Baas Charlie, he used to climb all over the house, your age," he said.

"Must run in the family. Good-night."

"Good-night."

Mrs Oliphant was snoring, louder than the bombers or the wind. Jean was waiting by the window, anxious and cross, and expecting to snuggle on the parlour settee, but he made her put on an extra jersey and walk with him in the roaring woods for an hour while he talked about roles he would one day play, and how he would tackle them. Her lips were rubbery cold when he kissed her good-night.

The climb back up went easily. The linen-room window was still open. It was just before midnight when he got to his room. On his pillow he found a note in Mrs Mkele's handwriting. "Please to see Sir Arnold 10 o'clock a.m. Respectfully, S.M."

FIVE

There was no answer to his tap, but as he took hold of the handle it turned from the inside and the door opened. Uncle

151

Vole's nurse blinked at him with an outraged look, as though someone had just pinched her bum.

"Sir Arnold asked to see me," he explained.

She put a hand to her ear and pulled out a plug of cotton-wool. He explained again. She stood aside to let him through.

"Try not to tire him," she snapped as she left.

Uncle Vole looked younger. Perhaps the angle of the head on the pillow smoothed out some of the wrinkles, or perhaps what he had been saying to the nurse had brought a flicker of blood into the parchment cheeks, but somehow his whole face spoke of what it might have been in years gone by, all the way back into the obscurities of childhood. The room was summer-warm. Arms and hands lay inert on the counterpane, framing the body, which was so slight that without them it would have been hard to know where it lay beneath the bedclothes. A finger fluttered, summoning Andrew closer. The rheumy eyes glared up, then closed.

"Stupid cow," said Uncle Vole. "Stuffs muck in her ears so she can't hear what I'm telling her. Must have a good-looker, I told them. If that's the best they can do . . ."

"I suppose the young ones have been called up."

"If I was Adolf Hitler I'd have all that sort put down. Waste of money keeping them alive. Watcher want?"

"You sent for me, sir."

The eyes opened again, not glaring but peering, seeking for something in Andrew's eyes.

"I'm dying."

"Bad luck, sir."

"That all you can say?"

"If I said anything else you wouldn't believe me."

A long pause.

"Right. The bugger calls himself Charles. He's not my son. Spotted that soon as I saw him. Might've booted him out that very night. Thought I'd have a bit more fun with the pair of you. Wanted to see May's face when the coppers came for him."

"Did Samuel show you . . .?"

"Bit from that paper? Don't prove a thing."

"I thought . . ."

"Fuck that. I say he ain't my son, and Samuel says he ain't

152

neither. None of the others is worth a bugger. That's why I've hung on to Samuel. There's a nigger-trick he can do — they can't all, but he can. I've seen him stare at a heap of lumps like a sick goose and say 'Big stone in there, baas,' and I'd hammer the lump apart and half the time he'd be right. More'n once I had him tell me the Company Police were coming on a surprise visit and I've had time to get things straight for them. If he says the bugger's not Charlie, you can take it as read."

"What are you going to do, sir?"

The eyes closed as the old man rested. Andrew studied the line of the blue lips, the nose pointed like a sail. You'd never be able to afford a pause this long, he thought. You'd have to make it seem like one.

"Brandy," said Uncle Vole. "On the table here. Use the dropper."

There was a bottle, a glass and a glass tube with a rubber bulb at the top. Andrew poured out some brandy, sucked a little into the tube and fed it in between the lips. Another immense pause.

"I'm going to tell you a story," said Uncle Vole, still with his eyes closed. "I don't like you. Why should I? Nobody's ever liked me. But you're my sort — look out for Number One and bugger the universe. Might have told you anyway, one day. Want someone in the family to know. You're the one. Goes like this. When I was eleven I decided I was fed up. Fed up with my fool of a mother and my mouse of a brother and my Godspouting greasy father and everything else. Most of all fed up with Chapel. Came to me one morning, like Paul on the way to whatsit, that I was buggered if I was going to sit through that one more Sunday."

"Yes, sir. You told me."

"Shut up and listen. My brother held me down while my father laid into me with his belt on my bare arse and I swore at them the foulest I knew. My father must've gone off his rocker — he kept at it till I passed out, and I was five days in bed after, lying on my belly. Got the marks still. Feel 'em each time I go to the shit-house. But it didn't change my mind — all it did was make me promise myself by every oath I knew I'd get the best of 'em in the end, and I'd do it in a way so they'd think about it every day they lived, all the rest of their lives. Brandy."

Andrew dribbled another dose between the lips and waited.

153

"It wasn't my father I swore I'd do for so much as my swine of a brother. I knew I'd have to wait my time. Four years I sat through Chapel, foul-mouthing under my breath, thinking about it. First I knew I'd need money. When I was twelve my father put me into a ship-chandler's. I worked at that job like a good 'un. Stole what I could, but only when I knew it was safe. Spent a bit on whores — balls dropped afore I was thirteen — saved the rest . . ."

His voice was a scrape, barely loud enough to hear, with indragged wheezing every few words. When he rested Andrew gave him more brandy, imagining in his own throat the voice that would sound like that and yet be heard in the furthest seats.

"Didn't tell yer. Brother seven years older than me. Been others between, but they'd died. Got engaged. Older than he was. Chapel, of course. Plain as a boot. Father put him up to it. She'd a part share in a coal-yard coming to her. Father wouldn't let 'em marry till my brother was twenty-five. Three more years. I was fifteen."

Now the voice strengthened slightly, as if with remembered energies.

"Summer Sundays they'd go for a row on the river. Not alone, of course. Chapel. If her cow of a mother was stuck they'd take me. Only a kid, so that counted. He never touched her. I can see us now, him with his oily pink neck and his little bowler and his stiff white collar and his waistcoat with the watch-chain like Father wore, sweating at the oars, and her lolling under her sun-brolly at the tiller and looking at him and thinking how she was stuck with him cause it was her last chance, and me hunkered up in the bows, watching her past his head, thinking too. Brandy."

Revenge, Andrew thought. You get it a lot as a motive. Reading the lines you wonder what the point is. But here is this old man, dying, sending for me so he can have his revenge on my family one more time . . . The blue lips moved again.

"August nineteenth was her birthday. Tuesday, with a big party. Her Mum had to bake all Sunday, Sabbath or no Sabbath. A week before, on the Saturday, I took the twelve quid I'd saved and put it on a horse called Breaker. Came in at six to one. Then I knew it was my hour. There ain't no God up among the stars, that's all horse shit, but there's a little god

154

inside you and when he tells you Go you must go, or he'll be sour on you the rest of your days. I bought myself a passage to the Cape, ship sailing Monday. Not my own name. Booked another for Boston, sailing Liverpool, Tuesday, just the deposit. Used my own name for that. Bought a padlock, bottle of bubbly, pie, peaches, glasses, napkins, all the trimmings. Made sure of my boat."

A long pause, different somehow in nature. He wasn't simply resting but remembering, savouring.

"Sunday. Chapel in the morning, then dinner. Amy used to have dinner with her lot, then we'd go by and pick her up and on down to the boat-house. Between us and her we went close by the chandler's where I worked. Told Ozzie I'd a present for Amy's birthday I wanted him to have a look at. I'd a key to the shop, cause of being first in to sweep out. The old man had a store-room at the back, kept it padlocked, but I'd made myself a key. Saturday night I'd been down and changed the padlocks. Took him into the shop, opened the store-room. After you, Ozzie, booted his back and shut the door. Locked it, picked up my basket I'd hid under the counter, on down to Amy's, told 'em Ozzie'd be meeting us at the boat-house. Soon as we were out of the house I told Amy fact was Ozzie'd come over queer at dinner, but if I'd let on to her Mum she'd have been kept home to help with the baking. Sin to waste an afternoon like that, and the boat all booked. She didn't like baking. I was only a kid, wasn't I?"

More brandy and another rest, the lips pursing and falling back.

"Oh, it was perfect weather. It had to be — my little god was working. Bloody stiff pull in a boat that size, but I needed the room in the bottom. Ran in among some reeds I'd spotted earlier trips. 'What are you doing?' Got the bubbly out. Winked. 'Going to America Tuesday, so you've got to drink my health. Sorry old Ozzie ain't here too.' She was a stupid cow. Catch Ozzie drinking bubbly, on a Sunday too, even with the reeds to hide him. He'd have rowed straight home to tell Father. She didn't think about any of that, only the romance of me going to America and her being in the secret, and trying her first champagne. She might be Chapel, but I'd been watching her, Sunday by Sunday. She said it tasted like lemonade. Never knew you were supposed to get it chilled, so we drank it warm while I told her about America and how I was going to make my fortune and bring her back a necklace of real pearls. Best afternoon of my life. Brandy."

The rest was shorter this time.

"We had some pie and more bubbly. 'Now I want you to kiss me good-bye. I've never kissed a woman before and I want to know what it's like. Least you can do for a brother-in-law.' Didn't give her a chance to say no, just slid my arm round her waist and started in. 'That was nice, let's do it again.' She was waiting-ripe. Didn't take long to work her up. We tried drinking out of the same glass, and then we ate a peach together, juice running over our faces, down on to our clothes. Gave me an excuse to start taking 'em off — I'd paid a whore to show me how everything fastened — clothes women wore those days. Don't, she kept telling me, but I'd kiss her quiet while I undid the stupid little hooks and she never moved a finger to stop me. She was clay in my hands. I could've done anything I wanted with her, anything at all. Clay in my hands."

Rest.

"Didn't let her go till it was getting on dark. Four times I did her, each go better 'n the last, and each time I went in I put up a prayer. 'Give us a kid, little god. Make it a son.' Nobody came by. There was only us, and the reeds, and the boat-cushions in the bottom of the boat. Then I told her to get herself dressed and I pulled back to the boat-house, whistling under the stars, and her sighing and blubbing in the stern. You'll be all right, my girl, I thought. First you'll think you can get away not telling anyone, and then you'll find what's happening inside you and you'll think you're shamed for ever, but Ozzie'll marry you all the same, cause of the coal-yard. Father will see he does. Nothing to blub about. Walking up from the river I kept my arm round her waist and talked lovey-dovey about her coming out with me to Boston. Took her up past her house till we came to the chandler's. 'Got a present for you.' Pulled out the keys and told her where to look. There was a street lamp shone in through the shop window, so she could see. She was a stupid cow — she still didn't twig. Soon as she was in the shop I went whistling off to where I'd stowed my gear. Slept on a bench that night. Next afternoon I was leaning on the stern rail, looking back up the river where we'd been."

He stopped, exhausted, but a flutter of his fingers showed he had something more to say. Andrew waited, interested but still disappointed. It was too obvious. A scene like this should have something jarring in it, something almost wrong but still dead right . . . The story, he knew, had been told before, often. It had the same feel of being shaped by performance as Mrs Oliphant's account of her husband's death. Uncle Vole had brooded it into that shape over the years, told it round diggers' fires on the veld, in the pauses of poker sessions on *Diamond*, and then only in the private theatre of his skull. Now, for the last time, aloud. When he started to speak again rhythm and tone were different. This time he was telling Andrew something new.

"Soon as I started to make my pile I wrote and hired a nark back home, find out what had happened. Answer, Father hadn't made 'em wait after all. They'd married that November and they'd had a kid in May. A boy. My son."

The eyes shot open, glaring up with all their old malice.

"Your grandad."

Andrew simply nodded to show he'd understood. The eyes closed.

"Never had another, and I know why. Amy expected Ozzie to do for her same as I'd done in the reeds, and Ozzie wasn't up to it. In the end she scared him, so he couldn't do it at all. Still wasn't enough for me. I'd got to rub it in, so that they woke up mornings thinking about it and went to bed nights with it still buzzing in their brains. Took me a while to think how. Then it came to me. Something Samuel said, if you want to know. I decided when I'd made my pile I'd come back to England and build myself a house, no expense spared, close as I could get to Southampton, make a splash in all the papers so they'd know it was there, go on doing things, charities, all that, so my name would always be in front of 'em. Sir Arnold Wragge of The Mimms. Then on they'd never walk into their grubby little two up two down without their guts twisting inside them, thinking of me. That's why I built this home. That's what it means. That's why I've sent for the lawyer, to change my will. I'm leaving it to you."

Nunc Dimittis.

"Well, watcher got to say?"

"It's been very interesting, sir."

The eyes opened, furious.

"Watcher mean, interesting? That all you got to say?"

Andrew paused, mastering the rage inside him, keeping his face marble. The rage was intense, a focused blaze, far stronger than what he'd felt running up through the plantation when he'd heard Jean's scream and Brian's laugh. This old wretch, this useless left-over, trying to sucker himself on to Andrew, to attach the long loathsome trail of his own life, all the way back to that afternoon in the Itchen reeds, for Andrew to drag on through the years. It was not going to happen. Mum was dead. There was going to be no past. He let the pause stretch while the clock tocked in the corridor outside and the painful breath wheezed to and fro. At the twanging instant he spoke, icy but amused.

"It has been useful to me as an actor to listen to an old man on his death-bed."

Instantly, with no pause at all, the body beneath the bed-clothes convulsed. That spasm jerked the shoulders up and sideways, with the head seeming to lunge snarling for Andrew's wrist. The movement stopped. In fact it had been only a twitch of a few inches, but its suddenness and speed had given it that sense of violence, the last spurt of life's energies exploding out of an ember. The right arm scrabbled to support the body, failed. The body flopped back. The lungs dragged at air, choked on the indrawn breath. The face suffused blue-purple and lay staring at the ceiling.

After a couple of seconds Andrew took the right wrist and tried to find the pulse. None. With his index finger he pulled an eyelid down. It came at his touch and stayed. He closed the other eye and stood staring down.

We did that, he thought. Adrian and Andrew. We spoke the word, and it was done. A clean cut. No past. Gone.

He waited half a minute more, filled with the wonder of it, then turned and ran to the door. The nurse was standing along by a window into the courtyard, frowning at the crossword she was doing on the sill.

"Quick!" he blurted (worried, scared, only-a-boy). "Something's happened!"

She scuttered to the room, saw the still-purple face on the pillow, paused and went quietly over. She felt for the pulse, raised an eyelid and closed it, and stood back.

"He was telling me a story," he said. "Then suddenly he sort of choked."

"Now don't you go fretting — it was none of your fault. Could've happened any instant. A wonder he'd lasted that long."

"Shall . . . shall I go and tell my cousins?"

"And if somebody could phone up the doctor . . ."

"All right."

Cousin Blue sobbed gustily. Cousin Brown went to her desk and began a list of things to be done. Charles, after a few grave murmurs, stared out of the window. Andrew had found the three of them in the Boudoir, apparently in the pause of an argument. Now all he could do was wait. Jean would be coming along for a rehearsal in ten minutes, and he could slip out and explain . . .

Cousin Brown rose and left the room with the list in her hand. Cousin Blue dabbed her eyes, blew her nose and crossed to the window where Charles was standing. She put her hand on his shoulder, a gesture implying ownership as much as affection, and looked at the familiar view in silence. Cousin Brown came back into the room.

"How very peculiar," she said. "Please ring that bell, Andrew — two pushes. I telephoned Foley to tell him of Father's death and to ask him to come out as soon as he was able, but it appears that he had already arranged to do so this very afternoon."

"On a Saturday?" said Cousin Blue.

"Samuel apparently telephoned him on Thursday, saying that he was speaking with Father's authority. He would have preferred to come yesterday, naturally, but was told that was too soon. Furthermore, he was not to let any of us know that he was coming."

"Really!" said Cousin Blue. "It seems to me that Samuel is becoming a thorough . . ."

She stopped as the door opened and Samuel came quietly in.

"You rung, miss."

159

"Yes," said Cousin Brown. "I'm afraid I have some sad news. My father has died."

"We are all very sorry, miss."

"Thank you. And you have known him a long time and been a very faithful friend and servant. Would you please see that the others are told?"

Samuel nodded and turned as if to leave.

"One moment," said Cousin Brown. "I gather you spoke to Mr Foley on Thursday and made arrangements for him to come and see Father this afternoon."

"Yes, miss."

"And you asked him not to let any of us know he was coming?"

"Only what Baas Wragge told me to say," said Samuel, not at all defensive.

"But why? It seems very peculiar."

Samuel hesitated, looking gravely at the four of them in turn.

"He said to tell Mr Foley to bring out the old will," he said. "He was planning to change it."

"Oh, nonsense!" said Cousin Blue.

"I do not agree," said Cousin Brown. "All we know about the old will is that he made it when he was in a rage with Clarice . . ."

"Your silly little wife, Charlie," said Cousin May.

"Ah," said Charles.

"It would be entirely sensible for Father to make a new will," said Cousin Brown. "He would no doubt leave instructions for the clarification of Charles's position, and also make some provision for Andrew. Did he say anything to you about any of this, Andrew?"

"Andrew is hardly a reliable . . ."

"May!"

"Dear Andrew, I am not talking personally, of course. But anyone who thought he might inherit *rather* a lot of money would be bound to be a *bit* influenced . . ."

"It's all right," said Andrew. "I mean, well, actually he spent most of the time telling me about the row he had with the rest of the family. I sort of got the impression that he knew he was, well, dying, and he just wanted to rub it in he'd been in the right."

160

"Of course he was," said Cousin Blue. "That goes without saying. Samuel, I have to tell you that in my opinion you are grossly exceeding your duties and we are far from pleased with you. You are not to tell anyone else this ridiculous tale. You agree, Charles?"

"Er, well . . . isn't it all a bit late? I mean, er . . ."

"It is clear," said Cousin Brown, "that Father intended to do something for Andrew. That is no doubt why it wouldn't do for Foley to come out until this afternoon. Father wanted to speak to Andrew first. Samuel, did he tell you anything about how he proposed to change his will?"

"Yes, miss."

"Well?"

"He said for me not to tell anyone."

There was a long silence while they looked at him. Cousin Blue was about to break it when Samuel held up his hand.

"Baas Wragge is dead," he said. "No good me saying anything now."

"You know, I seem to think that's right," said Charles. "Let's see what's in the will, eh? Then we'll know where we are."

"Very well," said Cousin Brown. "Andrew, I think you had better stay here this afternoon. Mr Foley will no doubt wish to speak with you. And Samuel, I think you would be well advised to tell Mr Foley what you know, too."

"I must think, miss."

"I'd better go and rescue Jean," said Andrew. "She hasn't got a pass."

"Oh yes, of course," said Cousin Brown. "Now, Samuel, what time . . ."

Andrew slipped away. He had to wriggle through a sort of traffic jam on the stairs, where the GIs carrying the officers' personal belongings down from the upper floors had become enmeshed with others ferrying cases of equipment out of the lower rooms. There were still the same furious outbursts but their tone had changed. The frustration was now of hustle. I'll make her go alone, he thought. The trailers had looked like rubbish, back-row stuff. No harm in reminding her what it used to be like without me.

161

Old Mr Foley was a surprise — not all that old, for a start. Andrew had been expecting someone ancient, parchment-dry, with a reedy voice and gold-rimmed spectacles. He turned out to be around sixty, a large man with jutting bones, like a starved cart-horse. Certainly he appeared exhausted, with deep-sunk eyes and wet purplish lips. When he spoke the air in front of him was filled with spray. To Andrew he had the look of a visiting preacher, the sort about whom the chapel-goers murmur afterwards that he used to be a very fine man.

Altogether the scene was a bit like Chapel. The furniture in the Boudoir had been rearranged with Mr Foley facing his congregation across Cousin Brown's desk. His clerk, a nut-coloured little woman, sat at his elbow. The family were in the front seats and the servants behind. Flies tapped and buzzed on the window-panes. Orders and music — Cousin Blue's nice war-music — came faintly from the camp tannoy. Brief spells of sunshine shafted between speeding clouds. It was difficult to stay awake.

"Bit premature to read this," said Mr Foley, "but since I'm here, and it's here, and you're all here, and we don't want a lot of unnecessary speculation at a time of great uncertainty for us all, and there's the difficulty of getting everyone together . . ."

He drew a wheezing breath. The clerk took her chance to whisper in his ear.

"Yes, yes, of course," he said. "I'd best explain before I start that there are provisions in this will — my father drew it up . . . when was it? Oh, yes, 1922 . . . provisions about which my father was dubious from the first . . . whether they would stand the test of the courts, you understand . . . supposing it came to litigation, that is. Sir Arnold was absolutely insistent, it seems. Be that as it may . . . ahem . . . in view of recent events, let us hope . . ."

He glanced at Charles who was staring at his own shoes and did not stir. As the lawyer began to read, Andrew withdrew himself into his inner cave. The will was nothing to do with him. He would not move a muscle, breathe a breath, for the sake of a single penny of the estate. He would not even take an interest in the outcome. He let the words bumble against his mind like the flies against the window.

"*To Samuel Mkele, so long as he shall remain in service at The Mimms . . . To Mary Mkele . . . service at The Mimms . . . To Florence Lavender Franklin . . . The Mimms . . . The Mimms . . . The Mimms . . .*"

Endless commaless sentences. Jean would be at the cinema by now — he'd bike out and meet her on her way back. No rehearsal tomorrow. Church, of course. Black arm-bands? Uncle Vole's death was not part of the plan but it was perfectly timed, heightening the drama, the feeling of world-change, of time rushing away, of a moment to be seized and clung to — she would feel that. He would see that she did. And at a tactical level the domestic upheavals meant that he could see just as much of her as he needed, judging his point each time at which to sigh and say he'd better be getting back to the house, so that by the time she cycled off to milking tomorrow afternoon . . . He must find an hour somewhere to get the eyrie ready. It looked like being a colder evening than he'd hoped for. They'd need something to cover them . . .

"*. . . my son Charles Arnold Bellamy Wragge . . . using their utmost diligence in such inquiry . . . failing such proof . . . my grandson John Nicholas Wragge . . . conditional upon his residence at The Mimms . . .*"

As Mr Foley tired, his voice became hollow and dragging, a voice from the grave, muttering instructions — well said, old Vole, canst work i' th' ground so fast.

"*. . . predecease me, leaving no male issue . . . my house The Mimms . . . and all other structures whatsoever to be utterly demolished . . .*"

"No!"

Cousin Blue's shriek of protest shook Andrew from his trance and allowed his aural memory to reconstruct the rhythm of the preceding phrase and then to understand it. Mr Foley looked up.

"This is the provision about which my father was dubious," he said. "Rightly, in my opinion. It could certainly be contested in the courts by any interested party, though the litigation might prove lengthy and costly, so let us hope . . ."

His voice trailed away. He glanced towards Charles, as if expecting him to come to his rescue, but it was Cousin Brown who spoke.

"May we have this quite clear? My father left instructions that a search was to be made for my brother Charles, and if he was found then the estate was to be his . . ."

"After certain bequests and the settlements upon yourself and Miss May, yes, yes."

"If he was not found, then Nicholas was to be heir. And if Nicholas died before my father, leaving no children . . ."

"No *male* issue . . ."

". . . then May and I and the servants would still get our share and after that something called the Wragge Foundation was to be set up, and everything left would be sold and put into it, except that this house and all its outbuildings had to be pulled down . . ."

"Ridiculous!" said Cousin Blue. "He must have been of unsound mind."

"Nonsense," said Cousin Brown. "It was absolutely typical of Father. He hated women."

Yes, thought Andrew. The old poison-spitter, in his prime of malice, twenty-five years ago, just after he'd lost his lawcase to get his hands on Nicholas, standing on his terraces one evening, looking at his view, hearing a daughter's voice from behind his rose walk — May's simper to some shiny fortune-hunter, perhaps, or had it been Elspeth hallooing to her actors? — women, stupid cows, only good for a couple of functions. No harm in daughters, rounded the family out, wore the stones, gave the artist-johnny something to paint. But it was the house that mattered, and a man in it, a man with your own name, living on for you when you were a goner and his sons doing the same after. You'd have thought Charles had the right ideas about women, way he treated his sisters — what did he want to go marrying that Aussie cow for? Couldn't he have had her without? Had all the women he wanted on his allowance? Now there was only this brat, other side of the world. He'd come back for the money though, and boot his cow of a mother out for the money too. Must remember to put that in the bloody will. But suppose he went and died like Charlie . . . (May's simper beyond the roses. Elspeth's bray.) No! Nobody! Hang

164

on as long as you can, squeeze the utmost relish from your pile, then when you've got to go wipe the slate clean. Finish.

". . . all so dreadfully complicated," Cousin Blue was saying. "Such a good thing dear Charles came back to us in time, and we needn't worry any more."

"Yes, indeed," said Mr Foley. "It appears to have saved a great deal of trouble. Of course it would have saved yet more if Sir Arnold had lived long enough to clarify his wishes to me, but I have little doubt that it was to that end he sent for me at this juncture . . . Well, I think I have no need to read you the rest of this document, which concerns the detailed instructions for the establishment and running of the Wragge Foundation . . ."

He began to push back his chair, closing the meeting, but as he did so his face changed. A quick look of surprise, replaced at once by wariness, came over it. At the same instant there was a muttering from the servants. Andrew turned his head and saw Samuel standing and holding up his hand, palm forward, fingers spread, not asking for attention but commanding it.

Once in Chapel Miss Dandy, a quiet little spinster, had stood up just as the sermon was about to start and accused Mr Ruggles, the Minister, of breach of promise. Now in this other congregation Andrew felt much the same tangle of responses — embarrassment, shock, pity, inquisitiveness, relief from tedium and so on. You were aware of them before anything was said. It was the speaking-out-of-turn that aroused them — Miss Dandy, a woman, unmarried at that, and plain and poor too — Samuel, despite his long connection with the family still only a servant. Though he had been remembered in the will, the will wasn't for him. Andrew could sense that the other servants, Mrs Mkele included, felt the same social shock.

Ignoring them, Samuel spoke quietly but with complete confidence, in the Hampshire accent he normally used only below stairs.

"You haven't told us, sir, what and if this Mr Charles turns out to be not our Mr Charles after all."

"Really! Samuel!" said Cousin Blue.

Mrs Mkele whispered and tugged at the hem of Samuel's jacket. He put down his hand and eased her fingers loose, then stood waiting.

165

"Ahem," said Mr Foley, waiting too and looking towards Charles, who simply shrugged his shoulders and half-spread his hands.

"I think it would be as well to clear the point up," said Cousin Brown.

"Quite unnecessary," said Cousin Blue. "We must offer Mr Foley some tea before he goes."

Mr Foley turned helplessly to his clerk, who took the will from him, turned a couple of pages, pointed and whispered. Mr Foley sighed and whispered back. Andrew cursed. If this was going to drag on he wouldn't have biked out far enough by the time he met Jean coming back. He wanted her to feel his eagerness, to be sure of him, trusting . . . At last the clerk prodded Mr Foley back to his duty.

"The contingency in question," he said, ". . . of course Miss Elspeth is right . . . I shall have to look into it . . . naturally it is not covered in the will itself . . . I may have to take further advice, but my impression — please note that it is only an impression — is that the only parties who could bring a case disputing the authenticity of a claimant are those whose interest is affected, and since the other provisions of the will would stand the only such parties are the Trustees of the proposed Wragge Foundation. Most unfortunately the original appointees have all deceased, and, ahem, for some reason fresh Trustees seem not to have been appointed . . ."

"You mean that I, or Andrew here, or even Samuel, could not bring such a case?" said Cousin Brown.

"I think not, Miss Elspeth. That is to say you would have to contest the whole will, not merely Mr Charles's right to inherit. Any such move would involve extremely protracted and costly litigation. Let us most sincerely hope it can be avoided."

Again he pushed back his chair and half rose, but again he was stopped by a gesture from Samuel.

"It'd be something for the police, too, wouldn't it, sir?" he said.

This time Mr Foley completed his movement and rose. He passed the will to the clerk, who folded it and tied its pink ribbon round it.

"I doubt if the police would be interested," he said. "If the family recognize Mr Charles, which they appear to do, that

166

would satisfy them. They are extremely busy these days. There is a war on, you know."

The clerk tucked the will at last into Mr Foley's brief case and snapped and locked the clasp. Nothing for me, thought Andrew. Not a mention. Be free and fare thou well.

The mood stayed with him as he pumped up the drive, past the camp gate. A convoy of empty lorries was jolting across towards the wood. He could see men waiting in paraded lines beneath the trees. Some smaller trucks, closed and not canvas-topped, were parked near Sergeant Stephens's store shed, having their camouflage touched up it looked like, but then something on one of them slipped and a whole square of cloth flopped down, revealing a large white circle with a red cross on it. Of course, you don't let the heroes notice the ambulances, not on their way to the war. For once the notion didn't fill him with dread. The confidence, the sense of power and invulnerability that had welled up in him as he gazed down on Uncle Vole's dead body was strong enough to make him feel that when the time came somehow the same power would be there to rescue him from between the closing talons. And meanwhile there was Jean.

Twenty minutes later he crossed a crest and saw her already started down the opposite slope. He put on a spurt till the wind whined round his ears, and when he had made up ground he freewheeled, timing his descent so that they came swooping effortlessly down to meet in the valley bottom.

"Now you've got to climb the whole way back up," she said. "You should've waited for me at the top."

"Couldn't."

SEVEN

She had begun to sob, a gentle watery sound that blended with all the other noises of the evening, the bubbling call of a dove below, the crackle of the camp tannoy, and the drumming of lorry after lorry crossing the park loaded with soldiers. There had been thousands of them in the camp two nights back. Tonight all but a hundred or two would be gone. Tomorrow they would be across the Channel, fighting their way on to the beaches, and you and you and you would be dead.

Andrew lay on his back listening, with his hands beneath his head and the peeling dome above him. The canvas of the old cart-cover rasped on his naked shoulder-blades. Under the eiderdown, borrowed from Florrie's linen-room, Jean's fingers drifted over his rib-cage.

"You shouldn't've. You shouldn't've," she whispered.

All his choice then? No will of her own? So wholly in his power? Anyway, her fingers said she was lying.

The painted fingers on the ceiling were saying something too as they reached for the dove. There were yellowish lines to their left, loose curves. Hair. And the foot — that thing it was standing on was a scallop shell. Instantly all the other fragments of paint came into their context, spoke. There were three fingers of the other hand, covering a breast. An edge of floating gauze. A wave-crest. Venus, landing from the sea, new-naked. And there would have been satyrs in the niches, or nymphs. A bed, here, where the cart-cover was, against the blanked-off window — no wonder you weren't meant to see in from the house! The old goat!

He almost laughed aloud, but stopped himself. Mustn't spoil the mood. Her sobs were satisfying to both of them in different ways. And it wasn't the sort of joke she'd enjoy.

Perhaps it had been a young goat, though. Long before Uncle Vole, two hundred years ago, living in the house Uncle Vole had pulled down to build his new one, plonking this extravagant top-knot on to the squat old dovecote so that he'd have somewhere to bring his milkmaids to. No, not milkmaids, actresses lured down from London. They'd know what the room was — a private theatre, a wooden O, for a play by a cast of two who were their own and only audience. Now Andrew had staged it again, after all these years.

The discovery was immensely exhilarating. It wasn't a fluke. He had felt it the moment he'd first climbed through the hatch, had understood the essence of it in his bones, had refused other chances — the night she had slept in the Ivory Room, or last Sunday night, kissing good-bye at midnight through Mrs Oliphant's window — because he had recognized what this place was and known that the play must be staged here. The room was sacred to the act, built for this ritual, this triumph,

168

wrought by his sole power, his Art. To savour the moment more he let Adrian slip free, turn and look down cool and benign on the tableau, the yellow satin eiderdown, Andrew full face and smiling at the ceiling, Jean's ginger head in profile on his bare left arm . . .

"My brave spirit!"

The murmur set Jean off again.

"Oh, you shouldn't've!"

Rot. She had bought her own ticket for the performance. She had stood at the bottom of the ladder on the floor they had swept together, softly calling his name. He had raised the trapdoor.

"Come down."

He had shaken his head. She had climbed slowly up the ladder, looking into his face, seeing in his eyes what was going to happen, knowing it must because she wanted it too. That was important. It always would be. The triumph didn't lie in persuading them to pay for their tickets, but in causing them to experience all the exhilaration of the event, to be swept up, rapt, made into something more than themselves for as long as the performance lasted, and then to go home changed. All that he had done for her.

He slid his arm from under her head, rose on his elbow and eased her on to her back so that he could gaze down at her. The only undesigned element was the lighting, not the gold summer dusk he had asked for but almost better, a storm buffeting the dirty panes, a heavy, drab light but still enough to let him see the tender-to-the-touch look under the freckled skin, and the wet half-open lips and the greenish eyes blurred with tears. He bent his head to lick as much as kiss the salty lashes, but she nuzzled her mouth upward, looking for his. The wind thumped against the glass. Further off, but still part of its roar, the lorries trundled another load of Americans away to the tempest on the beaches.

"Do you keep count?"

"Of what?"

"How many of us?"

"I don't think about the past much."

"You like reading your press cuttings."

"That's different."

"You're only awake on the stage? Everything else is dreams, the sort you can't remember?"

"In a manner of speaking. We are such stuff."

Adrian was lounging in the corner of the sofa wearing a blue silk dressing-gown over shirt and slacks. The girl, in black jeans and black angora jersey, cuddled catlike at his side. It was after midnight. On the low table to his right lay the remains of the supper she had had ready for his return from the theatre — *raie au beurre noir*, a pear, a half bottle of Meursault, brandy. The fire murmured to itself. The attitudes of the couple had a composed look, not because there was any audience but because it was part of a deliberate exercise in relaxation after the tensions of a big performance. The girl's skill in conforming to the ritual was as important as her looks or her cooking. Perhaps Adrian's satisfaction, though he had not expressed it in words, had prompted the question.

"Do you want me to give you a list?"

"Course not. I'm not jealous, promise. Only sometimes, when you're not here, I'm sort of haunted. You know, when I was a little girl I used to sit in buses and things and wonder about all the people who'd sat in that seat before me, and it felt — I don't know how to say it — well, as if they'd left a sort of shimmer of themselves there, lives inside lives inside lives, like

170

an onion, and me in the middle. Don't you feel that sometimes?"

"I am far too conscious of my own uniqueness. I have never
given a moment's thought to any of your other lovers."

"There've only been three!"

"You have a life before you."

"I can't imagine anyone after you."

"Seriously?"

"Yes. I think so."

"Body and soul?"

"If you want them."

He did not answer, but with his free hand picked up a morsel
of broken roll, mopped it round the congealed butter on his
plate and chewed.

"Nice?"

"Excellent."

"I've got veal in cream and calvados for tomorrow."

"We're eating in town tomorrow. Will it keep?"

"Oh. Me too?"

"If you please. Benny is over."

"Oh. All right."

"You like Benny. He'll want to see you."

"Of course I do."

"I will instruct Robin to protect you from Louise."

"You don't have to."

"What is the matter? Tell me. Tell me."

"I . . . You'll be angry."

"Angrier still if you refuse."

"Oh dear. It makes me feel so stupid when everyone else . . .
I mean I know it's what you do, better than anyone else, and
this time it's special, terrific, everyone says so . . ."

"You disagree?"

"Oh no no no! That isn't what . . . I mean, that's *why* . . .
being so marvellous, and me sitting there, can't get out, *having*
to look . . . Can I stop? Please, A."

"You are sitting there watching my performance and wishing
it were over. It is my performance, not the play itself?"

"It's just worse with this play. I feel so frightened."

"Worse?"

"Please, A."

171

"Go on."

"Let me think . . . You see, it isn't *you*. It's something else up there."

"Some *thing*? Not some one?"

"That's right. You're magical at the someones. I can see that. I can feel it. But . . . but . . . I mean, for instance, this time, when Polly goes out thinking she's won and you get up from the table, and then . . . then you make yourself bigger than you are . . . that's not someone. That's some thing. I have to stop myself screaming."

"Some nights they do scream. You are lucky to have seen it. It is an instant which theatregoers will recall in their memoirs long after I am dead."

"But that's not . . . I mean, when they scream, they're frightened for them. I'm frightened for you. Where does it come from, A.?"

"What?"

"The something?"

He shrugged and sipped his brandy. Her explanation seemed to have appeased him. His left hand gentled the nape of her neck. He made his voice ironically portentous.

"It sleeps within its cave until I summon it forth. Thou earth, thou, speak!"

"Don't. I'm not joking. I really do get terrified. Like in nightmares. I sit there and look and look and I can't find you. Where've you gone?"

"I am there too, watching, invisible."

"I wish I could see you."

"And spoil my magic?"

"Not if it did that. That's the important thing."

"The only thing."

The calm of the ritual seemed to have been restored, intensified, after the brief rift. Perhaps her tribute to his power, by its very unwillingness, was the small sacrifice essential to the egotism of art. He put his glass down and lolled himself into the crook of the sofa so that she could lie with her head on his shoulder, her fingers teasing the braid of his dressing-gown.

"In one sense it is only a trick," he said. "The eye chooses how it sees things. A man standing twenty yards away from you ought to appear only half the height of a man standing ten

172

yards away from you, but the visual cortex makes the necessary adjustments. When I grow in that scene I do it by an alteration of posture which brings me an inch or two down stage without seeming to have moved, and the visual cortices of the audience are tricked into increasing my height. Of course there is more to it than that. Making the actual movements is not enough. Consciously or unconsciously the audience would perceive what I was doing and my height would not change. So I must by the force of my performance so obsess them with the stillness of the moment that they cannot believe that I have moved. The movement is the trick. The stillness is the art. As a matter of fact I learnt it by watching Samuel Mkele, though he himself was probably largely unaware of how he achieved his effects. His first entrance was a tour de force. He had been on stage all along, crouching among some seaweed-covered rocks and seeming to be one himself. His change from rock to creature took, oh, fifteen seconds. If you had stopped it halfway through he would have seemed to be still partly stone. He made it appear that in calling him forth I had by my power created him out of the rock.''

"And only just that once."

"Just that once. Just that once. It was enough."

"And then he was dead."

"Yes."

The syllable had a finality about it that seemed to have closed the conversation, but after a short pause Adrian picked the subject up.

"As a matter of fact I have been thinking about Samuel off and on throughout the last couple of weeks."

"Yes, I know."

"Know?"

"Well, sort of guessed. Only you'd said I mustn't ask."

"That still applies."

"I don't know if it counts, but just now, when you said 'It was enough.' What did you mean? You don't have to tell me."

"Have you ever heard of a man called Barrie Oakley?"

"I don't think . . . oh, sex-scandal? Before I was born?"

"He was killed in a drunken squabble in the mid-Fifties by his lover, a clever but lightweight actor called Jonny Price. Before the war he had been a successful and innovative producer, and during it he became a key figure in some of the official organizations which were supposed to keep the troops' morale up by staging plays and other performances around the world. My Cousin Elspeth arranged for Oakley and Price to come and watch my Prospero. Afterwards he was extremely encouraging. He wrote down the details of my call-up and said that he would arrange to have me transferred as soon as possible into one of his outfits. That indeed did happen. I spent three years technically in the army after my basic training and never heard a shot fired, and moreover I made a number of contacts that were invaluable to me when I was demobbed. So what I meant was that the one performance of *The Tempest* which we were able to stage before Samuel was killed . . ."

He froze. His error, his momentary loss of control (tiredness? the relaxation of guard in her company? subconscious need to have the thoughts that had been troubling him out into the open?) were so unusual that the girl froze beside him, waiting, tenser if anything than he was. He produced a casual light-comedy laugh, making it a meaningless sound out of his immense repertoire.

"Action is momentary — a word, a blow,
The motion of a muscle this way or that —
'Tis done, and in the after vacancy
We wonder at ourselves like men betrayed."

"You needn't tell me," she said again.
"I think I had better. The floor of the dovecote was thick with bird-droppings. I climbed the ladder beside Samuel's body to see if there was anything I could do. I then realized that the soles of his feet — he always went barefoot in summer — were clean, and the rungs on which I was standing were clean too. Automatically I looked down and saw in the droppings on the floor the imprints of American army boots. It was just after sunrise, with the light striking sideways through the flight-holes. The marks would have been barely perceptible in any other light, and then only from directly above. Samuel had told me only a few weeks before that he had been attacked by two soldiers from the American camp in the park, and one of their sergeants had warned me of the same possibility. The camp was a transit-point for troops leaving for France. I had heard one of

174

their regular convoys going off as I was walking towards the dovecote. You can imagine a group of wild young men, southern roughs, breaking out for this final hideous fling before going into action; if so, they would already be in France. There would have been enormous delays in finding them and bringing them to trial. At least it was clear to me that I must not allow myself to become an important witness. If that were to happen I might have to hang about indefinitely, and thus miss the chance that had opened for me with Oakley's offer of patronage. He was notoriously wayward and impulsive, not the type to maintain his interest over a period of months. My having found the body was already tiresome enough — I could not escape that. But in fact it all turned out better than I could have hoped. The official who interviewed me for my affidavit asked no questions about the footprints, nor about the door having been forced when Samuel had a key to the dovecote on his board. Of course I did not say anything, unasked, but if I had been I would have lied."

"They hushed it up? And you could've . . ."

He shook his head.

"I wasn't at the inquest, but evidence was given that Samuel had been seriously depressed, which was true. Charles added that while they were changing for the play he had dismissed Samuel for gross impertinence. I imagine he gave them to understand that Samuel had attempted some kind of sexual assault on him . . ."

"He couldn't have!"

"I'm afraid he could. We'd all seen them come out of the hut, both extremely agitated and Charles only half dressed. The play started almost at once. I don't know whether evidence was given about Samuel's performance, which as I told you was remarkable and to the naïve spectator might have seemed an exhibition of pure frenzy. It was of course perfectly under control, but even I was surprised at times by its vehemence, and Elspeth told me that the coroner had seen fit to animadvert on the unwisdom of involving a man of primitive race, without the sophistication to distinguish between role and reality, in a part such as that of Caliban. Suicide certainly appeared a logical verdict."

"You keep saying things like 'appeared'."

"Bed now, I think."

He waited for her to rise and pull him two-handed to his feet. Deliberately she pulled too hard, using the momentum to bring him into her arms. Standing, they were of equal height, but she relaxed her joints to give him an inch of domination. He smiled, but as he bent to kiss her the movement froze. They stuck in their pose for an instant before he took his right arm from round her and pushed their bodies apart so that he could feel in the gap between them, first just above her diaphragm and then with spider-creeping fingers tracing a line up to her collarbone. She endured his touch but was clearly troubled as he slid his hand inside the soft roll of her jersey-collar and hauled out a loop of the white lace of a training-shoe. She bent her head to let him lift the lace clear. As he continued to haul, the object that had caught his attention, intruding its hardness between their bodies, moved visibly up under her jersey, like a cartoon mouse running under a carpet. He eased it free and held it in his palm.

It was the hand-carved butter mould that had attempted to portray his own boyhood face. She had knotted black thread round the neck and tied it to the shoelace. He stared at the object for a couple of seconds, then closed his fist, turned his wrist, gripped the lace with his other hand and snapped the thread. With a movement of utter rejection, not bothering to watch it fall, he tossed the image into the fire.

"Oh, no!" she shrieked, and rushed past him.

He grabbed at her arm but, used to her total compliance, was unprepared for the violence of her movement and lost his hold. She flung herself down on the hearth, plunged her hand into the embers and seized the already flaming head.

This time he picked her up bodily, hefted her to his chest and strode round the sofa and across the room.

"Ow!" she mewed. "Ow!"

He kneed the kitchen door open, lurched through, dumped her on her feet in front of the sink, turned the cold tap full on and pushed her still-clenched fist under the stream of water.

"Keep it there," he snapped.

There was a plastic bowl in the sink, full of the pans in which she had cooked his supper. He lifted it out and tilted its contents splashing and clattering on to the floor, then set it beneath the tap. She was grey with pain, and crying. As the bowl filled he took her arm, more gently now, and eased it below the surface, leaving the tap running. She shouted as he forced her clenched fingers open.

"Please, A. Please!"

Black embers floated up, bobbling around in the rush of water, and then a larger morsel. He paid no attention, letting her fish the knob out with her unburnt hand; the top of the disc and one side of the head were charred dark brown. He fetched the kitchen stool and made her sit sideways to the sink so that she could keep her whole forearm under the water. He took his dressing-gown off and wrapped it round her shoulders.

"How does it feel?"

"Ow, it's sore. I'm sorry, A. I'm sorry."

"Keep it in the bowl. I'll be back in a minute."

In the living-room he checked a number on the card by the telephone, pressed the buttons.

"Fritz? Adrian Waring. Woke you up, I'm afraid. Listen, a fairly serious burn to a hand and forearm. . . . Yes, I did that at once. She's still got it under water . . . Tripped and fell into the fire . . . I'd be more than grateful . . . One second — it's clearly hurting considerably . . . I've got Codeine . . . Thanks, old boy. See you then."

He went to the washroom, took pills from a cabinet and set them to fizz in a tumbler which he left on the table by the sofa as he crossed the living-room again. In the kitchen he soaked a teatowel, wrung it, lifted her limp arm from the bowl and gently wound the cloth around it, bandaging the bundle with a dry roller-towel and finally a plastic bin-liner.

"Other arm round my neck."

"I can walk."

But she did as she was told and let him lift her from the stool and carry her to the sofa.

"I'm sorry, A. I couldn't help it. Really I couldn't."

"So I gathered. Drink that. Fritz will be here in ten minutes."

He fetched a rug to cover her, then went back to the telephone. This time he needed to find the number in a pocket diary.

"Louise? . . . I won't apologize — we all know New Yorkers have evolved to do without sleep. It's Adrian . . . How very kind of you. Let me guess. A designer sponge? . . . Then I'll

177

wait and be astonished. How was the trip? . . . And Benny . . . That's good to hear — what did you see? . . . No, I haven't had a chance. A bit stodgy? . . . That's why I'm calling — we may not be able to make it — we've had a mishap — I won't go into details . . . Well, I can't at the moment be sure. I think my understudy might be very good indeed, if Benny would be interested to watch a young man seizing his chance . . . Oh, I would be desolated to disappoint you both, and it may well be all right. I really called to ask about your movements tomorrow, so that I can get in touch when our problem is clearer . . . Right . . . Got that . . . Right . . . Oh, I shall know before then . . . No, you're wrong — I had to take three days off from *Misanthrope* in '81 . . . Very kind of you to say so, my dear . . . I'll be in touch in the morning."

He put the receiver down and turned. She had thrown the rug aside and was starting to rise but he squatted beside the sofa and pushed her gently back.

"You mustn't, A. I'll be all right. I won't even have to cook for you. It can't be serious — it was only a couple of seconds. I could come with you if you like and wear a sling, only you'd have to think of a story."

"You tripped and fell in the fire."

"All right. It's not hurting nearly as much. It'll be gone in just a few days."

"Superficially. There is a phenomenon called shock."

"I'll be all right."

"Yes, I think you probably will."

"Then . . ."

"But I cannot yet be sure whether I shall."

He rose and stood looking down at her, warming his calves and hams in the ember-glow, until they heard a car come scrunching up the gravel.

ONE

"Shoulders back, chin in, head against bar, heels on the ground — right . . . You bending at the knees, lad? . . . Then five three and a quarter's the best we can do for you . . ."

"Hm . . . Usual childhood illnesses? Polio? . . . Know your father's height? . . . Runs in the family, evidently — nothing wrong with that . . ."

"Here's one just right for the midget submarines! Only joking, lad. You want the navy you got to volunteer, and you're too late for that."

Queue to have your chest thumped and listened to. Queue to piss in a bottle. Queue for eye-test. Tempter at your elbow all the time — epilepsy, myopia, nameless wheezings . . . No! When you were seventy you needed to be able to count on your fingers the performances you had missed through illness. Summon such a familiar now and it might nestle inside you through the years. Pure superstition, but real. He couldn't. He let Adrian rattle off the bottom line of the eye-chart.

Then another wait, this time sitting in a sideroom till a second batch was ready to join them in the written test.

" 'ow much choice've we reely got, sarge?"

"Sergeant to you, lad."

Interest woke at the voice. The sergeant was Education Corps. Andrew had been wondering how you got into that. Gold-rimmed specs, twenty-fivish but balding, born to become a teacher. And the voice . . . it was the tone, not the accent, a Midland whine. There was a deadness about it, as if it was numb with the repetition of its own arguments. Know-all, unbeliever, preacher, fanatic, assassin of Czars, builder of glistening cities . . . One day . . . If only . . .

"Sorry, sergeant."

179

"You've got just as much choice as they feel like giving you, if you want to know. Just now I wouldn't say you'd got much. Armour's been suffering over in France, and the way they're running this war it'll go on suffering, and that means they have gaps to fill. Drive a car and you'll find yourself learning to drive a tank. Twenty-twenty vision and you'll be finding out how the gun works. Anything else and you're a fitter, no matter how cack-handed you turn out. That's how they do it in the army. It's what we call a microcosm. If you don't learn anything else you'll learn what the world's really like behind the Saturday football and the Sunday sermons. Them and us, that's the army. Them and us, run mad."

Bicycling the familiar route in the unfamiliar early afternoon Andrew felt not unhappy. He had dreaded the medical, the gateway to his nightmare, but the actual event had been almost neutral. The presence of so many others all going through the same process, none of them liking it, some much more bewildered than he was, had diluted his terror, making it not much different from the others' nervousness. Now there was almost a month before call-up. He had Jean and the play to take his mind off it . . .

The day was hot and still, with the first reaper-binders clattering round the fields, fighters and fighter-bombers going over a few at a time but all the time. Though the rush of the invasion still crammed the main roads, along the lanes it might almost have been peace again, only without motor-cars and signposts at the road-junctions. He was in no hurry, so walked the steeper hills.

Then everything changed. It was at the crossroads in the woods, where the big ammo-dump had been established under the trees. Each time he had passed it on his week-end trips the seemingly endless ridges of stacked shells had been there, looking as though they were part of the landscape — in a couple of months the leaves would fall and cover them and begin to rot, and in a few more winters they would have become ancient earthworks, there for ever.

The first two ridges were gone.

On his way out that morning he had noticed the lorries turning in to the site but, with his mind on the nightmare ahead, had not been struck by them. Now . . . It was the speed of the work which appalled him. Lorries were backed up to the third ridge every few yards, with a gang of soldiers at each tossing the shells up and stacking them away. Hundreds of thousands of shells. Shells, anti-tank . . .

Andrew had little idea what an anti-tank shell looked like, but in a blink of terror he saw another forest, pines this time, and the uniforms of the soldiers grey, but the shells were the same, hundreds of thousands of them. Many would never be fired. Most that were would miss, but that still left thousands and thousands doing what they were made for . . . twenty-twenty vision and you'll be finding out how the gun works . . . in its steel shell, its trap, trundling between French hedgerows . . . and out in the orchard somewhere another gun-crew, grey uniforms, the sights lining up . . .

He did not remember crossing the main road. He found himself fifty yards up the lane beyond it, standing on the pedals, slogging frenziedly at the slope. He dismounted, wheeled the bike in among the trees and tried to vomit his terror up. Nothing came.

Back on the road he walked on, pushing the bike. When he had first freewheeled into the shade ten minutes ago he had enjoyed its coolness, but now he felt deadly chill, and even when he trudged up into the open again the sun seemed not to penetrate beyond his shirt into the ice inside him . . . thrilling region of the thick-ribbed ice . . . cold obstruction . . . sweet sister, let me live . . .

He felt utterly deserted, naked, helpless. Adrian had gone. Adrian had never existed, of course, had never been anything more than a child's imaginary playmate. There was nobody, nothing . . .

"I thought you were never coming."

Leaning forward on the handlebars, hypnotized by the front tyre's monotonous reel towards the chalky tarmac, he only knew she'd been there when she spoke — been there all along, sitting on the road-bank with her bike beside her watching him since he'd trudged out from under the trees. She rose, brown and carefree. She was wearing her Land Army uniform, breeches and open-necked shirt.

"Why aren't you milking?"

"I swapped Saturday with Dolly. The binder broke, so she can do it."

Without giving him time to get rid of his bike she put her arms round him. The slope of the road made her inches taller than him.

"Come to mother, then," she said.

With the cross-bar against their hips the pose was uncomfortable. She broke off, laughing.

"Cheer up. You're supposed to be glad to see me. Was it foul?"

"Not really. Everyone's got to do it, I suppose. Only . . ."

"That's never any help. Let's find somewhere a bit private."

She picked her bike up and walked beside him over the crest of the hill. Twenty yards down a track led off through a broken gate. There was a lark, invisible but singing, high over the thistly rabbit-nibbled pasture, and they could see thirty miles north over a landscape blue and still with summer. The track ended in a chalk-pit with a shepherd's hut on wheels, unused at this season, parked on one side and on the other some rusting farm machinery tangled with briars, but in the middle bare white chalk, too barren for growth. They leaned their bikes against the hut and kissed again. She made herself small for him, holding him tight but pliant to his movements. Her face softened, her eyes became misty. Since that first evening in the eyrie above the dovecote they hadn't kissed seriously in broad daylight — it had always been at least dusk before the Cousins were in bed and he could climb out and steal up the drive to the lodge. Now he was suddenly aware how she had changed in those weeks — no, not changed, but unfolded, opened, at least for him, letting him discover what had been there all along, far more than his original picture of mere childish freshness and romantic sop. She had her own taste, her own odours, which he was the first to explore.

"Keep your mind on the job," she said, pulling her head away with a joke frown. "It's me doing all the work."

"I was thinking about you."

"You think too much."

Their lips locked again. Her fingers clutched and nuzzled, felt their way in and up under his shirt. There was someone on the rim of the chalk-pit, looking down, benignly amused. Only

Adrian, come back. Her right hand slid round between them and felt for her belt-buckle.

"No good," he whispered. "I haven't brought anything. Didn't expect . . ."

"Bother."

The hand had a will of its own. She counted days.

"Let's risk it," she said. "Just this once."

"Well, now we're quits."

"Uh?"

She looked past his head to the shaggy rim of grass above the white walls of the pit. They lay naked, belly to belly on the narrow strip of their clothes they had spread to protect them from the rubbly floor. The sun baked down. Even in the shade of the hut it was very warm.

"It's a sort of amphitheatre," she said. "Like the one at The Mimms, only steeper. Glad there wasn't an audience. Do you know . . ."

"What?"

"I was thinking. All that stuff about being certainly a maid and so on, and how vital that is . . ."

"Prospero needs it to make his magic work. It's sort of in the rules."

"But I used to feel so stupid saying it — I mean when it was true — and now it isn't I shan't turn a hair. I'll rather enjoy it, I think. Isn't that funny?"

"Told you so. What did you mean, quits?"

"Did I look like anyone?"

"When?"

"Just now. Come on, guess. At the flicks. We argued about her all the way home."

Dorothy Lamour? Nothing like, and anyway they hadn't. The week before? *Somewhere I'll Find You* — can glamour compensate for ham acting? Discuss.

"Oh, her . . . I could have told you apart in the street."

"Don't be clever. I want to know. Did I?"

"Give or take a freckle, I suppose so. A bit."

"I was trying to. For you. It was a present."

"Thank you very much. Is there anyone you would like in exchange?"

183

"You've given them all already, except one. I know I can't have him."

"Who?"

"Andrew Wragge."

Before he could answer she rolled him on to his back and pinned him down. He was off the clothes and the gravelly chalk bit into his shoulders. Her green eyes looked down into his.

"The invisible man," she said. "I was thinking about us, waiting. I came out because I knew you needed me. I felt it last night. You were so frightened. The real you, the person inside. Poor darling, I thought, I'll bike out and meet him and cheer him up. And then you didn't come and you didn't come and I started to think. About us. I've always sort of supposed you'd go into the army and do your bit and then the war would be over and you'd come back and we'd get married and that would be that, like it is in the flicks, but then, sitting there waiting, I suddenly understood it wasn't like that. This is part of the war. It'll all be different when it's over. We'll be different too."

Four planes, Beaufighters, drummed north above, going back from whatever they'd crossed the Channel to do.

"It was like when somebody switches on a light in a dark room and you suddenly understand the shape of the furniture you've been bumping into," she said. "I wonder if you love me at all."

"I love you."

"Yes, but who's saying that? I know what it's like to love somebody because I love you. I know how much it hurts. I don't think you do. I don't think you can. You've sort of arranged yourself so that nothing can hurt you. You can't risk really being in love. You'll always have to act."

"So does everyone. Lovers have to act being in love, just like Hamlet has to act being Hamlet. That's what the play's about."

"It isn't a play. That's what you're never going to understand. You're a magician. You think your magic's real. I suppose it is. You wanted to see if you could use it to seduce me, didn't you? And it worked. You didn't cheat. You kept telling me you were only acting, only I was too stupid to understand. But just now it was the other way round. I was acting Lana Turner for you just now, on purpose, thinking about it, the way you do. And you weren't, not this time. You

184

needed me, didn't you? Not just wanted, really needed. That's what I meant about being quits."

He lay inert. Their faces were inches apart. Her breath was moist and sweet, like one of her cow's. Her soft weight pressed on his chest, forcing the sharpness of the pit floor into his back. The joint heat of their bodies made the sweat stream down his cheeks. He had no strength in any of his muscles to throw her off. But Adrian was back, close now, hovering above them.

"If you're a magician then I'm a witch," she said. "I'm going to put a curse on you. It goes like this. One day somebody else is going to understand you, and love you in spite of understanding you, like I do. And you won't know what to do."

He summoned his selves together and bent his mouth into a smile.

"Was it a good-bye present?" he said.

She lowered her head and licked the tip of his nose, a long stroke like a cat grooming its kitten, then rolled away.

"Just a present," she said. "But don't you forget — from now on I know your secret, Mr Magician."

T W O

Stooking looked idyllic, from a distance. Now that the harvest had started Andrew worked at the farm most days. It was expected of him, not just by Mrs Althorp, greedy for unpaid labour, and Cousin Brown with her strong sense of duty, but by everybody, himself included. You were free, so you gave a hand with the harvest. As well as the usual farm people there were often four or five others working in the golden fields, a couple of Italian POWs, an off-duty bobby, the vicar's son, home from Lancing, Jack to manage the horses — there was a war on, wasn't there?

Around nine o'clock — no point in starting till the dew had begun to evaporate — the horse-drawn reaper clattered round the edge of the field, leaving a swathe of mown oats laid flat. Two workers followed, raking them into bundles; behind them two more, each of whom picked up a dozen stalks, twisted them and used them as a cord to tie the loose bundle into a sheaf. It was a knack. Dolly did it without thinking, without

185

even watching what her hands were up to. Being no good at it Andrew took one of the rakes. There was a knack here too, in nudging the mown stalks into a gatherable bundle, which even Brian managed better than Andrew. All this in the quiet of the morning, with the dew-smells, and the cow-smells from beyond the hedge, Dolly humming at her work, the whirr of disturbed partridges flighting away, the coo of pigeons, the last bombers going home.

By about the time Jean came down after the milking there was a cleared lane all round the field, with the hand-tied sheaves laid under the hedge. Now the tractor could start, and the feel of the morning changed. The drub of its motor and the clatter of the reaper-binder — ten times louder than the simple horsedrawn bar, became the main noises of the day. Dave drove the tractor. Jean sat on the pierced metal seat at the back of the binder, controlling the height of the cutter-bar and lifting it for the turns. She had a cord that led to Dave's elbow which she could tug for him to stop before things went disastrously wrong behind him. The binder was old, much-mended, and broke down every third circuit, but Dave understood its moods. He would climb down, mumbling slurred obscenities, tug some tangle out, adjust something with a spanner, oil something else and start again.

Meanwhile the stookers, working in teams of two, picked up a sheaf under each arm, faced their partners as if setting for square-dance and plonked the four sheaves on their bases with the seed-heads leaning together. If they got it right the sheaves stood and eight more could then be stacked against them to make a stook, in line from the last and the right distance from the next line so that in a week a wagon could drive between them and the now-dried sheaves (if the weather held) be pitched easily up to the loaders. Stooking was not difficult work, nothing like as heavy as mucking-out, but after a couple of hours you became very weary, weary of the monotony, of the glare of the noon sun off pale stubble, of the strange refusal of particular sheaves to stand. Your arms rubbed raw along the inside. Patches of most fields were infested with thistles, so that each sheaf tortured the tender skin. Seed heads (barley was even worse than oats, everyone said) worked their way into your clothing to scratch at each move. Harvest mites chose your

186

softest places — under your belt, your arm-pits, crotch, the crook of knees and elbows — producing at first a pleasant mild itch which you soon learnt would be a furious irritation by midnight.

Worst of all, the work gave you time to think. There was nothing else to do with your mind while the slow hours passed and the island of uncut stalks dwindled and dwindled. Other times of the day you could read, or help Cousin Brown with the play (Andrew, in addition to being principal actor, had also the jobs of assistant stage manager, box-office clerk, messenger and wardrobe hand); nights, there was Jean, up in her room at the Lodge, or if it was warm enough wandering out under the stars and finding somewhere. But harvesting you couldn't help thinking, thinking and feeling, your days of hope closing and closing, your chances of escape becoming ever fainter.

Most fields were small enough to mow in one day. Dolly drove the tractor for the last few circuits while Dave and Mrs Althorp waited with shot-guns at opposite corners of the now cam-shaped island of stalks. The stookers stopped work and stood clear, some gripping staves. Out of the last unreaped yards the trapped rabbits bolted for the hedgerows. Guns banged. Stave-holders yelled, chased, thwacked. It was meat to add to the rations, a flare of fun after the dusty day. Everyone looked forward to it.

Three evenings after his medical Andrew was sitting on a fallen tree at the top of the Five-acre, watching the rabbit-drive. Jean had gone off for the evening milking. The late afternoon sun shining through the dust of harvest hazed the whole scene brown-gold. He made a rectangular frame with thumbs and forefingers and looked through it, choosing shots for an imaginary film. When he had the prestige he would insist on directing his own films. One day . . . If . . .

A twig cracked in the copse behind him. He twisted and saw Sergeant Stephens push his way out between a couple of elder bushes and raise a hand in greeting. Yes, of course. This was where he came to leave Cousin Blue's butter for Samuel to fetch, and later came down to collect his payment. He didn't seem at all put out to find himself observed, but climbed by the protruding roots up on to the bole of the tree and walked out along the trunk, stepping easily over the couple of strands of

187

barbed wire which the men who'd fenced the camp had thought enough at this point. Owing to the tighter security since the invasion Andrew hadn't seen him for several weeks.

"Hello, sergeant," he said.

"Hi. Thought I'd come take a couple of snapshots, send to the folks back home. You don't see this kinda farming around there these days. We cut a mile at a time, combines, four of 'em in a row. This looks like something out of a picture book."

"Are you a farmer?"

"My dad was, only he went bust in the depression and we moved to the city."

He lifted his camera and looked through the viewfinder.

"Too far off," he said. "OK if we move down a little? Where's your girl?"

"Milking. Please don't mention she's mine if you get talking. Mrs Althorp doesn't like it."

"Sure, no problem."

They walked down, the stubble crackling under the sergeant's enormous boots. He took several pictures, of the binder, the stooks, Mrs Althorp in the act of firing.

"That dame can handle a gun," he said. "Better than a lot of our guys out in Normandy, way things are going."

"It seems to be taking ages."

"The Krauts can fight. Best army in the world. We're taking one in ten casualties already, and the closer we come to Germany the tougher it's gonna get. The Russkies won't have it any easier, even if they are going great guns right now. Once they're on German soil . . ."

"We've got to win in the end."

"Sure."

"When, do you think?"

"Winter of forty-five, maybe. That's the Krauts. After that it'll be the Japs. You ever think what it's going to be like taking the Jap mainland? One in ten casualties will be nothing."

"I've had my medical for call-up."

"You'll be in time, kid. You're not going to miss a thing."

"I'm more interested in things missing me," Andrew heard Adrian saying, while he shrivelled inside.

"Have those lawyers finished messing with the old man's will?" asked the sergeant.

"It doesn't look as if anything's going to get settled till the war's over and young Mr Foley comes back."

"Jesus!"

"Did Phil find any more out?"

"Phil? You didn't hear about Phil? He was the one in his ten."

"The one . . . That's awful. When?"

"Week after D-Day. Say — I haven't told your nigger friend."

"Why on earth . . .?"

The sergeant sighed.

"Well, first off I guess I felt bad about old Phil. I'd staked him, remember? It was my dough. So when I saw that clipping he sent I figured I was on a loser. I called Phil back. If I'd kept him on the job he'd be alive now."

"Yes, but . . ."

"Your friend, he's kind of crazy, huh?"

"He's different."

"Yeah. Obsessed, I'd call it. Look, suppose I tell him I'm calling Phil back, what's he gonna do?"

"Offer to pay the expenses himself? He's got a bit saved up. But you could always explain that you can't get Phil more than a few days' leave."

"Sure, and *then* what's he do? Hire a private dick of his own, I'll bet. Now, you gotta understand, I do things my own way in this camp, but I can't afford to have guys nosing around asking questions. I can't afford some guy asking about Phil, saying he was in Hull early June when he shoulda been here, right? I could be in bad trouble. So I stalled. I thought if I give him time to think about it, your friend would come around. He asks me, any news from Phil and I tell him no. But he keeps on and on. Then he starts to think just because there ain't no news from Phil that means Mr Charles ain't telling the truth. Phil would've found something else by now, supposing it was there to find. Right?"

"So you started making things up?"

"Yeah, an old lady who was in the shelter . . . Jesus, all I want is to get the guy to lay off! Why can't he see reason? You ever seen that clipping? Ain't that enough?"

"The trouble is my uncle told him something the morning he died. I think he probably said that Charles wasn't his son and he

189

was going to change his will to make sure he didn't get anything. Nobody'd believe Samuel if he just said so, so he's got to try and prove it somehow. I don't think he'll ever give up."

"Jesus! What am I gonna do?"

"I suppose I could talk to him. I'd have to tell him the truth. I could explain about you not being able to afford having people asking about Phil's leave. He'd understand that. He's lived in England most of his life. He knows how things work."

The sergeant shook his head gloomily and rewound the spool of his film. It seemed an absurd small mess for somebody so competent and wary to land himself in, but of course it wasn't only questions about Phil's leave he was worried about. Questions of any sort would be very unwelcome. It crossed Andrew's mind to wonder whether the episode Samuel had told him about, when it looked as if a couple of GIs were going to rough him up in the drive but the sergeant had turned up providentially and rescued him, hadn't perhaps been staged to try and warn him off. But then why had the sergeant not cut the link completely by refusing to supply Cousin Blue's butter?

"Yeah, I guess that's the best plan," said the sergeant. "Provided he lays off — that's all I want."

The last swathes went down. The last sheaves tumbled from the binder. One little rabbit, barely a month old, lolloped a few paces and sat cowering until an Italian POW picked it up and stood teasing the back of its neck and gentling its flattened ears beside the line of corpses.

"There's always one who gets lucky," said the sergeant.

Make it me, thought Andrew. Oh, make it me.

THREE

"It was really very effective," said Cousin Brown. "It stuck at the dress rehearsal and I dreaded it would do so at an actual performance, but in the end it behaved perfectly and the audience applauded the effect every time."

"Provided I don't touch it," said Andrew. "Props tend to go wonky for me."

There was no harvesting that morning because it had been

190

raining off and on since dawn, so between showers Cousin Brown had taken Andrew down to the Amphitheatre to help her fetch out the banquet-table for Act Three from the shed behind the larger Green Room hut where the props from past productions were stored. One at each end they carried it on to the stage. Andrew stood back to look. From the front it appeared to be a table draped with a gorgeous cloth, but though eight foot long it was barely a foot wide, and the cloth was cleverly painted board, hinged halfway up. From beneath it Cousin Brown fetched out a number of L-sectioned objects, made of plywood, and started to set them up, clicking them into place and attaching to each a spring which stretched down into the surface of the table. On the forward-facing surfaces were painted the items of the feast, a boar's head, a luminescent jelly, a grotesquely turreted pastry and so on.

"Rex Whistler designed it, you know," said Cousin Brown. "He did all our magical effects for the production. Stoddart, who used to be our general handyman until he volunteered, was marvellous at building things like this. Now both Rex and Stoddart are dead. How strange and sad war can be."

Andrew's distrust of the object as a gadget liable to stick deepened into horror. The lives, the performances, gone. This *thing* left. The fact that audiences had applauded it deepened his loathing.

"Now, you see," said Cousin Brown, "Ariel, dressed as a harpy sweeps into the banquet just as the nobles are reaching for the food. He claps his wings over the table and 'with a quaint device' the banquet vanishes. I have him standing here, behind the table, wings spread wide. The nobles start back — he really does look rather horrendous, you know, in Rex's jokey manner — Ariel brings his wings together. There is a thunder-clap to drown the clicks, and . . ."

She had been going through the movements as she spoke and must at this point have touched a lever below the table with her foot. The painted dishes rattled down, pulled by their springs, and the shorter feet of the L-sections shot into view, with boulders painted on their undersides. At the same time the top half of the cloth flopped down and the front of the table became part of the same barren outcrop. A dismal seagull perched at one end.

191

"Isn't it fun!" cried Cousin Blue's voice. Andrew turned and saw her standing with Charles at the top of the tiers of seats.

"Wasn't Rex too clever!" she said. "I adore that sort of trick — *much* the best part of the play, don't you agree?"

She fluttered her eyelids at Charles and then held out her arm for him to help her down the flight of steps between the seats. He did so a little perfunctorily. It wasn't that their relationship had changed, quite, but their performance of it had, a bit like that of actors in a play which has run too long but shows no sign of closing. Nothing could happen until Uncle Vole's will was sorted out, and nobody knew when that would be. Cousin Blue was holding a buff government envelope in her other hand.

"Something's come for Andrew," she said. "It looked important, so we thought we'd bring it down."

Andrew's heart thumped. He took the envelope and stared at the address. No possible mistake. The handwriting, niggling but characterless, spoke of the ordinariness of the event. That clerk might have written a couple of hundred envelopes that day before he reached this one, almost at the end of the alphabet. Each one vital to the addressee, all indifferent to the clerk, another day of John Smiths, Number x, Some Road, Blankton. Death would be like that clerk, choosing you not because your name was Stoddard or Whistler but because you were next on his list. He opened the envelope and read the instructions.

"It's my call-up," he said. "The thirty-first."

"But there is no . . . of *this* month, do you mean? You said it was not till September!"

"That's what they told us at the medical."

"Heavens! And we shall barely have ended our run! What a mercy it is not a day sooner!"

"Nonsense," said Cousin Blue. "We would simply have told them he couldn't be spared. I'm sure they would have understood. But don't you think it a pity, Charles, that you aren't doing the play down here, the way we always used to?"

"And how would we get an audience out here in wartime?" said Cousin Brown.

"Why — we have one ready-made! Let's ask the Americans!"

"Absurd. Besides, all the dates are already booked."

192

"But you're going to have dress rehearsals — why don't you have one here? Please do not sigh at me like that, Elspeth."

"My dear May, from what you have seen of the Americans, from the so-called music they choose to play over that dreadful instrument, do you seriously believe they will wish to spend their time watching . . ."

"That's just what you said about my tours of the house, and look how successful they were. If Andrew were to have a word with his friend Mr Stephens . . ."

"Really!" said Cousin Brown. "Who is producing this play, may I ask?"

"We are, of course. It's always been a family thing. Charles and dear Andrew are acting in it and you are directing and now I'm helping to get an audience. All together. Quite like old time. Charles?"

Cousin Blue had presumably made the original suggestion on the spur of the moment, merely for the sake of interfering with already settled arrangements. Now she was enjoying Cousin Brown's irritation. Andrew mentally drew himself aside. The flimsy letter fluttered in his fingers. It had a temporary feel about it. It didn't have to last, only three weeks. Then it could go to the paper collection and be pulped and become another drab summons for someone else . . . Three weeks to do what he chose because he chose it, his own master . . .

"Don't you think, Andrew, it would be jolly to put on just one teeny wee performance down here?"

"Of course he does not. Now, May, I must ask you to stop interfering. We have more than enough to get done. Andrew . . ."

Cousin Brown paused, waiting for him to turn, but he stood looking up over the tiers of seats towards the head of the valley. All the lines of the landscape focused on him. The stage was meant for him, made for him. He would never get another chance.

"I suppose it's impossible," he said, deliberately filling the syllables with longing and regret.

"Now, really . . ."

"Pretty good acoustics," said Charles.

He had characteristically retreated up the steps during the argument and wandered along one of the lines of seats. He

193

spoke as he was starting down again.

"We were very lucky," said Cousin Brown. "Edith Evans told me they were the best she had ever heard, outdoors, and several other good judges have said the same. But it is still quite ridiculous . . ."

She stopped. Charles had climbed on to the stage, turned and struck a pose. He began to declaim:

> "And Crispin Crispian shall ne'er go by
> From this day to the ending of the world
> But we in it shall be remembered,
> We few, we happy few, we band of brothers."

Cousin Blue clapped.

"Let's give it a go, eh?" said Charles, not directly to Cousin Brown but giving instructions to anyone who happened to be in earshot. It was the first time Andrew had heard him speak with this kind of authority, though there was still an edginess in the drawled phrase, as if he felt this might be a moment of crisis, a step he had to take but didn't know if he'd get away with.

"There!" cried Cousin Blue. "That's two to one!"

"Well, all I can say is . . ."

"Wasn't that the bell?" said Cousin Blue. "Shh, everyone."

She must have had very keen ears. Even in the silence the distant tinkle could only just be heard. Cousin Brown shaded her eyes. One of the maids — Florrie, Andrew thought — was standing on the Top Walk shaking her hand above her head. He couldn't see the bell.

"Two rings, I think," said Cousin Brown.

"No, only one," said Cousin Blue. "It was for you, Elspeth. Andrew dear, go up and wave to Florrie to show her we've heard."

"It was two rings," said Cousin Brown.

"I think you're getting a bit deaf, darling. Perhaps that's why you talk so loud."

"Very well, we will both go. Charles, if you would be kind enough to help Andrew pack the banquet away . . ."

They unfastened the items of the feast, stowed them beneath the table and carried the whole contraption back into the shed. As

194

they walked up between the ruined lawns Charles said, "I've been wanting to talk to you. Don't get much chance with May around the whole time, eh?"

Andrew mumbled sympathetically.

"Bloody nuisance about this will," said Charles. "Old Foley seems to have made a complete mess of things. But let's assume it'll sort itself out in the end. I'm afraid Father didn't get round to making any provisions for you — daresay that was why he'd sent for Foley day he died, pop something in."

"It doesn't matter. I'll be all right."

"Every chance you will, dear boy. If you want my opinion, you've got the talent all right. Still, no harm in having a bit of a financial cushion, especially while you're starting. Otherwise things can be bloody rough. I know what I'm talking about. So I just wanted to tell you that as soon as this will business is sorted out I'll get the lawyers to draw something up, see you're all right."

"That's very kind of you," said Andrew.

"Not at all. Plenty to go round. I shan't miss it. You've taken the whole rum business very well, to my mind. I mean, supposing I hadn't shown up . . ."

"It was always a sort of fairy-tale. I never really believed it."

"Bit like that for me too . . . Life's a rum do . . . Tell me, any idea what the row was about, the one that started it all off?"

"I think it was something to do with a girl."

"Not surprised. The old boy had a weakness there, all right. His fault, I take it."

"He did it on purpose to settle a grudge with his brother. That's why he built the house too, to rub it in."

Charles shook his head, frowning.

"Never been able to understand that," he said. "You get it a lot in the classics — what's the point? Never played the Prince myself — done Horatio a couple of times — supposed to be every young actor's dream, but I don't think I could've taken the chap seriously."

Andrew liked Charles and felt comfortable with him, partly because Charles in his vague way seemed to take it for granted that Andrew was already a professional actor. In addition to that there was an unspoken set of complicities — the men of the family against the dominating women, the late-come outsiders

195

against the Cousins who had lived their whole lives at The Mimms, and, subtler than either of those, a shared understanding of each other's right to present an outer self to the world, perhaps quite different from their inner selves. Whether Charles was an impostor or not, he still had almost thirty years of hidden life behind his new façade. It was odd that he should reveal such a glimpse at this moment. Perhaps he had something else he wanted to say, but was trying not to rush it.

Two things struck Andrew. First he had been shown a possible way to find out some of the truth about Charles. How many productions of *Hamlet* had been staged between the wars? A hundred? Trace all you could. List the Horatios. You'd have a very good chance of netting at least one of Charles's. You could go to agents, look at photographs. You might even start with Cousin Brown's diaries — perhaps that was the performance she faintly recalled, and asking her would jog her memory . . .

The second thing was that he wouldn't do anything about it. It was what Charles had just said that decided him. Revenge. Uncle Vole's malice had been built into this house, binding its mortar, nailing beams and floorboards. Once you knew the story you couldn't forget it. That was why he'd insisted on seeing Andrew before he changed his will, to make sure that he would continue to live and breathe the old grudge, both victim and perpetrator. The house was a trap as Samuel had said. It waited for its victim. Andrew had escaped that morning by speaking with the power of Adrian's voice, but the trap still gaped.

Now along came Charles, and stood at the entrance. Why stop him? Why even warn him? He was immune to Uncle Vole's malice. He could breathe the air of The Mimms, sleep in its sheets and not be poisoned. Best of all, in a way, if he was an impostor. Break the chain. Close the circle. Finish.

Charles cleared his throat.

"Better spell it out, I suppose," he said. "What I was saying just now about setting you up financially — it all depends on getting the will sorted out."

"Yes, of course."

"Something you might be able to help with there."

"Oh?"

196

"Tell me, what d'you make of old Mkele?"

"Samuel? I like him very much."

"Talked to him about any of this?"

"Well, not recently. It's been a bit awkward."

This was true. In fact, since their one meeting in the woodland garden the night before Uncle Vole's death Andrew hardly remembered speaking to Samuel alone. It was impossible at rehearsals, of course, and though he used to breakfast in the kitchen on days when he was helping at the farm the atmosphere there had changed. Before Samuel's intervention at the will-reading the servants had talked openly among themselves about whether Charles was "our Mr Charles", taking sides — Florrie, for instance, saying it didn't matter either way, because he was a nice gentleman who'd had a hard time and he was due for a bit of luck — but amicably, feeding each other crumbs of evidence, for and against. It was a welcome topic, a change from the weather and the war. Since that day, though, Mrs Mkele had made it clear, largely by the weight of her silences, that Andrew, for all his privileges as "family", would only be welcome in her kitchen so long as he minded what he said and asked about.

"Awkward, I dare say," said Charles. "Can't make the fellow out. I wasn't sorry when he brought that business up when old Foley read us the will. He might have done it a bit more tactfully, but as Elspeth said it was best to have it in the open, and cleared up. But since then . . . Not that he isn't perfectly respectful, does what he's told and so on. But he's still brooding on it. What's more he wants me to know he is. He's never said a syllable, but I can tell."

"What do you want me to do?"

"Let me put it to you man to man, what I'm driving at is this. The important thing is to get Father's will cleared up. I can't hang around waiting for young Foley to come back, so I'm getting a lawyer of my own and I'm going to tell him to take things out of old Foley's hands. May will back me, and I dare say we can bring Elspeth round. The one thing we can't afford is to have somebody go spreading it around that I'm a fake. I can quite see that when I first turned up some of you must've thought that was a possibility, but I'd think it ought to be clear by now. Of course old Mkele's getting on a bit. Father's death must have been a great shock to him. I'm not saying the courts would give a deal of weight to what a fellow like that says, if that's the particular bug that's biting him. But none of us wants the matter to come to court in the first place. Once the whole pack of lawyers get their hands on it it'll take years to clear up and cost the earth. Why, I can't even guarantee what I just said, that there'd be enough to go round to spare a bit for you. It'd be a damned shame, but there. You follow?"

"All right. I'll do my best."

"Good lad. Let's not beat about the bush. You try and get it into his head that if he goes on the way he's been doing he'll have to go."

They had reached the point where the winding path up the slope joined the Top Walk. Charles halted and turned, with the Africa statue towering above him. His head was craned slightly forward and he stared at Andrew with a faint version of Uncle Vole's furious glare — over the last few weeks he seemed to have picked up or fallen into a number of the old boy's mannerisms. Only the malice was missing. The look said, "Well? Is it a deal?"

Andrew gazed back. It was a perfectly fair offer. It didn't even prove that Charles was a fake, that he should make it — the real Charles would have been just as anxious not to get the estate enmeshed in an endless law-suit. From Andrew's point of view it was almost ideal — far better than inheriting the whole estate and all that it meant, trailing that with him — rooms, statues, servants, memories — through his career; better too than Cousin Brown's offer of support, which would have been better than nothing, but carried the bargain that she should somehow have her own long-thwarted career inside him. This way he would owe no one anything.

The sky darkened. Raindrops streaked the stone of the statue.

"Let's get in," said Charles. "You don't want it to look as if I've put you on to him."

"That's all right. There's a book I was reading to him but we never got through. I'll finish it off this afternoon — there won't be any harvesting — and we'll just get talking."

"Good lad."

Mrs Mkele was alone in her parlour listening to *Variety Bandbox* while her fingers knitted without help from her mind. She was clearly in no mood to be interrupted.

"Sambo?" she said. "He'll be in the winecellar." She turned the volume up.

Andrew went back along the corridor. Now that the Americans were gone these lower regions of the house seemed echoingly empty, but subterranean voices reached him from one of the inner doorways. He went in, through the narrow vaulted chamber where he had once found Samuel doling out the family butter ration. The voices, Samuel's and Hazel's, came from the larger space beyond. They were not speaking English. He paused to listen. It was a language lesson, Samuel saying a few words in the form of a question, and Hazel repeating them, slightly altered to give the answer — *Is this the old lady's cooking-pot? No, that is not the old lady's cooking-pot.* That sort of thing. He coughed, and the voices stopped.

When he went through into the main cellar he found Samuel stretched on a camp bed. A paraffin lamp glowed on the shelf of the wine-bin above him. Hazel had retreated and become a shadow at the edge of its sphere of light. Beyond her, and far into the dark, row upon row of faint crescents gleamed where the beams of the lamp were reflected from the bottom of Uncle Vole's hoarded wine-bottles, his buried treasure, no use to him now. The air was dry but chill, and Samuel was wearing a dark overcoat of heavy serge, which made him look somehow a bit like a POW. He had swung himself up on to his elbow at Andrew's entrance.

"Don't get up," said Andrew. "I didn't mean to interrupt. Was that Zulu?"

"Something to do on a wet day," said Samuel apologetically.

"Pity there aren't any scenes for you to rehearse together."

Andrew had long got over his initial dismay at the casting of a child as Ariel. Hazel was intensely shy, but a naturally graceful mover, and Cousin Brown had drilled her all summer, teaching her dance-like movements and a strange, metallic, bloodless

voice all in extreme contrast to Caliban's violent earthy gesticulations and bellowings but despite that echoing them at times,
attempting to imply that the pair were spirits of the same
inhuman creation.

"She learns pretty quick, don't you, lovey?" said Samuel.
"No harm in her knowing a bit about where I come from. After
all, she comes from there too, some of her."

"Pretty difficult for her to imagine. I mean, it's so different
from this."

Samuel grunted and lay back, staring at the ceiling.

"There was a morning," he said. "Listen to this, lovey.
You'd better know. There was a morning at the diggings. I'd
been there eight months, working for Baas Wragge, and I'd
made me enough money to buy a good rifle, which is what I'd
come for in the first place. So when we lined up for our pay that
morning I told Baas Wragge I was leaving. He said to stand to
one side while he settled with the others. We were outside his
tent. It was just before winter, cold, with a thick mist. I stood
shivering in my blanket and waited. Then he beckoned me over
and I went and stood in front of his table."

He sat up and began to act the characters in the remembered
episode. He hunched his shoulders, poked his head forward and
glared up.

" 'You're not going,' says the baas. 'You're staying with
me.' "

Now he straightened his back and looked down, puzzled,
hesitant.

"Remember I seen plenties of Baas Wragge's doings. I know
him for a liar and a cheat. 'Gainst that, he's a white baas and I'm
a black boy, so I stood there trying for to make my neck shake
my head to tell him no, but the neck it was gone all stiff.

" 'What do you want to leave for?' he says.

"I tell him I'm going to buy a gun and go back to my kraal
and be a big man there with a good wife and a fine hut. What
else for am I a man?

" 'Me too,' he says. 'Me too.'

"He sits there for a bit, like he's gone into a dream, and then
he starts to talk. He tells me that when he has got enough
money from the diggings he's going back home, and he's going
to build himself a palace bigger than a hundred huts and be chief

of his tribe, and I must go with him and stand behind his stool and be his counsellor."

Samuel stopped acting and became a tired old black man sitting in a cave under a Hampshire hill. He smiled up at Andrew and shook his head, still helplessly puzzled by his long ago decision.

"Often I think of that morning," he said. "Why did I answer yes? It was like a voice inside me, speaking for me, before I could tell Baas Wragge no. I see pictures of myself, sitting in front of my door with my rifle across my knees while my wives pound the mealies behind the hut. But 'stead of that I tell him yes. I give him my whole life.

" 'You won't regret it,' he says. 'I'll see you're all right.'

"Kept his promise too. Not many promises of his you can say that of. Hazel, lovey, you understand what I been saying?"

The child murmured in the shadows.

"My whole life I gave him that morning," said Samuel dreamily. "Plenties of times after that I might've stopped off, but somehow it never came to it, and after a bit, what'd I have done for myself, supposing I had? Gone back to my kraal? My kraal was burnt by the Boers. The boy who wanted the rifle, he was dead too. My whole life. That's what your Granny can't understand, lovey."

He shook himself and spoke directly to Andrew.

"Mary Jane and the rest, they're at me to stop bothering about this man says he's Master Charlie. You remember, night before Baas Wragge died, that cutting Phil sent?"

"Yes, of course."

Samuel reached into the breast pocket of his coat, took out a battered black notecase and drew from it the piece of paper with the cutting pinned to it, both now becoming flimsy with handling. He stared for half a minute at the to him meaningless print.

"Took it in and showed the Baas," he said. "He weren't interested. Day before that he'd got me to send for Mr Foley and tell him to bring the will, but he hadn't said what he was planning. Now he made me tell him again what I'd arranged, and he asked if you was in the house, and he says to tell you to come and see him ten o'clock next morning. And then he says to me, 'I'm changing my will, Samuel. I'm leaving the house to that actor brat. This other fellow's not my son.' He'd asked me what I thought pretty well soon as the man showed up — you remember, you helped me put him to bed? Morning after that — and I'd said, but he'd never told me what he thought himself. Only I knew he knew — it was just he couldn't bring himself to do anything, 'cause that'd have meant admitting he was dying. Now he goes and admits it. 'I'll be gone soon,' he says. 'Three more days is all I'm good for. I'm not having that fellow take over. He's not my son. I'm not having May getting her hands on everything.' Never knew why he hated women the way he did. 'When's Foley coming?' he asks. I told him again. He didn't say anything a long while and I thought he'd fell asleep, but then he says, 'I should last that long. I should last that long. If I don't, then it's up to you. Now get out.' So I went and looked for you and when I couldn't find you I got Mary Jane to write a note and I put it on your pillow. When I saw Baas Wragge next morning he didn't say much about any of that, only asked if you was coming. I reckoned he sounded stronger and I thought he'd last out till the afternoon, and more, but he didn't."

"Did you tell Mr Foley or anyone about this?"

"No good, not unless I can prove something. Who's going to listen to an old black boy? That's why Mary Jane and the rest are so against me. 'You'll never prove it,' she says, 'and in any case it's better all round if you don't. What does it matter if he isn't the real Master Charlie, provided he's keeping us on?' That's what they say."

"The same applies to you, doesn't it? I mean, whatever you think in private, if you accept this man as Charles then you can go on living here. And if you managed to prove it wasn't him it wouldn't do you any good. Mr Foley seemed to think that bit of the will wasn't legal, but if it is then everybody would have to leave. And if you don't prove it, but just go on hoping to find something against him . . ."

"He'll kick me out."

"I'm afraid so."

"Mary Jane, she won't come with me, neither."

"Hadn't you better give up?"

"Can't do that."

"Look, if it's for my sake . . ."

The old man shook his head.

"My whole life I gave him. I'm the only one he ever did trust."

Samuel reached out with his left arm and with wavering fingers beckoned into the dark. Obediently, but reluctantly, Hazel came and settled against his side. The arm closed round her for comfort, his, not hers. Aware of her role the child put her hand in his and let his fingers clasp it, but at the same time, as if trying to withdraw herself from his pain into some distraction she eased the cutting from his other hand and started to read it through. Andrew shared her feelings but found he couldn't withdraw. He hadn't realized this would ever happen to him again, not after Mum's death and his deliberate choice that night, with Mr Trinder's help, of heartlessness, of not becoming entangled in anyone else's needs or emotions, not ever again, from then on. Now he remembered the first rehearsal in the Institute, how when he had called Caliban from his cave — 'Thou earth, thou, speak' — more than a voice had answered, choices had been made, everything that had happened since then had been changed by that moment. It wasn't just a sense of fellowship between two performers, though Samuel, given a white skin, other chances, might have become an actor, world-known, somebody you were privileged to have met. The power was there. It was that which mattered, that which must not be denied or betrayed. It might be different from the power Andrew knew he would one day command — Samuel needed no Adrian, no second self, to make himself wholly Caliban, or the Othello or Lear he had never in fact been allowed to portray — but it was the same in one way. It was the only thing that mattered, the only thing to which you must stay true. Here, in this real cave, Andrew was forced to accept the bond.

"What do you think, lovey?" sighed Samuel.

"Look," she said. "It's a flower show. Like at the Institute, when Nanna won all the baking."

She had folded the cutting back and showed him the photograph. He stared at it vaguely. She cocked her head and frowned at the paper it was pinned to.

"Funny . . ." she said.

"What do you think, lovey? Did I better give in?"

"Can't you be friends with Nanna again? I don't really like it in here. I feel all shut under."

Samuel sighed again, shaking his head to and fro and gazing up at Andrew for help.

"Did Sir Arnold tell you why he wanted to leave me the house?" said Andrew.

"Just he was going to. That's all."

"Well, what he told me was that I was his great-grandson. He had a grudge against his elder brother, so he seduced his fiancée on purpose and got her pregnant and then went off to Africa. The brother married her and pretended the baby was his own. Sir Arnold told me he'd built this house to rub his revenge in. He said he'd got the idea from something you'd said to him — that morning you were just talking about, I think it might have been. He wanted to leave me the house so that I could go on living here and keep his revenge alive for him after he was dead. He told me the story so that I'd know all about it. I told him — well, I told him I didn't want it. I was going to be an actor. In fact, I told him in a way which made him so angry that he tried to sit up and choked and died. I did it on purpose — not making him die, I mean, but making him angry. It came to the same thing. Do you understand?"

Samuel nodded slowly. Hazel beside him gazed up at Andrew, her wide clear eyes glistening with the sideways glow of the lamp.

"I think the story's over," said Andrew. "It's come round on itself and it's time to stop. I don't know if it's any use, but when Sir Arnold said he was making me his heir he didn't really mean heir to his money and all that — he meant heir to his life, don't you think?"

"Maybe so."

"Well, in that case I can let you off your promise to him, can't I?"

It seemed, now he'd said it, a pretty feeble argument, but Samuel sat grunting faintly to himself, a quiet but still painful noise, like a tree groaning in the wind as the gusts wrench at its innards, gradually tearing it in two. Hazel reached up and stroked his cheek.

"Can't you be friends with Nanna again?" she said. "Can't you? Soon?"

204

"Look," said Andrew. "I'm being called up in a fortnight. I'm not looking forward to it, and you can say that again. At least I'd like to feel I'd got this part of things settled. Couldn't we say that if nothing new's come up by then, then you call it a day? I release you from your promise and you accept that Charles is who he says he is. Whether it's true or not doesn't matter. He's acted himself into the part OK. You can too."

Samuel sat shaking his head, but then somehow the movement converted itself into a questioning tilt of the neck, as though he were trying to get rid of a stiffness in the vertebrae.

"And if, before you go . . .?" he muttered.

"You find something? I can't think what, but if you do, and it really proves he isn't Charles . . ."

"You are the heir to the life. You just said it."

"I suppose so. Well, in that case I'll back you up."

Once again Samuel sat silent, thinking, then nodded decisively.

"Then I still got a chance," he said. "All right."

"OK, it's a deal. I really came down to ask you if you'd like me to finish reading you *Nada*. There's about a couple of chapters to go."

"Hazel done that for me. She's beginning to read pretty good, aren't you, lovey?"

The tone told Andrew that Samuel had made his decision and would stick to it. Things were going to be all right. The discomfort and awkwardness caused by the rift between the Mkeles would go away. Samuel could stop sleeping alone in the cellar. The wound would heal. Andrew felt an unusual sort of pleasure at what had happened — this was something he had brought off by himself, being himself, without any help from Adrian. With anyone except Samuel it wouldn't have mattered, but it did.

It was almost as though Adrian had been waiting for him in the corridor, unable for some reason to enter Samuel's cave. He shook his hand in mock self-disapproval. Mustn't get involved like that. Can't risk it, though it had worked out OK this time. More than OK. He'd done exactly what he said he would. He'd delivered his side of the deal with Charles.

The rain-rehearsal on the Institute stage finished just before ten, and the cast dribbled out from the apparent midnight of the blacked-out hall into the bright dusk of double summer-time. A large flight of bombers was drumming its way south and Peter Boller was standing on the steps looking up at them with a just-lit cigarette between his lips, not caring that he was half-blocking everyone else's way. He had come out from Southampton that afternoon and would be staying for six more days of rehearsal and then the five performances. He glanced down at Andrew.

"Got your papers yet?" he said.

"Yes. The thirty-first. Warminster."

"Same here. Fred Yates says that means tanks."

"Basic first."

"Anyone's fit will be tanks, he says. You'll be just what they're after — plenty of headroom."

"They'll fit you in somehow. Curling up by numbers."

As the bombers dwindled another wave could be heard throbbing from the north.

"Fred says it'll be Burma, once we're trained," said Peter.

"The Ed. Sergeant at my medical told us they'd need replacements for the chaps they're losing in France."

"Oh, that can't last that long. Look how the Russians are getting on. And with any luck the Japs will pack it in when Germany goes."

Andrew shrugged. No, he thought. One in ten casualties would be nothing, Sergeant Stephens had said. What did he mean? One in two? Which two? Peter and Andrew, one of them? The toss of a coin? Then . . . Peter alive, posturing and strutting through his career, while everything that had been Andrew dissolved into the floor of some German wood? Obscene. A whisper rustled in his mind. Let it be him who's the one. Little god, let it be him.

He saw Jean waiting for him by the bikes. The pony-traps clopped towards the steps.

"You get a ride," he told Peter. "Where's your bag? See you at the house."

"Will we get something to eat?"

"Oh, I should think so."

They pushed the bikes side by side up the dusty street while the traps climbed slightly faster, fifty yards ahead now. In front of the almshouses a woman in a yellow headscarf was pumping water into a bucket.

"Evening, Mrs Archer," called Jean.

The woman looked up with a ferocious bright glare, small blue eyes in a million-wrinkled face. She said nothing and returned to pumping.

"She's the village witch," whispered Jean. "Dolly told me always to say hello to her in case she turns the milk. In any case, we witches have to stick together. I'm going to get her to teach me to ride a broomstick soon as rationing's over."

"What's rationing got to do with it?"

"You're supposed to rub them with baby-fat, but we modern witches use butter."

Andrew grunted. He was getting a bit tired of the witch joke. Since the afternoon in the chalk-pit Jean had exploited it in various ways, not just as a joke but in a shifting, sometimes half-serious way, to remind him that their relationship had changed. He might have started absolute master, dominating her by his secret powers, but now she had found a weakness, so she had some say too.

"I'm sorry I winked," she said. "I just wanted you to know what I thought of Peter. I didn't realize you'd be furious."

"Just don't do anything like that again."

"He really is pretty dreadful, isn't he?"

"Glad you think so."

"What were you talking to him about just now? On the steps?"

"Nothing. Oh, call-up. He's in the same batch as me. We were guessing how long the war's going to last."

"You made your Sir Arnold face."

"Did I?"

"Don't pretend. I know you terribly well. Better than you do, some ways."

They mounted when they reached the top of the hill and pedalled slowly through the cooling air. After a few minutes

207

they overtook the traps and drew ahead. Jean seemed to have lost interest in his conversation with Peter. She hadn't really wanted to know, only to tell him she'd seen it had mattered.

"Isn't Mr Mkele terrific?" she said.

"That's the word."

"Was I all right?"

"Charming, fresh, lively — *Sunday Times*."

"Oh, good. I never imagined how much I'd be enjoying it. Still, I'm glad it's only a week. I don't understand how real actors keep it up for months — being Miranda, I mean, newborn each time, like a little calf staring at the world."

"You've got Peter to stare at."

"At least he's handsome. It's just everything else about him."

Suppose he told her straight out . . . but he'd promised Cousin Brown a happy Miranda . . . you couldn't tell — there was so much more to her than he'd realized when they'd begun.

"Do you mind if I don't come to the lodge tonight?"

"Oh?"

"I've got to start concentrating."

"I thought you were already."

"Not enough. I think about you, I worry about call-up, I wonder what's for supper, I day-dream about when I'm on in the West End . . . Now until next Saturday all that's got to stop."

"All right. Actually I'm due to tell you you can't come for a bit."

"Bad luck."

"My fault for being a woman."

They reached the top of the drive. It was darker under the trees. A convoy coming from the other direction was swinging in through the gates. They waited, straddling their bikes. As each lorry took the turn its hooded headlights swept across them. Andrew imagined other endings. They wouldn't always be like this — the women would be different, for a start, stupider or cleverer, experienced, dreamy, tempestuous, childish; there would be stormings-out, chilly dismissals, champagne parties, fadings away; whole worlds of other endings.

In a gap in the convoy she reached towards him for a quick kiss. He let it happen, still thinking about endings.

"That wasn't much fun," she said.

"I told you, we've got to concentrate."

He was looking at her, clear and then dim and then clear again in the headlamps. Her face stiffened.

"I'm not going to let Miss Elspeth down, whatever happens. When I've started something I see it through. You ought to know that."

"You're going to be very good."

"You don't have to wait. See you in Fogg's Corner, after milking."

"OK, good-night."

"Good-night, darling."

The last lorry churned in, followed by the tail-end jeep. As Andrew freewheeled down the fumy tunnel between the banked rhododendrons he discovered that something had happened inside him, new and strange. It was to do with breaking off with Jean, giving her up—more than just a sense of freedom or relief at having got it over. A pocket of energies he didn't know were there was welling out, feeding his powers, just at the right time. Anything was possible.

There was a hold-up at the camp entrance. Twenty lorries stood in a line down the drive, their engines drumming. They were all empty. Early next morning he would hear them leaving the camp on their regular run, taking another batch of young men off to the battlefields. Their bulk almost blocked the drive, but they had left just enough room down their offsides for him to whistle through.

S I X

"Today's the big day, then," said Jack. "Quite like old times, eh, Mary? Got a spare egg for Master Andrew? He's going to need his strength."

"Hens been off their lay," said Mrs Mkele.

"Quite like old times, I say," said Jack.

"Hardly that," said Mrs Mkele. "Old times there'd have been forty in the house, and marquees for the suppers, and champagne and dancing till all hours after, and none of the upstairs out of their beds till twelve next morning, 'stead of which we've got poor Master Andrew gobbling his porridge crack of dawn and then off to the harvest."

"What about poor old Jack, then? Same with me."

"All you got to do is rattle that thunder-sheet. Funny to think nobody coming from London. Not a soul. We used to have hundreds."

"Least we're doing one down on the right stage, even if it is only for a pack of Yanks."

"Pearls before swine," said Mrs Mkele.

General Odway and his staff had been gone six weeks now and she had her own kitchen back, besides several bits of equipment which the American cooks had simply abandoned, rather than bother to account for, but her enmity towards these allies had not lessened.

"There's some gets on with them well enough," said Jack, winking at Andrew over his mug. The wink was a measure of the change below stairs. Mrs Mkele was still the dominant figure, but her command was not automatic. It was something to do with the rift between her and her husband, as though she had derived her authority from him in some mysterious way, and now could no longer claim it on that basis but had to assert it for herself. Jack's wink and its meaning would have been unthinkable two months back. Mrs Mkele paid no attention.

"I'm giving my Hazel a lie-in," she said. "It's a lot for a child."

The bell on the board jangled. She glanced up to see which disc was jiggling.

"Back door," she said. "Who's that, this hour? Give Sambo a yell, Jack."

"Sam! Oi! Sammy! Back door!"

"Finished your porridge, Master Andrew? Plenties more if you wanted it. Here's your fritters then. Sorry about the hens."

Mrs Mkele waddled over with the plate. The fritters were potato cakes with onion and parsley fried into them, crisp outside, gooey in, full of taste. For some reason they made Andrew think of Mum, though anything she'd tried in that line would have been soggy, greasy, flavourless. He hadn't thought about Mum for weeks. Though in the old days his day-dreams had always included her, set up in comfort somewhere, at his first nights, pasting up the scrap-albums of his career, she was now part of the past. It was sad that she wouldn't be there for the performance, but it was right. The sadness was right, adding a necessary flavour to the event. If she'd still been alive, and coming today, the whole thing would have been different. The process of becoming Adrian Waring and ceasing to be Andrew Wragge would have been more difficult, messier, less definite. Dad must be dead too. Rotting in a grave in some jungle. Andrew had no way of knowing this, but he was sure it was true — it was the shape things were meant to be. The deaths were right. They fitted in. They gave him something he hadn't had before — just like the break with Jean. He didn't understand how, any more than you can understand why a scene in a play has to be the shape it is. All you can say is it must be, because it is art. His life, life as Adrian Waring, was going to be like that too.

Samuel came into the room, silently because out of habit he still went barefoot and didn't need his floor-polishing slippers at this time of year. He was carrying a small dark brown envelope.

"Telegram, then?" said Jack.

"For Miss Elspeth," said Samuel.

"Florrie'll take it up on her tray," said Mrs Mkele.

"Big day, then, Sam," said Jack.

"Very big day."

"Mr Charles get to bed all right?"

"He got to bed, same as usual," said Samuel in a dead voice.

Mrs Mkele swung from the cooker and slapped her palm on the table.

"Now, that's enough of that," she said. "Sick and tired of it all, I am, and I'm not having it spoken of again, not in my kitchen. You got the horses to see to, han't you, Jack? You too, Sambo — there's plenties to get set, never mind there isn't forty in the house. Off you go, the both of you."

For a moment it was almost as though the spirit of the permanently furious GI cooks had returned to haunt the kitchen. Jack winked at Andrew as he rose and left. Samuel looked at him too, gazing blank-eyed for several seconds before he turned for the door.

Lower Park — the area below the camp, with the dovecote at its centre — was the last to be reaped. It was barley, which was bad

211

enough, but in addition there was a broad strip parallel to the camp fence that was mottled with thistles, whose fluffy seed-heads and dark green leaves stood proud of the level crop. And most of the south-east corner was laid flat by the down-draught from the woods. Three Italian POWs were helping, two of whom teamed up to stook with Dolly and a girl from the village, and since Brian would only work with Mrs Althorp, that left Andrew to pair with the third Italian, who sulked throughout the morning, listening to his friends having all the fun and sometimes going over and trying to persuade one of the others to swap places.

The work was hot and slow, painful along the thistly stretch, but for once the teams almost kept up with the reaper, which was delayed by the flattened patch on each circuit. Jean arrived quite early and took over on the rear seat from Jack, who went back up to the house. Around half past ten Cousin Brown came striding down across the stubble with a sheet of paper in her hand.

"I have some most promising news," she said, and gave Andrew the paper. It was the telegram that had come that morning.

"MEET FOUR TWELVE PETERSFIELD STOP HAD BETTER BE WORTH IT SCREAMER LORD HOW WISH FILTHY WAR WOULD GO AWAY SCREAMER LONGING TO SEE DEAR OLD MIMMS STOP SORRY READ ABOUT YOUR DAD STOP B."

"Barrie Oakley," said Cousin Brown.

"Golly!"

"I wrote to him ten days ago asking him to come if he could. He always loved the Amphitheatre, so there was just a chance once we had decided to do a performance there. This is typical. He never makes up his mind about anything until the last possible minute. That is why I did not tell you sooner — I did not want to disappoint you."

"That's marvellous!"

"It is quite a chance for you, Andrew. He will probably bring Jonny Price."

"I'd love to meet him. Thank you very much. I say, did you tell him my name?"

She looked surprised.

212

"I think I just said 'a young cousin'. Does it matter?"

"Well, I hope you don't think it's stupid . . . you see, I want people to think of me as Adrian Waring. Right from the start, I mean."

"Yes, of course. You do not even wish to be introduced as Andrew Wragge?"

"If that's all right."

"I will try to remember."

She left. Andrew worked on in a dream, glad now of the Italian's silence and surliness. The long repetitive hours, stooking over the crunching silvery stubble, were just right for his mood — not that he spent the time being Prospero or repeating his lines or thinking about the play, though occasionally some little nuance of tone, some pause, would involuntarily float into his mind and he would then consider it briefly before rejecting it. That was all settled. Better not mess around now. Mostly, though, his mind stayed blank, so that by the end of the morning he wouldn't have been able to remember a single definite idea that had been there.

He went back to the house for luncheon. With the harvesters breaking off at noon and the cousins not lunching till one, he ate alone. Again, that was best.

His Italian had persuaded one of the others to swap places for the afternoon, and the new man wanted to be friendly, but Andrew rebuffed him, so he spent his social energies shouting to whichever of the other two was nearer, clearly relying on the privacy of language to tease his friends with earthy remarks about the women, who themselves joined in by asking with less than innocence what he was saying. In the end the one who had been working with Andrew all morning came striding over and embarked on a face-to-face quarrel with gloriously Italian gestures and poses. At any other time Andrew would have watched, absorbing each detail, but now he blanked the scene out and stooked on alone. The quarrel ended with his morning's companion returning to work with him in welcome sullenness.

Halfway through the afternoon the binder broke down, more seriously than usual, so that the stookers reached the point where there were no more sheaves for them to stack and Dave was still wrenching and cursing at the innards of the machine.

The other two Italians, apparently a little ashamed of their behaviour, made a peace move by calling to Andrew's partner to come and join them where they sat with the women. He scowled but went over. Andrew stood alone, staring over the half-cut barley, with the stubble in the foreground and then the wall of bare stalks and the browner heads sloping smoothly away towards the dovecote. Footsteps crackled to his left. He turned to see Jean striding towards him. He made his smile welcoming but purely social.

"I've got to talk to you," she said. "There isn't time now. He's almost got it going."

"Can we leave it a few days? Till the play's over?"

"Don't be stupid, darling. You'll be going away straight after. Something's happened. I mean it hasn't."

"I'd . . ."

"Listen. I know it's no use before tonight. I can cope with that. And I don't want to muck things up if I can help it. But you can't expect me to . . ."

She paused, staring at him, her chin set. Beyond her Dave straightened from the binder and began to wipe the grease off his forearms with a twist of straw.

"I'll come up tonight," he said. "Usual sort of time?"

"You'll still be too worked up. You'd better sleep on it. You know what it's about, don't you?"

"I suppose you're sure?"

She gazed at him, not angry, hardly hurt. Almost amused, in fact — studying him, the sort of person who, knowing her so well, could still ask a question like that. He realized that she had stopped loving him. Anyway, she was sure. You could set the calendar by her, she had said last time.

"Listen," she said. "I'll get the milking done early tomorrow and not clean up. I'll be free by half past six."

"OK. At the stile?"

Dave turned. His unarticulated shout floated across the stubble. She shook her head, then nodded it towards the dovecote.

"Down there," she said. "Quarter to seven. Don't be late."

She turned and ran back to the binder. The tractor-engine roared, the blades clattered and the sheaves came tumbling out on to the stubble. Andrew slotted himself back into his job, using its rhythm to blank his mind once more so that the energies could go on gathering into the well of his inner self. At half past four Cousin Brown came down again to make sure that Mrs Althorp didn't try to keep her cast at work a minute longer than the agreed time.

SEVEN

A hazed August evening. Bodies still sweaty with harvest, aching with the long day, tender with the scratch of thistly sheaves. From beyond the yew hedge the voices of the audience, their main note clearly American, restless, an irritable patch in the smooth calm of beechwoods and the sweep of unmown lawns. Everything weary, leaves still green but with a deadish hue, the tussocks of grass half fallen, stems pale, seed shed. A kind of ache in the air, in the slant dull light, a yearning to have all this world over and swept away by the scour of winter.

"Did you hear?" someone whispered. "We've taken Paris. It was on the six-o'clock."

Cousin Brown had decided to begin her production with Ariel beckoning the whole cast to cross the stage in procession. Those needed for the opening scene were to peel off and take up their positions. Prospero, who was to remain on stage throughout the performance — sometimes asleep, sometimes watching in trance the action on stage, sometimes conducting or reacting to it — crossed to his cave down right while Caliban, his entrance concealed by the procession of courtiers, huddled invisible among the weed-covered rocks down left. The mariners posed in their mime of ship-work while the rest of the procession passed out of sight. Prospero summoned Ariel and mimed the transfer of powers that would allow him to wake the tempest, Jack rattled his thunder-sheet. The mariners woke into movement and the play would begin.

Sweltering in his heavy robe, with his tome under his arm, Andrew waited by the fresh-clipped arch. He had been first dressed because he needed to be alone, out of the fret and dither of the Green Room hut, away from the postmaster's tedious wishes of good luck and Charles wittering round searching for

215

his missing hose. The rest of the procession started to line up, the courtiers in velvets and golds, the mariners drabber, Trinculo in motley — Cousin Brown had amassed a biggish wardrobe over the years. Jean came and stood beside him, wearing a pale green floating tunic with a gold ribbon crossing between her breasts. Cousin Brown had erased her freckles, making her pink-and-white, with crimson half-pouting lips.

"You're going to get some whistles," he whispered.

She nodded, unperturbed.

"You're still coming?" she said.

"Yes."

She accepted his promise by practising her Miranda face at him, demure but eager. He smiled and turned away. She would understand he didn't want to talk.

The next ten minutes were crucial. He had to get them right. It wasn't only a matter of making a good impression on Mr Oakley — that was something practical, possibly useful, more likely a dead end. A career was certain to be full of people who could have helped but were too blind or busy to see their chance. The main thing was different but far more vital. It was already announced, clear and unchangeable on the playbills, in the programmes. "Prospero: Adrian Waring."

Tonight he was born.

In conversation he had been casual about it — might as well start some time — but inwardly it had become all-important. No more come-and-go of Adrian at need, to outface problems, to get girls and other things he wanted. Now he was going to take his place before the world and become real. For this birth he must prepare so that he would walk on stage filled with his energies, robed with his powers. There would be hundreds, thousands of other performances through the years, but they all depended on getting this one right. The jeering note of the GIs' chatter was a threat but also a test, exhilarating. If he got it right they would be silent for him.

Self-absorption did not mean unawareness — quite the opposite. He was conscious of everything, the itches and scratches of his skin and the ache of muscles, the silence of woods and lawns, the nervous gathering of the cast, the need to warn Jean about the whistles. If he had chosen he could have tuned his hearing and picked out the voice of a single soldier

216

beyond the hedge, caught every syllable, understood not just the present meaning but all that had happened to cause that present, far back into some small-town boyhood . . .

He heard a muffled yelp and turned to see the door of the Men's Green Room bang open and Charles burst out, half dressed, clutching the waistband of his hose at knee-level. At least he'd found them. He dropped his cloak and circlet on to the grass and finished pulling the hose up over his shirt-tails. His attitude expressed outrage, shock, fright. All the cast had turned at his yell and were watching, so they all saw Caliban come sidling out behind him. Impossible to think of him as Samuel, he was already so invested with his part, the grimaces, the gestures, the crab-like scuttlings. Cousin Brown was going over to speak to Charles. Caliban rushed past her, beyond his proper place in the procession and up to its head, where he seized Andrew by the arm and tried to drag him aside. Andrew resisted. The dark brown skin under its monster make-up seemed to be suffused almost purple. The eyes bulged. Andrew turned his head away. Cousin Brown was speaking to Charles. Charles said something, contrived a half-smile. Cousin Brown picked up the coronet and cloak and waited to help him dress.

"Baas! Baas!"

At least he kept his voice low. It was not his butler tone, nor Caliban's, but the nigger-talk he had used with Uncle Vole.

"Not now," muttered Andrew.

"You are the heir. You promise me. Send and fetch the wife."

Andrew did not hesitate, did not even choose. The voice was already in his mouth, as it had been the morning he had killed Uncle Vole. He looked coldly down.

"Be quiet. You can tell me tomorrow."

The contorted mouth opened to plead again, but now from beyond the hedge came a rasp of crackles, a magnified cough, a voice through a loudspeaker.

"Now, men, hear this. It is a great privilege, a very great privilege, for us to be here. Time to time you fellows get bitching about this war we're fighting. You ask your pal what the hell good we're doing over here, right?"

"Right, lieutenant," called a voice. Others laughed.

"OK, guys, take it easy. Now I read some place how Bill

217

Shakespeare who wrote this great play spoke the same way we do, with a good American accent. That doesn't prove he was an American, but it shows he wasn't only an Englishman. He was both. And this play of his . . ."

Caliban — Samuel — had not moved but still stood pleading, a violent agonized pose, the half-gripped hands held forward as if about to rip their way in, through the role of Prospero, through the public presence of Adrian to the inmost cave where Andrew had his secret being. Let him in, pay any attention at all, acknowledge his right to plead, and the focused powers would start to scatter. Andrew pivoted his own head away and allowed his body to follow it round. He felt fingers grip the elbow that held the tome against his side. Without looking down he raised his other hand and prised them loose. The cast were watching, mostly baffled but Charles now warily, out of the corners of his eyes. Cousin Brown marched up the line, took Samuel by the hand and led him to his place. Andrew faced the empty arch, seeing and hearing nothing and everything. The alien voice crackled to its peroration.

He waited for his long-planned life to start.

EIGHT

After seven weeks' practice his fingers and toes knew the route from Florrie's linen-room without conscious thought. The only strangeness was to be climbing down in the dawn, not up. The sash slid without a sound. Elbows on sill, reach with right foot for hopper-head of rainwater down-pipe, stretch right arm round corner to decorative bobble, swing body sideways and round into vertical slot, chimney down that, reach with right foot again — a blind bit, this — out and round for sill of Samuel's pantry . . .

What?

Slither. The crackle of something plummeting into bushes. Craning, he could see where the leaves still trembled in the shrubbery below. He reached with his foot again, found the place, but wrong — greasy and unsafe. Retracting the foot and holding his body in tension he peered down at the tilted sole. A yellow smear. Even before he had reached down to touch it and

218

then sniffed at his fingertip he had guessed what it was. Last night at the party . . . Cousin Blue's lost treasure. The missing butter.

Very peculiar. Somebody must have put it there. After Samuel had closed the shutters, or he'd have seen. He'd have done that just before the play and there'd have been people in and out of the pantry after. One of the other servants, taking the below-stairs schism into new areas of spite? Cousin Blue herself, so as to be able to berate Samuel and thus remind him of his place after his triumph as Caliban? Wouldn't she have done that more publicly? They'd been in the pantry when Andrew had rushed in for a wet cloth — Charles had spilt his wine over Jonny Price's beautiful pale blue suit — God knows how many coupons. Cousin Blue with her back to him, low-voiced but vehement. ". . . stolen by one of these strangers," she was saying. "Nevertheless I *will* have butter . . ." And then she'd stopped until Andrew had scurried out, cloth in hand.

He shook his head, refusing the mystery. It was part of the past, nothing to do with him any more. He eased the shoe off, gripped the laces in his teeth and with one bare foot climbed on. Round on to the sill, down on to elbows, reach with left foot for hopper-head of sink outlet, and down that pipe into the shrubbery. He could see the butter dish lying upside down a few feet down the slope, but he left it there. Perhaps on his way back he would retrieve it and take it to Samuel, give the old boy a chance to explain what he'd been so upset about last night. That was another bit of the past, but worth tidying up in order to be shot of it. Same with Jean.

He walked up the steep path to the front terrace and then immediately right down the stone stair that led towards the woodland garden. As he sat on the lowest step to put his shoe back on the air changed. Sunlight caught the topmost branches of the trees and moved steadily down. Dawn became day.

The woodland clattered with birdsong. He took deep, deliberate breaths of the dewy air, feeling marvellously alive, free, uplifted. The black, cold well of terror at his centre was gone, drained clean away, and in the space where it had been was thrilling hope. No, more than hope, certainty, foreknowledge of a life of glory. By his own powers he had wrought the change, he and Samuel, sweeping them all up — Hazel, Jean,

Peter and the others, drawing out of them energies they never knew were there, so that the impossible audience was stilled and swept up too. And Barrie Oakley had been there to see, and had understood what had happened. Halfway up the valley an engine started, then another and another, as the dawn convoy readied itself to carry its seven hundred GIs away to the war.

Startled by the squeak of the gate rabbits flickered back into the wood as he came out into the field. The shadows of the stooks lay long in the barely risen sun, making a striped pattern across the silvery stubble. The harvest had kept going last evening after he'd left and the barley was reaped right up to the dovecote, which now stood naked apart from a fringe of nettles round its foot. Its shadow ran all the way to the camp fence.

There were still about ten minutes before Jean would show up, he guessed. He'd come early, on purpose, so that she shouldn't have the slight advantage of having been kept waiting. Not that it made any difference. The whole thing was her fault, that afternoon at the chalk-pit. She'd known his resistance was at its lowest. She kept saying how well she knew him . . . well, in that case she'd know he wasn't going to marry her. Money? Cousin Brown would stump up — she'd have friends too, actresses who'd got into the same sort of mess and could tell Jean who to go to . . . Anything, provided it was tidied and done with.

A pigeon was cooing in the further wood and a couple of doves were out on the sills of the flight-holes, muttering in their deeper, bubbling note. Now the noise of engines from the camp strengthened as the first lorries started grinding across the valley, parallel to his path but in the opposite direction. The symmetry prickled his skin. Seven hundred men going one way. He, alone, the other. Tomorrow they'd be in France. By next week the chosen ones — you, and you, and you — would be dead. They would die with their own memories, which made them what they were — childhood in a prairie town, or a particular girl, or some quarrel or moment of shame, some drunken night — but in one or two misting minds a paved stage which was supposed to be an island, people in fancy clothes who were supposed to be courtiers and sailors, a magician who for two hours had made those suppositions solid. A memory to die with.

He had fitted the big iron key into the lock before he noticed the splinters on the jamb. An instant later he felt the slight give in the door itself and heard the scrape on the threshold stone as he pushed it further. The metal block into which the lock-tongue slotted had been wrenched loose, screws and all. The door had been forced.

Poachers after dove-meat? GIs from the camp? Lovers desperate for a place — but the nights had been fine and warm and the woods were private enough. He tiptoed up the narrow spiral stair.

"How did it go?"

"Very well. Benny sends his love."

"Really well? You weren't . . ."

"Apparently not, judging by the fact that two of the audience screamed just after Polly's exit. How's the hand?"

"It hurts when I think about it. I'm not really interested in *them*. I want to know about *you*. Were you all right?"

"I'd like some hot milk with rum in it. Give yourself something. We're not going to bed for a bit."

"It's half past two."

"I know."

"All right. You'd better come and get it. I might spill with a tray."

He fidgeted while he waited for her call, interrupted the flow of the water-clock, fingered about among her collection of treen, made adjustments to the fire. At the sound of her voice he crossed rapidly to the kitchen but slowed his pace at the door. He came back behind her, carrying both mugs which he put on the table by the sofa. He adjusted the table, then finally settled with her into their tableau with himself propped against the wing of the sofa and her nestling between him and the back. He lifted her mug to her left hand and tasted his own.

"Not enough rum. Don't move. It's probably just as well. Now, listen. Driving up this afternoon I came to the conclusion that I was going to have to break it off with you. By the time I was dressing it had become a definite decision. It is not, as you are aware, the first time I have broken off a relationship such as ours. Usually I have enjoyed the process, or at least experimented with it, arranging for it to happen in ways that might be useful to me. Not this time."

222

He paused and drank, studying her over the rim of his mug. Though her face was smooth with youth it was so structured — small snub nose, mobile mouth, too-round eyes — that it implied the sad and puzzled wrinkles you see in monkeys. Time would bring them. She was watching him dry-eyed but her tension showed in the hardening of the mouth-muscles.

"I was trying to remember when you stopped calling me Adrian," he said.

"After your birthday party."

"How do you know so precisely? Somebody . . . Priscilla?"

"She's one of the haunters, isn't she?"

"Uh?"

"Before me."

"I doubt if she'll haunt you in the kitchen. She never set foot there. Bitch. Did she tell you it wasn't my real birthday?"

"Wasn't it? August the twenty-fifth?"

"It is the birthday of Adrian Waring. Let us go back to your calling me by the ambiguous initial."

"I saw she was trying to stir things up so I only did it a little at first. I sort of guessed you mightn't like it if I actually asked. I'll stop if . . . It's too late, isn't it?"

"Was it a deliberate choice on your part, to cover both names?"

"It just felt more comfortable."

"Because it covered both names?"

"I suppose so."

He put his mug down and lifted her bandaged hand on to his lap, meditatively fingering the criss-cross folds.

"You seem incapable of the saving lie," he said.

"Of course not! I'm a terrible liar! You know that!"

"Not this time."

"I'm sorry . . . darling Adrian . . . oh dear . . ."

"There is an important scene in *Nada* in which the narrator has to convince Chaka that he is telling the truth. Chaka is an appalling monster, prepared to sacrifice whole tribes, whole regiments, to his egotism. One of his decrees is that no son of his may live, but the narrator has rescued a baby boy, who becomes the hero of the story. Chaka suspects this to be the case, and makes the narrator hold his hand in the fire while he swears that it is not. He does so, saving his own life and the child's at the cost of a permanently withered hand."

"That's quite different. I didn't even think. Mine's going to be well in a week, Fritz says."

"Besides, the man was lying all along. You know, I do not think I am quite the monster Chaka was."

"Of course not!"

"Certainly what appears to be my egotism is considerable. Equally certainly I have caused sacrifices to be made. People have suffered, because I needed them to. You will have met people who think that I have let them down badly, or deliberately betrayed them."

"I never listen."

"Much of it is true. I have more than once prevented actors who thought me their friend from getting parts they desperately wanted. Outside the profession I have exploited whoever I needed to and refused to be exploited in return. In my own way I have been as ruthless as Chaka. The difference is that I have been equally ruthless with myself. Nothing and nobody, myself included, matters, compared to the performance. That is the only thing that counts."

"You don't have to tell me. I'll go whenever you want."

"An analyst, depending on his creed, might trace my behaviour to my relationship with my mother, or my lack of stature, or whatever. My own rationale has been that I must have no impediments to my career, no ties of duty, friendship, affection, need. I must slide through the seas with a clean keel. But privately I have been aware that there is more to it than that.

"There has been another kind of sacrifice — or rather, such events, in addition to the hackneyed sense in which I have been speaking of sacrifice, have sometimes also been sacrifices in the original meaning of that word, magical acts which endow the operator with powers not his own. To that extent I am like Chaka, whose authority was fed on the deaths of his victims. Of course I do not believe in powers out there, invisible forces, angelic or demonic, that can be summoned by word and ritual to do my bidding. Despite that what seems to happen can most truthfully be described in terms of magic. The spirit I conjure is mine, the deeps from which I call it forth are me. Perhaps all that is taking place, physically, is the transfer of a few molecules

224

across a millimetre of my brain, but when that has happened the powers are there. The audience respond. They know."

"Magic does sometimes work."

"I can remember the place and hour at which I first half-knowingly performed the ritual. Dusk. A lane in Hampshire, under beech trees. We waited, leaning on our bicycles, to allow a convoy of American army lorries turn in to the driveway. I let the girl understand that our affair was over. Five weeks ago I received a letter from her daughter — our daughter, though we did not at the time realize that she was pregnant — saying that she had recently died of a brain haemorrhage. The girl had made no attempt to get in touch with me in the intervening years, though I learnt from other sources that she had refused an abortion and insisted on keeping the child. She had married and had more children, and as far as I am aware had led a reasonably contented life — she certainly had it in her to do so. Despite that my daughter's letter was extremely bitter, rancorous, an un-healed suppuration. It did not touch me at all. I felt no guilt. Instead, I imagined myself free-wheeling down the drive behind the last lorry, beginning to sense that something new and important had happened, a reinforcement of my powers, somehow connected with breaking off the affair. Deliberately, to emphasize my own confidence in that still being the case, I chose to take you to a sale at the house where all this happened. I wanted to prove to myself my own right to have behaved as I had."

"Won't she tell Hickey or someone? The daughter, I mean?"

"I think it quite likely. My public credit may suffer a little, but my private accounts will be in the black. The episode was necessary — in a certain sense crucial. Do you understand?"

"Sort of."

"Such sacrifices have occurred a number of times since then, not always or only concerned with the women I have lived with. To be merely bored with a companion is not enough. There must be a genuine sense of giving something up, of moving on, of loss. I should certainly feel that at your departure."

"Me too."

"Well, that's what I decided must now happen. I went on tonight with my mind made up. The house was full, the performance went well, everybody was very kind, Benny enthusiastic as only he knows how, it is clear that I can make my own terms for Broadway — but I knew from the first scene that it would not do. I felt no relief, no cleansing of my keel, only loss. All I had done to make the performance work was to draw on my reserves. This has never happened before."

He paused but she said nothing, waiting, sucking repetitively at her lower lip.

"What happened last night was a magical act. Not on my part, but on yours."

"It wasn't anything. I was just stupid. Don't let's talk about it. I feel so ashamed."

"You have altered the rules. The old rites have lost their force, and I must attempt new ones. We will therefore proceed to summon the dead."

"You're acting."

"It is my only means of telling the truth, the embodiment of an inward apprehension in visible form. My name is Adrian Waring. That is who I am. I took the name by deed poll when I came out of the army in 1947. Before that there was a boy and a young man called Andrew Wragge. He died, as he had always foreseen he would, during the war, not instantly from a bullet or shell, but over a period. I remember the time and place at which that death began, standing behind a yew hedge, turning away from an old man who was pleading to be heard. Now I am going to bring him back to life. That is to say I am going to attempt to explain how and why he chose to make that particular betrayal, inevitable in its way, but still the one sacrifice I seem never to have convinced myself was acceptable. It will take some time."

"As I ran down the dovecote stair my thoughts were wholly of myself. I could get rid of Jean for the moment by telling her what I had found — unless she wanted it to be known that we had arranged the meeting she would have to leave the scene at once. I could be as brusque as I chose. There would be no more performances, so there was no longer any need for a happy Miranda. Are you still awake?"

"Course I am, but I do think you ought to stop. You don't want to croak tonight."

226

"The voice will stand it. Much more important to me than Jean was that I must reduce my own role as a witness as far as I could, so as not to delay my call-up or in any other way disrupt the arrangement Barrie Oakley had said he would make. All I would admit to was going out for an early stroll, noticing the forced door and finding the body. Jean in fact insisted on seeing for herself — she suspected me of trying some kind of trick — but having done so she left. I ran up to the house, woke my Cousin Elspeth and told her what I had found. But even before I spoke to her I had begun to be aware that if I had listened to what Samuel had been trying to tell me the night before he would still be alive. I worked out most of the details over the next few days, but I still said nothing, and when it came to the inquest, as I told you, I maintained my silence. Charles gave evidence that he had dismissed Samuel for gross impertinence while they were dressing for the play; Mrs Mkele said that he had been very depressed since his old master's death and was not asked to say why. Perhaps she too chose not to rock the boat. At any rate, the motive for suicide must have appeared more than adequate."

"Poor old man. But it's a long time ago. You couldn't've done anything, could you?"

"I could have listened. I had promised to do so."

"I meant after. He was dead. Telling people wouldn't . . ."

"That is the rational response. You might also say that I could not have known that my refusal to hear what Samuel was trying to tell me would lead to his death. Rationally, that is true. But we are not dealing in rationalities. It is not my refusal which, in your phrase, has begun to haunt me. It is the manner of my refusal. I killed him with the same voice as that with which I killed my uncle, my great-grandfather. I should have spoken to him in my own voice. He would have understood."

He fell silent. The fire was almost out and had ceased its murmur. The faint ripple of the water-clock was the only sound until, somewhere outside, a blackbird piped up, anticipating day.

"Are you still awake?" he said again.

"I'm thinking. It wasn't the Americans. Who killed him, I mean. If it was them, you wouldn't've felt . . ."

"Yes. It may be morally absurd, but that is so. My actions

227

and motives would have been no different, but my refusal to listen to Samuel would no longer have been a link in the chain of events that led to his death."

He paused again. This time, for once, it was she who took the initiative.

"You'd better tell me or you won't get to sleep."

"Yes, I suppose so. I feel extremely reluctant. Well, you remember that I told Trinder about the Wragge fortune and the missing heir? He already had dealings with Stephens, and must have told him. Stephens took advantage of the tours of the house to photograph the family portrait, which showed Charles as a young man. With that to go on — Trinder had theatrical connections — they were able to find an actor of the right build to impersonate Charles, and by the device of having him lose his memory they avoided the pitfalls such as the Tichborne claimant, for instance, encountered. Thanks to May's enthusiastic reception he was provisionally accepted by the family. This may seem surprising, but he did in fact put on a very good show. Since Sir Arnold refused to give an opinion the one active objector was Samuel, so in an effort to prevent him making his own inquiries Stephens pretended to take my side and send a private detective to check on the story. I don't imagine the man ever left the camp.

"Then Sir Arnold's condition took a turn for the worse. He accepted at last that he was dying and sent for his lawyer so as to change his will and leave his estate to me. Samuel made the arrangements but did not know what the changes were to be. Hoping to influence the decision he must have asked Stephens whether there was any last-minute news from the detective, telling him that it was urgent, perhaps even why. At any rate Stephens and Trinder attempted to bolster Charles's story by providing a forged newspaper cutting which appeared to verify an important detail. Newspapers are printed on both sides, of course, so they used an old photograph of a flower show on the back. Trinder's tame printer may have had it lying around his works, or he may have worked part-time for a local paper. It was the best they could do. They had very little time, so little that Trinder took the risk of getting me to bring the cutting out that week-end.

"I don't know whether May saw the cutting, but if she did I

think she would have spotted that January is an improbable season for a flower show. She was extremely sharp. At any rate, I am fairly certain that she knew from an early stage that Charles was an impostor, and may even have worked out or wheedled out of him that he was in collusion with Stephens. She was determined that she was going to stay at The Mimms and oust Elspeth after her father's death, and had recognized Charles as a suitable tool to achieve this. Once the will was read it seemed to be in everyone's interest that Charles would inherit."

"Except yours."

"I had no legal title. Mind you, I doubt if the stuff about the demolition of the house in the absence of a male heir would have stood up if it had been contested in the courts, but that would have involved huge costs, long delays and great uncertainty. In any case, Charles bought me off with a promise of support once the will was proved in his favour. At the same time he got me to use what influence I had with Samuel to persuade him to give up his opposition. I did so. We agreed that if no new evidence had come to light by the time I was called up, then Samuel would accept Charles as Sir Arnold's heir. I, casually since I didn't believe it would happen but still quite definitely, promised that if he found such proof I would support him. He told me he still had a chance. I thought he was speaking just of a general faint possibility, but I now think he meant there was one particular thing he wanted to try. He waited for his moment while they were dressing for our first performance of *The Tempest*.

"You remember May had got out an album of early photographs to remind Charles of things he was supposed to know, and this then disappeared? Charles changed the subject abruptly when May started talking about its loss, but by that time she had already asked one of the maids about it. So Samuel would have known. There was one particular photograph which showed Charles, as a child, naked. When the supposed Charles came out of the dressing-room he had not finished pulling up his hose, and he was in a state of outrage and fear. It is clear to me that Samuel had worked out why the album was missing, had concealed Charles's hose so as to delay him and thus be left alone with him, and had then pretended to find the missing

229

garment. While Charles was putting it on he had seized his underpants and exposed his genitals."

"No! A birthmark? But . . ."

"The essential element in the ritual by which a Zulu boy was accepted as an adult warrior was circumcision. I did not know this at the time, of course, in fact I looked it up only last week. I simply assumed that Samuel had seen something which both he and Charles knew proved that he was not the child in the photograph."

"I don't see. Couldn't it have been done after?"

"Yes, but not the reverse. The child in the photograph had been circumcised. I don't remember this as fact, but it is clear to me that it must have been so. It was a common practice among the English classes to which the Wragges presumed to belong by the time Charles was born. No doubt their doctor advised it. Some thought it hygienic, especially for children in the colonies, but the original motive, believe it or not, had been to discourage masturbation."

"Did it?"

"To judge by Philip Roth, no. So what Samuel must have seen was that Charles had not been circumcised. With the album gone that was still not proof. May had told me that they were not normally let run around naked, and in any case she and Elspeth would have contradicted each other's evidence. So Samuel's first thought was that we must send for the real Charles's wife.

"In fact the verification of Samuel's proof is irrelevant. The important point is that Charles knew. We performed the play without an interval and I was on stage throughout, but Charles was off for long periods. May of course fussed to and fro. He would have plenty of chance to take her aside. Stephens was in the audience — she could have talked to him. After the play Charles stuck to me like a leech — I thought it was because he was interested in Oakley and Price. At one point I found May making a fuss about her butter, which she said had been stolen. Stephens must have told her that she must somehow arrange for Samuel to go out and meet him that evening, which she did by hiding the butter out on the windowsill of the pantry — I trod in it as I climbed down. They may well have calculated that Samuel would seize the chance in any case — since he had been prevented from talking to me, Stephens was his other best hope of help. Anyway he went, and Stephens met him, heard what he had to say, asked if he had told anyone else and, learning that he had not, laid him out. Stephens was immensely strong. I remember him lifting Jean into the back of a truck as if she had weighed nothing.

"I think it possible that he had worked out his scheme in advance, not for this particular moment, but provisionally; he had been bothered by Samuel's persistence for some time. The stake, remember, was enormous. I do not mean that when he first mentioned lynching to me, or when he came on the tours of the house, that he was already thinking of murdering Samuel, only that the potential was there and continued to grow. What he needed was something from which to hang his victim, ground soft enough to take the imprint of boots — he had a supply of them in his stores — and a means of reaching both the gallows and the ground below it without leaving the impression of his own unusually large feet. The dovecote provided all this. He could hang the body from the beam and then rotate the ladder, standing on the lowest rung and pressing the individual boots into the droppings on the floor. No doubt the result would not have stood up to close forensic inspection, though he had very bad luck in my finding the body so soon — a day or two more and the rungs would have been covered with bird-droppings again."

"But after all that they said it was suicide."

"My own guess is that it wasn't an out-and-out cover-up, rather a case of tactful under-investigation once the verdict of suicide became plausible."

"What happened after? Do you know? The sergeant and Mr Trinder and everyone, I mean."

"By the time I came out of the army Elspeth was living at Charles Street. I used to stay with her when I was in London, and she was very useful to me in other ways, getting me introductions, giving me money and so on. In the end she became somewhat over-possessive, or so I told myself, and I stopped seeing her. Until then she kept me in touch with events at The Mimms. Charles and May succeeded in appointing fresh lawyers and having the will proved. I imagine that at that point Stephens and Trinder expected to be able to cash in on their investment — I can't be sure about that since Elspeth of course didn't know of their involvement, but I know what May's defence was. It was characteristic. She let Charles go back on the bottle. The cellars at The Mimms were still extremely well stocked, and she saw to it that she controlled access to them. Charles became totally dependent on her. According to Elspeth she treated him like a trained dog, rewarding or punishing him according to performance. When Stephens and Trinder made their attempt to cash in she called their bluff. If they exposed Charles they would get nothing. She must have known that Stephens had killed Samuel, and wouldn't have hesitated to accuse him of doing so, and accuse Trinder of fraud — Charles would have told her of his existence, and everything else. The point was that she had less to lose than they had. All three men could at least have gone to prison for conspiracy to defraud, and Stephens might have faced the death penalty. Knowing her I have no doubt that she saw the blackmail attempt off. Next she had the entail of her father's will broken by Act of Parliament, and then got Charles to make his own will entirely in her favour and organized his affairs to reduce death duties, but interestingly she seems to have done her best to keep him alive well beyond the seven year period. She enjoyed her power over him, I think. It was a sort of revenge on her own father. She lived to be ninety-one. The sale we went to was consequent upon her death. Incidentally, she had never let Charles pay me the allowance he had promised me. Elspeth, on the other hand, when she died in the late Sixties, left me almost everything she possessed. About the others I know nothing, except that Mrs Mkele suffered a stroke while I was still in the army and became completely paralysed and helpless. I don't know when she died. That's all."

He yawned, looked at the water-clock and rose. The girl made no effort to follow him, though the timer had switched off the central heating hours before and the fire had burnt down almost to ash. He stood looking down at her.

"Do you have anything to say?" he said.

"I don't know. Has it helped, telling me?"

"I shall find out this evening, perhaps. Let's go to bed."

"I'm too cold to move."

He bent and without apparent effort, though she cannot have

been much lighter than he was, lifted her from the sofa and straightened, holding her to his chest as if posing for a cartoon of a bridal couple entering their first home. After a moment, instead of carrying her through into the bedroom, he lowered her deftly to her feet. The water-clock whispered in the silence.

"I shall have to stop doing that sort of thing one day," he said.

"Don't."

"Wheel-chair parts. Fogeys on benches."

"Please don't."

"We seem to be a reasonably long-lived family. Eighty or ninety years of total self-dedication in the case of old Sir Arnold and my Cousin May."

"You're different."

"Miser leans against the wall and becomes generous."

"What's that about?"

He let go of her and created by his stance an invisible vertical surface against which he seemed to lean while a look of senile benignity suffused his face.

"It is said to be a Restoration stage-direction," he said. "Some playwright hacking his way out of his fifth act. I have never found it in print."

"I don't believe it."

"The transformation? No more do I — but I could make an audience believe it if I chose."

"I don't want you to. If I've got a say, I mean. Are you going to send me away?"

"No. Not yet. Not for some while."

"And I can go on calling you A.?"

"Um. You realize that we have now invested the letter with a meaning? Three weeks ago it was almost anonymous. Now each time you used it you would be making an assertion about who and what I am."

"It's just a way of saying I love you."

"Love whom?"

"You."

He shrugged, hunched, spread his palms and became for an instant his classic Shylock, rejecting mercy as unreasonable. With a twitch he shook the role off him and straightened.

"All right, in private," he said. "Let's go to bed. Wake me at

233

half past eleven. I'm meeting Robin at half past two to decide how much we can screw Benny for, and then I'll have an hour in the gym and then there's some bloody Dutch woman coming for an interview . . . Do you feel up to coming to watch this evening?"

"If you want me to."

"I don't suppose it's ever crossed your mind to wonder what sort of job Prospero made of ruling Milan when he got home . . . It might be a help, knowing you're there."

"All right."

ABOUT THE AUTHOR

Peter Dickinson, the son of English parents, was born in Zambia. He returned to England at age seven, and attended Eton and Cambridge. After serving for seventeen years as assistant editor of *Punch,* he turned to writing books at age forty. Since that time he has become well known for his detective novels and children's books. Several of both kinds have won prestigious prizes, including the Crime Writer's Association Gold Dagger and the Carnegie Medal for children's books. Among his more recent books are *Tefuga, Death of a Unicorn, Hindsight,* and *The Last Houseparty.*